Una Horne lives ... eland.
Trained as a nurse, s... amily
... p.
... ve
... he

... rd
... of
... m

Also by Una Horne

A Time to Heal
Under the Rowan Tree
Come the Day
Bright is the Dawn
Lorinda Leigh
When Morning Comes
The Jewel Streets
A Blackbird Singing
The Marble Clock
The Ironmaster's Girl
Child of Sorrow
Early One Morning

The Pitman's Brat

Una Horne

PIATKUS

All the characters in this book are fictitious and any resemblance to actual persons,
living or dead, is purely coincidental.

Copyright © 2004 by Una Horne

First published in Great Britain in 2004 by
Piatkus Books Ltd of
5 Windmill Street, London W1T 2JA
email:info@piatkus.co.uk

The moral right of the author has been asserted

A catalogue record for this book is available from the British Library

ISBN 0 7499 3573 1

Set in Times by
Action Publishing Technology Ltd, Gloucester

Printed and bound in Denmark by
Norhaven Paperback A/S, Viborg

Acknowledgements

I wish to thank Adam Lamb for his advice on the history of mental health in the area and especially Winterton Hospital in the period after WW2. Also my sister Margaret and her son-in-law Stephen Luke for their help. Durham Records Office is, as always, a valuable source of information to me.

Any errors are of course entirely my fault. I have combined fact with fiction for the sake of the story.

To Jonathan

Part One

Part One

Chapter One

Chapter One

'Stay there and watch Annie.'

'Yes Mam,' said Cath obediently and held on tight to Annie's hand as the four-year-old began to whimper and tried to get away to follow her mother. Cath was eleven and knew better than to disobey but her heart thumped as she watched her mam walk across the grass with baby Timmy wrapped in a shawl in her arms. Even at eleven Cath knew what was happening for it had happened before; even as she struggled with Annie, she was filled with dread and her large dark eyes were brimming with tears. She tried to control them for her mam would be annoyed if she saw them and then she would be in a bad temper all day.

Sadie Raine strode across the grass in the Bishop's park and slipped behind the ancient stone wall of the deer house in the distance. Cath waited anxiously with Annie, quiet now and sucking her thumb, standing beside her. The tiny girl was shivering and Cath cuddled her thin frame to her; trying to impart warmth from her own body.

'Mammy coming back?' asked Annie, looking up at her sister hopefully. There had been so many times when she had been left with Cath for hours. Once it had been morning before her mam came home. Now she had a terrible fear of being abandoned.

3

'Yes pet, she'll come back,' said Cath. She dragged Annie a few paces to one side from where she could see the path, which led away from the deer house on the opposite side. After a moment or two she saw a man carrying a bundle and hurrying away down the path and then her mother appeared, walking over the grass towards the two little girls. Her head was down for she was stuffing something into her worn imitation leather handbag so she wasn't looking at them.

'Mam!' Annie succeeded in breaking free and ran to her mother but Cath was frozen to stillness with her grief. She stared at her mother mutely.

Sadie grabbed hold of Annie and dragged her, running to keep up, after her. She stood before Cath and stared down at her angrily.

'Aw, don't look at me like that, you cheeky little monkey. And don't start crying neither or I'll give you something to cry about!'

'You gave our Timmy away,' said Cath. 'You gave him away for money.'

'No, I bloody did not,' Sadie retorted. 'I've just sent him to a nice house where he'll be looked after till your dad gets back.'

In spite of herself, Cath couldn't stop a sob escaping and Sadie raised her hand to her.

'Don't start that twisting, our Cath. I had to do it; any road the money I get from your dad isn't enough to keep three kids. He's been away for two years now, leaving me on my own and I have to manage as best I can.' Sadie grabbed hold of Cath with her free hand and, with a small girl on either side, marched along the gravel drive that led from the park to the arched entrance. It was dusk and on one side the bulk of the ancient castle loomed darkly while on the other the land sloped away to the trees and bushes shrouding the River Gaunless. Sadie paused outside the gates.

'Howay then, we'll have a nice cup of Oxo and a cracker

4

in Rossi's before we get the bus home. It'll do for your suppers. You'll like that won't you?'

The three of them trailed up Newgate Street to the small café and Cath sat with Annie in one of the booths while Sadie went to the counter for the drinks. Cath had a great weight of misery pressing on her; she felt sick. She loved Timmy, he was only two months old and she had had the looking after him most of the time. She fed him with National Dried Milk and changed his nappies for if she did not he got a sore bottom, for her mam didn't like to change him. But she was only eleven and she knew she didn't always do things right. Maybe Timmy would be better off with someone else but by, she missed him already.

She looked across to where her mother was leaning on the counter chatting with the girl who was serving. Then a man came in and stood beside Sadie and even Cath could see how she perked up, her face brightening. The three cups of Oxo were ready on the counter but Sadie lingered as the man bent and spoke to her.

'Mam!' Annie began to cry and Sadie looked across at her children and the smile left her face.

'All right, I'm coming,' she said grumpily and the man turned away, losing interest.

Cath dipped the cracker in Annie's Oxo and fed it to her sister before sipping her own drink. Across the table her mother lit a cigarette and fiddled with her cup handle.

'Leave her be, she can feed herself,' snapped Sadie suddenly noticing what Cath was doing. 'Hurry up an' all, the bus goes in five minutes.'

Both children hurried to finish up the meagre meal. They were hungry and unlikely to get any more supper. Though there might be bread and dripping in the pantry at home, Cath thought hopefully. And she could make up some of the National Dried Milk that was left now Timmy had gone.

Timmy had gone, Timmy had gone. Cath thought about

it all the way home on the bus and walking from the bus stop to Eden Hope Colliery village. She thought about it as she lay in bed beside Annie and waited for her mam to come back from the Black Boy pub in Winton. By, how she wished her dad would come back from the war.

The Middle East, that was where he was with the Eighth Army. If her dad had been here, Mam would never have sold Timmy or the other baby, the one Mam hadn't even given a name. A poor little thing he'd been who never cried. Did Mam not like boys, was that why? Cath didn't understand but then, nothing grown-ups did made sense to her. Why didn't Daddy just come home? They needed him. She remembered how Mam had met her out of school and rushed her and Annie on to the bus for Auckland. Cath had thought they were going to have a treat. Marina's mam sometimes met Marina out of school and took her to Auckland for a treat and Marina, who was her best friend, told her all about it next day at school. They went to the pictures or to the Store tearooms for tea and it all sounded so exciting to Cath. Well, Mam had taken them to Rossi's today . . . But what about Timmy? Cath dropped off to sleep abruptly, worn out with the happenings of the day.

'Catherine Raine, you're late again,' Miss Robinson stood at the top of the steps leading into the school hall as the last of the lines of children marched in from the school yard. Miss Robinson wore half-glasses and she looked severely over them at Cath as she ran into the yard. 'Why are you late this time?' she asked.

'Please miss, me mam slept in—' Cath began.

'Never mind your mother! Can you not get out of bed for yourself? A big girl like you?'

Cath had no answer to this so the result was she started the first lesson of the morning excluded from class and had to walk round and round in the hall for fifteen minutes until Miss Robinson let her in.

'Catherine can't get out of bed herself in the mornings,' the teacher said as Cath slid into her seat, her head down against the sniggers of her classmates. The truth was she did feel guilty anyway for she had slept in and on top of that she had to dress Annie and give her a cup of milk and a piece of bread and jam before she could get herself ready for school. Mam had gone out yesterday evening. She had put on red lipstick and rouge and told Cath she wouldn't be long, she was going out with Marina's mam. But she hadn't come back until what seemed to Cath to be the middle of the night. When Annie woke up screaming in the dark Cath had taken her into bed with her and in the end the little girl had gone back to sleep. But then, early in the morning Cath woke up and Annie was lying on top of her; she had wet the bed, and was crying again.

'For God's sake see to the bairn, Cath,' her mother's voice came from the other room, 'I've got a hell of a headache and she's making it throb.'

Cath was exhausted by the time she was allowed to stop tramping round the school hall and slip into her seat. Her head kept drooping over the list of sums in the arithmetic lesson and she was was glad when it was playtime and the milk was handed out for her stomach was rumbling. Some children didn't like the luke-warm milk and pulled faces about it; Cath could only wonder at them.

Cath felt the morning would never end but of course it did and she walked home for her dinner. She walked on her own for Marina was off school with the measles and Marina was the only one to make friends with her. The others were told to keep away because she had nits. In fact, hardly anyone in the rows talked to her mam either but Cath didn't know why that was.

The few tumbledown houses at the end of the rows were older than the rest and a little apart from them. Cath lived in the very end one. The gate was rickety and there was a mark on the flags where it scraped on the stone and it wouldn't open all the way. Cath got through it and trudged up the yard to the back door. To her surprise, the door opened and her mam stepped out.

'Your dad's home,' she said and then, in a sort of hiss, 'if you say out about our Timmy, anything at all, I'll leather the hide off your backside, do you understand me?'

'Yes, Mam.'

In contrast to her quiet words a wild excitement was flaring up in Cath. She looked past her mother into the kitchen but she couldn't see him.

'He's away down the garden,' said Sadie. 'Go and tell him the dinner's ready. Now mind what I told you though.'

There was a smell of something cooking in the oven and any other time Cath's stomach would have been rumbling at this unusual happening but now all she could think of was that her dad was home and hunger was forgotten. She pushed past her mother and through the house to the front door, which led directly into the long strip of garden. Alf Raine was standing by the gate at the far end, looking out over the old wagon way and pit heap, now overgrown with straggly patches of brown grass. He had little Annie in his arms and she had on a clean dress and even a cardigan.

'Daddy!' Cath cried as she raced down the stony path. But she slowed down as she got close to him, overcome with a sudden shyness. He was a stranger and not at all the daddy she had pictured in her mind for so long. He wasn't big enough, why he was no taller than any of the other men in the rows. But he held Annie with one arm and held out the other to Cath and grinned and then she knew him and he took her up and held them both, one on each shoulder.

The khaki cloth of his uniform scratched against her bare legs but she didn't care. She grinned back at him and touched his cheek.

'You're a funny colour, Daddy,' she said and he

8

laughed for he was tanned almost to a mahogany shade by the Tunisian sun, in sharp contrast to Cath's white skin.

'Man,' said Annie, digging her finger in Alf's chest as she tried to explain to Cath who he was. 'Nice man.'

'No, it's not a man, it's our daddy,' said Cath and Annie looked blankly from her sister to the man.

'Man,' she said firmly.

'Howay, the dinner's ready.'

Mam was standing at the front door with a big spoon in her hand and she was smiling all over her face in away that Cath couldn't ever remember her doing before.

'Right then run,' said Alf and he put the children down on the path. 'I'm a A-rab and I'm going to get you, run!'

The girls ran, Cath holding on to Annie's hand and practically dragging her along. Both of them squealed and shouted as they ran.

There was corned-beef stew for dinner and even chocolate after, for Alf had brought back food points and a ration card and a parcel of iron rations. The chocolate was in the parcel and there was cheese, hard American cheese, and biscuits. The chocolate was dark, hard and bitter too but Cath enjoyed it anyway. But in no time at all the dinner hour was over and it was time for Cath to go back to school.

The afternoon took for ever but at last it was time to join the crocodile of children to walk to the main gates where, holding Annie by the hand, her daddy was in his soldier's uniform and Cath was so proud of him she thought she would burst.

'Good afternoon, Mr Raine,' said Miss Robinson, smiling broadly, she who never ever spoke to Cath's mother, or Marina's mother either come to that. 'On leave, are you? My, it's a long time since you were home, isn't it?'

'Yes,' said Alf tersely and tapped the side of his nose as though to say 'Careless talk costs lives', which was a

9

notice on the window of the bus that went into Auckland from Eden Hope every hour. It always made Cath wonder what talk was careless: only some talk it must be because usually the women on the bus talked all the way to the town.

But her daddy had turned away from Miss Robinson to her and he walked away holding a girl with each hand and swinging his long legs so that Annie, in particular, had to run as fast as she could until he noticed and swung her up on to his shoulder and she squealed with delight. When they went in the back door Sadie was getting dressed before the fire.

'Have you been to bed, Mam?' asked Cath anxiously. 'Are you feeling bad, like?' Her mam and dad looked at one another and laughed and laughed until Mam suddenly sobered.

'I expect nowt comes of this, Alf Raine,' she said. 'I want no more babbies in here. You should have been more careful.'

'Aw, stop worrying,' he replied. 'What do you expect a man to do when he comes home after all that time? I'm no monk, you know.'

Annie had been laughing with her mother though she didn't know what about; she was happy because the others were happy. But suddenly she said, 'Timmy? Timmy baby.'

Sadie grabbed her arm and pulled her roughly to her. 'Shurrup!' she said sharply and Annie's face crumpled. Cath moved from one foot to the other in agitation.

'Don't—' she began in distress, looking from her mother to her father. He had taken little notice of what Annie said but after seeing Sadie's reaction his face darkened.

'Timmy? Who the hell is Timmy?'

'Nobody, take no notice,' said Sadie. 'Annie doesn't know what she's talking about, man.' She gave Annie a shake, which was a mistake, for the little girl started to wail and try

10

to get away and Cath, expecting her mam to smack Annie, began to cry.

'Who the hell is Timmy?'

Her daddy sounded really angry and was shouting now and Cath trembled, all the happiness of the day dissipated.

'I told you, he's nobody,' Mam shouted back at him and he moved across the kitchen and towered over her. Mam shrank back and let go of Annie and Annie ran to Cath and clung to her. 'He's just a neighbour's bairn, Alf,' Mam cried.

Alf turned and took hold of Cath, holding her by each arm.

'Who is Timmy?' he asked her and his grip on her arms was hard and hurt and Cath sobbed and Annie clung harder to her legs and screamed. Alf let go of Cath's arms and she cuddled Annie to her.

'Our baby!' Cath shouted, desperate to stop him hitting her mam. Alf turned to her.

'Our baby?' he asked and his voice was low and menacing.

'It's not,' Sadie asserted. 'I – I was just looking after it, that's all.'

'Mammy selled Timmy,' said Annie and Sadie shrank back again, away from Alf's lifted hand. He turned suddenly and stalked to the back door.

'I'll get to the bottom of this,' he muttered, 'One way or another.'

'Alf!' Sadie ran after him as he strode down the yard and grabbed hold of his arm. 'Where are you going? I didn't sell your bairn, man, it wasn't—'

Alf stopped and turned to face her. 'Not mine, wasn't he?' he said and shook her off so roughly she fell to the brick-paved yard. His face twisted into a cold grimace. 'You're nowt but a whore,' he said and walked out and on, down the street.

'Is he coming back, Mam?' Cath, who was standing in the doorway, asked, as Sadie got to her feet.

'It'll be your fault if he doesn't,' Sadie snapped and

thumped her on the shoulder so that the little girl stumbled and almost fell. 'What did I say to you? Not a word to your dad, I said. Get in there now and see to your sister or I'll sell you next.'

Chapter Two

'What're you drinking?' asked Jack Lowe. 'Pint, is it? Give the lad a pint, Lance, on me.' He'd just walked into the bar of the Workingmen's Club and Institute, his close-cut hair still damp from his bath before the fire. He'd been on back shift all day and was late getting out to the club as the shift had been on a couple of hours overtime. He had been tired and drawn when he opened the door but seeing his old marra, Alf, sitting in the almost empty bar he had cheered up immediately.

'You not won the war yet, Alf?' Jack asked as Lance put foaming pints of Federation brew before them. Alf shook his head regretfully.

'Not yet.'

'Make the most of them, there's not much more left,' said Lance as Jack handed him a shilling and eightpence.

'Aw, howay, man, the lad's been two years in the desert,' Jack protested.

'Aye well, I mebbe can spare him another one,' Lance conceded. 'But there's a war on, you know.'

'I should think he knows all right, you daft bugger,' said Jack.

During this exchange Alf had not spoken, simply nodded to the other men.

'By, Alf, you look as miserable as sin for a chap as

13

has just come home,' said Jack. Both men lifted their glasses and swallowed deeply of the amber liquid. 'You weren't injured, were you? Is that why you've come home?'

'Naa,' said Alf. 'I just got a spot of leave before we go on to – well we're not supposed to say where.' The beer swirled round his empty stomach and he belched. He made an effort to be sociable though his thoughts were full of suspicions. If Sadie had been up to something, and mind, the worry had been with him for two years because of how she was, she needed a man; if she had, he'd murder her, he bloody well would. But could he take the word of his bairns? At least he knew they were *his* bairns, both of them looked like he did, with dark curly hair and brown eyes set in heart-shaped faces. His mam, bless her, had used to say he couldn't get out of fathering them bairns even if he wanted to.

'Well, you don't look as though you're enjoying it.'

Alf looked up and smiled. 'Aye I am, man, I am. I was just thinking about Sadie. It was a long time for a lass on her own with two little bairns.'

Jack began to feel uncomfortable. He looked away; up at the ceiling, tobacco-coloured now, it hadn't been painted since before the war. He gazed across at Lance who was rubbing a glass with a teatowel, his fingers going round and round.

'Quiet tonight,' said Lance, glancing up as he felt Jack's eyes on him.

'Thursday,' said Jack. 'Any road, they'll know you're running out of beer. When's the brewery wagon due?'

'The morn,' said Lance and resumed his polishing. 'Mind, it's been known not to turn up.'

'Hell's bells,' said Jack. All three men were quiet as they contemplated the weekend without beer but Alf's mind soon returned to worrying on about his wife. They were worries a lot of the men who fought with the Eighth Army in the Middle East had. And occasionally one of

14

them got a 'Dear John letter' as the lads called them. Well, now he knew what that felt like.

A couple of miners walked into the bar and ordered pints from Lance. Lance pulled them before pinning up a notice behind the bar. NO BEER LEFT, it said. The newcomers entered into a spirited conversation with the steward.

'Have you heard anything about our lass?' Alf asked Jack, now they had a degree of privacy.

'What do you mean exactly?'

'You know. Was there any talk? While I was away, like?'

'Aw, Alf, I don't listen to talk. There's plenty of gossiping old wives in Eden Hope without me adding to them.'

'Howay, Jack, don't be so cagey. I have a right to know.'

Jack sighed. 'I told you I know nowt,' he said. 'Living over the end of the rows as she does, your lass.'

'Well, our bairns said something about a babby. Timmy they called him.'

'Oh aye, I did hear she was looking after her sister's babby. The wife said something about it.' Betty, his wife, had smiled knowingly as she remarked that Sadie said it was her sister's child. Sadie had disappeared for weeks before coming back with the baby. Been over to Shildon to look after her sister, or so she had said. 'Our Patsy's badly,' she had said. Betty had seen Patsy in the queue for pig's trotters at Manner's the butcher, in Newgate Street in Auckland, and she hadn't looked as though she was expecting.

Jack's thoughts were interrupted by the arrival of Dr Orton who had come to deliver a lecture on 'First Aid in the Mines' to the off-shift deputies and aspiring deputies. He looked about and realised the bar had been filling up with men come to hear the doctor.

'I'll have to go now, Alf,' said Jack, 'I'll see you before

15

you go back.' He looked relieved as he filed out of the bar to the back room after the others.

Cath was lying in bed hugging Annie close to her for warmth. Annie slept with her now more often than not and her little body was a comfort to Cath. Even though it was the beginning of June, the weather was still cold and damp.

Cath was tired out but somehow she couldn't go to sleep. Her dad had gone away again and it was all her fault. If she hadn't said anything about Timmy, her dad would have stayed at least until he had to go back to the war. That was what Mam had screamed at her and she knew it was right. Cath cuddled Annie and sobbed quietly. She didn't hear the footsteps coming down the yard to the back door but suddenly the back door opened and he was there, she could hear his voice plainly floating up the stairs. She was filled with a wild gladness. Mam wouldn't shout at her again, not while Dad was here and she wouldn't shout at Annie either. Cath dropped off to sleep as the voices downstairs became a dim murmur in her ear.

'We'll go into Auckland to the pictures, I think,' said Alf. It was Saturday morning and Sadie had Annie on her knee while she pulled on her socks and buttoned her sandshoes. Cath looked quickly at her mother.

'Can we, Mam?' she asked and Sadie nodded.

'Why not? If you've the money to pay, Alf, I've nothing to spare. The bairn needs shoes, these are getting a bit tight for her.'

'Well, we'll get some in Newgate Street,' Alf said grandly and Cath heard the chink of silver as he turned coins over in his trouser pocket. 'You got enough coupons?'

'Oh man, it's not the coupons I'm short of, it's the money,' Sadie replied. 'I don't get a living wage from the

16

army, you know.' For a second or two the smile disappeared from Sadie's face as she once again made her old complaint.

Alf was tempted to say other soldier's wives seemed to manage on it but he bit the words back. Today they were going to enjoy themselves. He had decided to believe Sadie. He had nine days left of his leave and he was going to spend it with his family, he had decided. *Cinderella* was on at the Majestic once again and the kids would love it. And he and Sadie could sit holding hands in the dark. She'd like that.

It was a magical day, thought Cath, as she sat in the darkened cinema. They had gone in out of bright sunlight and she couldn't see anything at all when she first went in. Nothing except the screen and the flickering images and bright colours that is. She couldn't even see her new sandshoes except for a light blur when she looked down. Both she and Annie had got new sandshoes and they were lovely. Annie had cried when Cinderella's stepmother was on the screen and Daddy took her on his knee and comforted her and she went to sleep.

Outside the picture house once more the family walked down Tenters Street and along Newgate Street to the market place. Mam bought penny dips at the butchers and they sat on the low wall outside the church where the iron railing had been sawn off to go for the war effort. Grease and brown gravy ran down Cath's chin from the penny dip but she pushed it up into her mouth and swallowed it. She didn't want to lose a drop.

They were still sitting there, listening to a stallholder who was making one last effort to sell his vegetables, when Cath's Aunty Patsy came walking along, laden with bags and tottering on high heels on the cobbles.

'Well, fancy seeing you lot,' she said. 'I didn't know you were back, Alf. On leave, are you? I've missed the bloody bus back to Shildon now, the next one doesn't go for two hours.' She plumped herself down on the wall beside Cath.

'Give us a bite of your dip,' she said, grinning at the little girl. 'Go on, give us a bite.'

Cath looked at the small piece of bread stained with gravy she had left in her hand before offering it sorrowfully.

Aunty Patsy grinned even wider. 'Why, thanks pet. But it's all right, I was only funning. I already had one. Are you not speaking to me, our Sadie?'

Sadie hadn't said anything to her sister yet, just stared at her in alarm. 'Hallo, Patsy,' she said now. 'We have to go, anyroad, the bus will be coming.' She jumped to her feet, still holding half a penny dip.

'No it won't,' Alf interjected. 'It's not due for another fifteen minutes. We've loads of time to get to the bus stop.' He looked from one sister to the other and knew there was something wrong. 'How are you doing, Patsy? Sadie said you weren't too good after the babby.'

'The babby?' asked Patsy, mystified. 'What babby?'

'Why, Timmy, I think Sadie said you called him, didn't you?'

'Timmy? But that was—'

'Howay, we have to go for the bus,' said Sadie. She grabbed Annie by the hand and began to back away. Turning to look back she cast a murderous glance at Patsy. 'Now, Cath, come on,' she said and Cath ran after her. She knew better than not to when Mam spoke in that particular voice.

'That was what?' Alf probed.

'Aw, nowt. I mean that was a long time ago, I'm fine now,' Patsy improvised. 'Well, I'll see you again no doubt, mind you don't catch a German bullet over in Egypt or where ever.'

'Aye. Ta ra Patsy,' said Alf and hurried after his family.

'What was that all about?' he asked Sadie in a low voice when they were settled on the bus. They each had a little girl on their knees for the bus was full, with people standing in the aisle packed like sardines.

'What?' countered Sadie.

'We'll talk about it when we get home then,' Alf said. A stout woman was leaning over him and Cath, her basket pressed against Cath's side. 'Watch what you're doing, missus,' he told her.

'I'm doing my best,' she snapped but pulled her basket away from Cath.

When the bus reached Eden Hope Colliery they struggled to the front and alighted at the bus stop at the end of the rows. 'You take the bairns home, I fancy some fresh air,' said Alf.

'But where're you going?' cried Sadie. She was terrified of the way he looked at her when he thought she wasn't watching and the way he avoided looking at her directly. 'The club isn't open yet.'

'No, well, I'm off for a walk, that's all.' Alf strode off along the path that led between a sand pit and the clay pit where the old brickworks had used to be.

'But it's getting dark—' Sadie started to say but he was already too far away to hear her or if he did he made no response. The girls were tired and deflated as they walked the slight rise by the rows and across to home. The late evening sunshine shone golden on the old bricks of the outhouses, making the coal dust sparkle like stars where it had lodged between the bricks. Usually Cath liked to watch it but tonight she was too tired and dispirited, even though it had been such a lovely day.

Alf walked through the play field, which bordered Eden Hope. In spite of the huge slag heap to one side it was beautiful. On the other side of the valley, the bankside rose towards Shildon, the pastures still green and dotted with cattle; the hawthorn in bloom, whitening the green with may. On the side he was walking the field gave way to woods and he walked on between the trees, coming

19

out eventually by the rabbit warren, the Bunny Banks, as the bairns called the place.

He thought of the arid sands of North Africa, by, the searing heat. The Arabs, poor sods, caught between the Germans and the British. There were worse places to be than Durham, he reckoned, even Durham in the depression as he remembered it before the war. Alf sat down with his back against the sun-warmed bricks of an old ventilation shaft, which stuck up in the middle of the field like a sore thumb. There weren't just rabbits burrowing beneath this ground. His thoughts rambled on idly as the sun sank below the trees and a cool wind sprang up. And at last he allowed himself to think about Sadie and his girls.

He had to go back, report for duty first to Durham City along with his mates and then they would all be packed off by train to the embarkation point, somewhere on the south coast. To North Africa first, then it would be Italy, probably Sicily he guessed. What old Churchill called, 'The soft underbelly of Europe.'

Well, he didn't mind that. He had been looking forward to having another bash at the Germans and at least it wouldn't be quite so hot as it was in Egypt. But Sadie couldn't stand it, he knew, and she would go off the rails again. And in spite of everything, he didn't want to lose her or the bairns. No, if he was at home he could keep an eye on her, couldn't he? And hadn't he done his bit any road? The fighting Durhams, as Monty called them, were well respected in the Eighth Army for their courage. That's what Captain Teasdale told them in his pep talks, any road.

It was getting dark – it must be ten o' clockish because of double summertime. Alf got to his feet and rubbed down the back of his trousers. Time to go home. He reckoned there was only one thing to do. When he reached the back yard he opened the coal-house door. His tools for the pit were hanging on nails on the wall; his large round shovel, his pick and his axe. He hesitated a moment, then took his pick and swung it before he could think any more about it.

Chapter Three

It hurt a lot, Cath could see by Daddy's face it hurt a lot. Sweat ran down his face and he was breathing funny, gasping. Sometimes he groaned but he didn't shout again, not after the first time. Cath stood at the bedroom window and watched him. She had to move the blackout curtain to do it but it didn't matter, there was no light on in the room. But Mam had ran out of the kitchen, leaving the back door open and the beam of light showed her daddy, on his back in the yard, leaning up awkwardly because his foot was pinned by his pick between two of the bricks of the brick-paved yard. Behind her Annie was crying but for once Cath ignored her. She was crying herself.

The ARP warden came to the gate and shouted, 'Close that door, you're showing enough light to lead the Jerries straight here!' Mam shouted something and he came into the yard.

'Oh, my blessed aunt!' he exclaimed. 'Don't move him, missus, I'll ring for the ambulance.' He was almost out of the gate when he turned back. 'Close that door, any road.'

It was an age before the ambulance came and by then Marina's mam had come and a deputy off-shift from the pit with his first-aid box. He loosened the bricks trapping the end of the pick and covered Alf up.

'Get it out o' me, please,' Alf pleaded but the deputy shook his head.

22

'Nay, man, I cannot.' He looked up at the window as a movement caught his eye. 'Missus, go and see to your bairns,' he told the shivering Sadie. 'They shouldn't be watching this.' But she stood, unmoving.

'I'll go,' said Betty Lowe. She had come over to see if she could help as the news spread round the village. She went upstairs and lit the gas mantle on the wall above the fireplace in the bedroom. Both children were out of bed, both sobbing hysterically. For all it was a summer night they were shivering, perhaps with shock.

'Howay now, pets,' said Betty, move to compassion at the sight of their tear-streaked cheeks. 'Into bed with you both and Aunty Betty will tuck you in.'

'I frightened,' Annie whispered.

'Don't be frightened, pet, it'll be all right,' Betty soothed.

'What about me dad, Aunty Betty?' Cath asked, reluctant to leave the window.

'He'll be all right,' Betty repeated, though she couldn't see how he ever could be. 'They'll take him to the hospital and mend his foot.'

I only hope they can, she thought, as she lifted little Annie into bed and Cath climbed in after her. 'Cuddle up, petals,' she advised them. 'Try to go to sleep. I'll stay here with you.' She sat down on the edge of the bed.

The children warmed each other and Annie fell asleep with her thumb stuck firmly in her mouth. Cath's eyes were closing when she was suddenly alert at the noise of an engine outside. Just for a minute she thought it was an airplane like the ones there had been in the raids when the Germans tried to bomb the pithead up the street.

'What's that?' Cath cried, with new alarm.

'Nothing, go to sleep,' said Betty. She got off the bed and went to the window and lifted the blackout curtain just enough so that she could see out. 'Oh, it's the Union ambulance come to take your dad to the hospital. They'll soon make him better now.'

23

The Union ambulance was only supposed to be used for miners hurt in the pit but Alf was one of their own, wasn't he? Even if he was a soldier now.

In the yard, Alf cried out once as they lifted him, together with the pick minus its handle by now, onto the stretcher, and carried him into the ambulance. After a minute or two, Cath heard it drive away and her mam and Marina's mam came into the house. She could hear them talking downstairs in the kitchen.

'Will he lose his foot, do you think?' Marina's mam was asking.

'Bloody hell, no!' cried Sadie and Cath started shivering again.

'Go to sleep, like I said, pet,' Aunty Betty said as she leaned over and tucked the worn blanket round Cath's thin shoulders. 'I'm going downstairs now, you'll be all right, won't you? A big girl like you?' Cath nodded and hugged Annie tighter to her. Annie whimpered but did not open her eyes.

'Keep your voices down,' Betty snapped as she walked into the kitchen. She looked hard at Sadie. 'You don't want to frighten the bairns to death, do you?'

Sadie's face looked as young and tear-stained as Cath's. 'What am I going to do?' she asked. 'Why did he do it?'

'He didn't do nowt!' snapped Betty. 'Don't you go saying he did. The pick slipped, that was all. He was going to bring some coal in and the pick slipped off its hook on the wall. That's what must have happened.'

'But we had a bucket of coal in,' wailed Sadie.

'Aye, mebbe you did but *they* don't know that, do they?'

Betty stared at Sadie's tear-stained face, her red, swollen eyes. Little Cath had more brains in her little finger than this stupid cow, she thought savagely. Everybody in Eden Hope and beyond knew about her carrying on while Alf was away in the Middle East. She just couldn't do without a man, that was her trouble. If Alf had done this to himself, and Betty wasn't prepared to admit he had, then it was her fault. He must have heard something. Lord knows there were plenty of rumours going about the place.

'Mind what I tell you,' she said, 'both of you, mind. Or, as sure as eggs is eggs, they'll throw him in the glass house until hell freezes over.'

'I won't say nowt,' said Etty Smith, Marina's mother. Her eyes sparkled with excitement. 'Are you staying, Mrs Lowe? Because if you are, I'll cut along home, check on the bairns.'

'Aye, I'll stay for a bit till Jack comes in any road.' Her own children were almost grown and all right to be left in the house on their own.

After Etty had gone Betty stoked the fire and put on the kettle. 'Likely a good strong cup of tea will do you good,' she observed.

'I wanted to go in with Alf but they wouldn't let me,' Sadie sniffed loudly, took a rag from her pocket and blew her nose.

Betty reached up to the high mantelshelf for the tea caddy and spooned a bare teaspoonful into the teapot. She was mindful of the fact that two ounces was all you got on the ration.

'You can go in the morning,' Betty said. 'Or, I tell you what, you can telephone the hospital first thing. I'll come along to the telephone box with you.' She poured two cups of tea and added condensed milk. It was sweet and so saved the sugar ration. The two women drank their tea in a silence punctuated only by Sadie's sniffs and an occasional coal hissing as tar escaped and flared. 'Now you'd best try to get some sleep.'

'I'll never sleep,' Sadie said mournfully. But she rose to her feet when Betty did and followed her to the door. 'You'll call for me then?'

'Aye, eight o'clock sharp. Mind you're ready, I haven't got time to waste.'

'I will be,' Sadie promised. After she had locked the door she went upstairs to bed and fell asleep immediately, worn out, she felt. In spite of her promise, Betty had to knock her up next morning, just as she had expected to.

'Watch the bairn, Cath,' Sadie shouted up the stairs as they went out; Sadie with tuppence clutched in her hand for the telephone call.

Alf was in bed in the men's surgical ward in Durham County Hospital when the Red Caps came marching smartly in unison down the ward until they got to his bed, before they split up and went one to each side of him. It was ten o'clock in the morning and two nurses were dispensing cocoa from a large enamel jug. They paused and turned to stare at Alf and the Red Caps, as did every other patient on the ward.

'Private Raine,' said one. His head was turned towards Alf and Alf knew he could see directly into his brain. The soldier was a sergeant and the peak of his cap came down almost covering his eyes so that, abstractedly, Alf wondered how he could see anything at all but yet he knew he could.

Alf felt sick. His foot throbbed so much he could feel the pain right through his body. The surgeon had had to remove the pickhead in the theatre while Alf was under a general anaesthetic and now the foot was swathed in dressings and a cradle kept the bedclothes from it. In spite of all this, Alf tried to sit up to attention but the movement sent strong waves of pain through him and a groan escaped him before he could stop it. The Red Caps ignored it.

'Cocoa, soldier?'

The nurse was standing by the bed, a mug of cocoa in her hand, her eyes bright with interest. Alf reached out a hand for the mug but put it back as the sergeant glared at him.

'He doesn't want any, nurse,' he said.

'I think he should have it, Sergeant.' Sister was standing at the end of the bed suddenly. 'Private Raine is under our care and has not recovered from surgery.'

26

'He will not be under your care for long, Sister,' said the sergeant. 'He will be transferred to a military hospital as soon as it can be arranged.'

'That will depend on his condition and is up to the doctors,' snapped Sister.

'I am still on leave,' Alf ventured. 'I've been two years in the desert.' He glanced around the ward at the other men, mostly men injured in the pit. 'I didn't do anything,' he told them. 'It was an accident, the pick fell off the wall and pinned my foot to the ground.' The men looked away, at each other or down at the bed. Alf could tell most of them thought it was unlikely.

'There will be an inquiry, Private,' said the sergeant. 'If you can prove what you say—'

'Please leave now,' said Sister in a no-nonsense sort of voice. 'Nurse, call Dr Moran.' In a movement that surprised the sergeant she got between him and her patient and laid her hand on Alf's brow. He felt hot and clammy and his cheeks were a peculiar sickly white, while his pulse was fast and thready.

'But—' said the sergeant.

'Now,' she grated at him.

'We will wait in the corridor,' he replied with dignity.

The two Red Caps marched down the ward to the entrance where they took up a stance on either side of the door to Sister's office.

Dr Moran walked past them with a brief nod and into the ward to Alf's bed. He was just a young houseman but he had assisted in theatre as the pickhead was being removed from Alf's foot and Mr Thompson, the surgeon, had done his best to repair the damage to the small bones and tissue of the foot. It was to be encased in plaster later in the day.

'Morning, Sister,' he said as he came in behind the screens put around the bed by the nurse. He proceeded to examine Alf. 'How are you feeling now, soldier?'

'Not too bad,' said Alf and winced as they laid back the bedclothes to look at his foot.

'It looks quite good, Sister,' the doctor said. 'No sign of infection though it is a little early for it.'

He gazed at Alf and felt his pulse. 'What do they want?' he asked softly.

'To move him to a military hospital, sir,' said Sister.

'Oh.'

Dr Moran carried on with his examination then replaced the cradle and pulled up the bedclothes. 'Two codeine tablets, stat,' he said and Sister called for the nurse to fetch them.

'Well, Sister,' the doctor went on, 'I don't think he should be moved today. I will have to have a word with Mr Thompson.' He did not miss he look of relief on Alf's face. 'I'm afraid you will always have trouble with that foot,' he said to Alf. 'You may not get back to the front, I'm sorry.'

As he walked down the ward he smiled slightly. The soldier wasn't sorry and he didn't blame him. But there were plenty of people who would, he knew that.

Behind him, Alf closed his eyes. He had thought he just might get away with what he had done but he was under suspicion right from the start. He remembered other times when men had injured themselves on purpose, desperate to get back to Blighty. And the contempt that came from the other men, the harsh treatment they received from those in charge. Oh God, how did he ever come to this?

In the café across the road from the hospital, Sadie sat at a table with a cup of tea in front of her and a plate with a piece of teacake spread with a sliver of margarine. She stared down at it. There were three currants in the slice of teacake, or perhaps they weren't currants, she wasn't sure. She took a sip of the watery tea sweetened with saccharin and put the cup down hurriedly. She would never get used to the funny after taste, she reckoned.

Sadie looked up at the clock on the wall behind the counter and sighed heavily. A Canadian airman sitting at the table next to her caught her eye and smiled tentatively.

Sadie turned her face away from him and he looked disappointed. The clock indicated it was a quarter to two. She could swear it had taken hours to go from half past to a quarter to the hour.

When she had rung the hospital early that morning they had told her she couldn't visit Alf until two o'clock. She had caught the twelve o'clock bus from the market place in Auckland, though she had known she would be early, but she couldn't wait any longer or she would have gone mad. Alf was 'comfortable', they had said. How could he be comfortable when he'd had a bloody great pick stuck in his foot? Sadie looked up at the clock again, it was ten to two. She got to her feet, slung her gas mask and handbag over her shoulder and went out of the café. Outside she took great gulps of fresh air then set off across the road and up the tarmac of the hospital yard, around the building to the main door. It was closed. There was a notice pinned to it: NO VISITORS BEFORE TWO O'CLOCK. The door was locked and there was a short queue of people waiting to go in. Sadie tagged on to the end.

When she at last got inside the building she followed the signs to Men's Surgical and went in. There was no sign of Alf. Sadie couldn't believe it. She walked up and down between the beds staring at each face.

'Who're you looking for, love?'

It was a pleasant-faced older man with his arm in a sling who asked.

'My husband, Alf Raine,' said Sadie.

'Eeh pet, he's gone,' said the man. 'They took him away, the Red Caps, I mean.'

'Took him away?' Sadie stared, unbelieving. 'Where?'

'You'll have to ask Sister, I reckon.' The man lost interest as a visitor, a plump middle-aged woman, came in and went over to him, kissing him on the cheek. Sadie walked out of the ward and knocked at the door of Sister's office. A few minutes later she was out on the street again, standing opposite the café not knowing what to do or where to go.

Catterick! He had gone to Catterick! It might as well be the moon, there was no way she could get to Catterick, not today. She was standing there, looking like a lost little girl, when the man in air-force uniform stopped in front of her.

'Is something the matter, lady?' he asked. It was the same one who had been in the café; he had Canada strips on his shoulders and wings over his breast pocket.

'Mind your own business,' she said but weakly. He smiled at her. 'Come and tell me all about it,' he said. 'I might be able to help. We could go and sit down by the river. It's quiet there.'

Sadie stared at him, hardly seeing him. But he was a man and his accent was lovely and he sounded real sympathetic. She nodded slowly and held out her hand to him. He tucked it under his arm as they walked down the hill to the path by the Wear, which meandered slowly around the promontory crowned by the cathedral.

Chapter Four

Keith Armstrong was a Canadian airman who flew bomber planes over Germany. Cath knew this because he told her when he came to the house to see her mam.

'My daddy is in the army,' said Cath, gazing at him beneath lowered brows.

'Is he, now,' Keith Armstrong said. He walked to the bottom of the stairs and called up to Sadie, 'Are you going to be long, honey? Only we want to catch the beginning of the film, don't we?'

'My daddy is a hero,' said Cath. 'Only he hurt his foot.'

'Did he? At the war, was it?' Keith Armstrong asked, as he turned back into the kitchen.

'No, it was in the yard,' said Cath. 'His pick fell on his foot.'

'Oh.'

'It hurt really bad,' said Cath for Mr Armstrong had a look on his face as though he didn't believe her.

'Good,' said Mr Armstrong and turned away as Sadie came down the stairs. Cath was confused but her mother was talking to her.

'Look after Annie, now, we won't be long,' she was saying.

'Is that OK? Leaving the kids?' asked Keith.

'They'll be all right. Annie is in bed and Cath is going up now. I'll lock the door, nothing will happen,' Sadie replied.

After they had gone Cath climbed into bed with Annie and snuggled up to her. 'Please Jesus help Daddy,' she whispered. 'Make his foot better soon and let him come home soon and the duration be over.'

Her mam had told her he couldn't come home, not for ages. 'He's away for the duration,' her mam had said. 'Stupid beggar.'

'He's not a stupid beggar,' Cath had said and got a slap for her pains.

At school, the others said nasty things about her daddy but Cath knew they weren't true. So she just didn't listen. He was a good man and he *was* a hero. What she didn't like was when the other girls started saying her mam had a fancy man. They would make a ring round her and skip and jeer and sing it out loud, 'A fancy man, a fancy man, your mam's got a fancy man!' The last time Cath had bunched up her fists and ran at the ring, bursting out and knocking Joan Prescott down as she did so. Joan had screamed and cried and Miss High had made her stand in the corner all afternoon with her face to the wall.

'It's not fair,' Cath had said mutinously.

'Remember sticks and stones,' Miss High had replied.

All afternoon Cath had repeated to herself, 'Sticks and stones may break my bones but calling cannot hurt me.'

Annie whimpered and stirred in her sleep. It was very dark in the bedroom and no light filtered up from the kitchen because, although Mam had left the gas on when she went, the penny in the meter had dropped and the gas had gone off. If Cath shut her eyes very tightly then she could pretend the light was on really so as not to be so frightened. Mam said she was soft for being afraid of the dark.

At last Cath felt drowsy and she drifted off to sleep. But then the siren at the pit started to blow and the wailing sound filled the room. Annie woke up and started to cry and Cath hugged her for a minute.

'Whisht, babby,' she said as she had done when Annie

was a little baby and Annie clung to her and cried for her mammy. Cath was crying too; it was ages since the siren went off but Cath knew it meant bombs would be coming and if one hit the house it would squash her and Annie. She climbed out of bed and pulled the pillows off and a blanket too and pushed them underneath, then did the same with Annie's but Annie didn't want to go and she fought back and screamed with fear.

Still, at last Cath had them both under the bed lying on the proddy mat and with the blanket over them. The siren had gone silent and nothing was happening and Cath thought maybe it was all right but then she heard the aeroplane, the engine loud overhead. Cath trembled and then she felt a sudden warm wetness as Annie wet herself and Cath's nightie as well.

The all-clear sounded, a long continous sort of whistle and Cath pulled Annie out from under the bed and took off her wet clothes though Annie was whimpering with fatigue and shivering too. She put a clean nightie on her and found an old dress to put on herself because she didn't have a clean nightie and they climbed back into bed. At least they were dry, Cath thought, as she cuddled in her sister. They were worn out and soon they were asleep.

Neither of the children heard their mother come back into the house, giggling a little and shushing the man with her.

'Quiet, man,' she whispered loudly. 'Don't wake the bairns. Our Cath's a proper little telltale and she'll tell her dad first chance she gets.'

'I'll be quiet as a mouse,' Keith promised and they tiptoed up the stairs past the open door of the children's room to the other bedroom at the front.

'Well, lad,' said the sergeant. He had marched down the ward and now stood by the side of Alf's bed looking down on him. Alf tensed and his foot throbbed right up to his hip and beyond. His wound was infected and they had given

33

him M and B sulphur tablets because the penicillin was reserved for the officers. He hoped desperately they would work though, he didn't want to lose his foot, did he? Sadie had a horror of any sort of disfigurement. He looked up at the sergeant through a haze of pain.

'Sergeant?'

'You're off the hook, lad,' said the sergeant. 'The powers that be have decided that there is insufficient evidence to court-martial you. You can count yourself bloody lucky, that's what I think.'

'I didn't to anything,' said Alf. 'I wouldn't. I was two years in the desert, wasn't I? I'm no coward, Sergeant.'

'Aye well, that's all right then,' replied the sergeant woodenly.

'What will happen now, Sarge?'

'Captain Rutherford will be in to see you, he'll tell you.'

Captain Rutherford was the man appointed to look into Alf's case. He was not Alf's commanding officer – he and his men had already embarked for foreign fields.

He'd be going home, thought Alf. That was what he had wanted, wasn't it? Now he wasn't so sure. He'd been a bloody fool, that was the truth.

'You'll be pleased to know you can have visitors now, Private. Your wife will be coming in.'

Alf opened his eyes. Sister was at the bottom of the bed.

'My wife cannot be coming right down here, Sister,' Alf replied. 'She has two bairns.'

'Catterick is not the end of the world, Private,' Sister replied before giving him two codeine tablets, smiling dismissively and moving on to the next bed.

It might as well be, thought Alf, as he closed his eyes again and waited for the pain to ease.

When he postman brought the letter from Catterick, Sadie stood with it in her hand, staring at it. She dreaded what it might tell her, that Alf was sentenced to prison for years, that he might even be going to die. Her heart thudded in her breast and her hand trembled.

'Is it from Daddy?' asked Cath.

'No, it's from the army,' said Sadie. The address was typewritten and the envelope a coarse brown, recycled paper. Sadie hated brown envelopes; they usually were bad news, like a bill or telling of a cut in the rations. But this was from the army and they might have stopped his pay because he was in such trouble.

'I'll open it if you like,' said Cath and held out her hand. But Sadie slapped it away with such a sharp blow that Cath's hand stung.

'I'll open it myself,' cried Sadie. 'Mind your own business, you sly little cat.' Cath rubbed at the red mark that had come up on her hand.

Sadie opened the envelope and took out the single sheet. She read it through slowly, mouthing the words, like a little child. Then she read it again as though she hadn't believed it the first time and smiled.

'Is Daddy coming home?' Cath ventured. Please God, let it be that Daddy was coming home. She clutched Annie who had come to her and was leaning against her leg with her thumb in her mouth.

Sadie opened her arms and grabbed at them both and danced around the room with them, laughing. 'They think it was an accident, a real accident!' she cried and laughed and hugged the two children. 'I can go to see him tomorrow.'

'Is he all right? Is he better, Mam? Can we go?' Cath asked breathlessly when the wild careering round the room stopped.

'No, you can't go, it's a long way is Catterick. Anyroad, I couldn't afford the fare for you an' all. And I don't think they let kids in. You'll have to stop at home and mind the bairn.'

Cath was crushed. She sat down and tried to hide her disappointment. Annie was still laughing with her mam though she wasn't quite sure what it was all about.

'Aw, don't look so bloody miserable our Cath,' Sadie snapped. 'You look like a wet week. Hadaway down the store and get a packet of biscuits, I've enough points left on the ration card. We'll have a bit of a treat after our dinner. Then you can mind the bairn while I go out this afternoon.'

She was going out with that Keith Armstrong, Cath knew it. Even though her daddy would be coming home soon. She walked down to the shop and stood in the queue with a sixpence clutched in one hand and the ration card in the other. The store had custard creams and the jammy biscuits with a hole in the middle and Cath dithered for a moment before choosing custard creams.

Mrs Holmes looked at her ration card when it came to her turn. 'You can have half a pound,' she said. 'If you have the money, that is.' She grinned knowingly at the women waiting in the queue. They all knew Sadie Raine and her spendthrift ways.

Cath handed over her sixpence, her face burning but she spoke up for herself. 'Half a pound for fourpence ha'penny, that's what it says. That's three ha'pence change.'

'Well,' said Mrs Holmes, 'so long as it hasn't to go on the slate.'

Cath ran back with the bag of biscuits, through the rows to Smith Street. Mam had made a sort of stew with corned beef and onions, carrots and potatoes and even put in a few dumplings. The dumplings were lovely, though a bit hard to chew because Sadie was unused to cooking much since Alf went away and she had no suet; but still, she added a bit margarine and the meal was lovely. She saved half the custard creams to take to the hospital for Alf.

'I have to take something, haven't I?' she asked and Cath nodded. 'Can I get some sweets with the change? We've plenty sweet coupons,' she asked. 'It's only three ha'pence.'

Sadie was in such a good mood that she nodded. She was putting on her eyebrow pencil at the time, standing near to

36

the fire to look up into the mirror over the mantel and it took all of her concentration to get the line straight.

It was a lovely day even though Cath couldn't go to see her daddy. After her mam went off on the bus from the end of the rows she and Annie walked back to the shop. They went along the short cut on the play field between the sandpit and the clay hole and along by the trenches the Home Guard had dug to practise in. Annie ran about and jumped and Cath warned her not to fall in one of the trenches and they they were out on the road. It was hot and tar bubbled up at the sides of the tarmac, black and shining in the sun.

They bought two ha'penny sherbet dips and a ha'porth of treacle toffee and wandered back home sucking at the sticky toffee. Cath thought about her daddy coming home and it was as good as the day when Russia came into the war and everyone was happy about it because Russia was so big and now she was on their side.

Sadie walked up the ward towards Alf and every eye in the ward was turned to watch her. She practically bounced rather than walked; she had touched up her hair with peroxide and it fell on her shoulders like Veronica Lake's and a Robin Hood hat with a jaunty feather sat over one eye. She had seen it in Doggart's window in Auckland and gone into raptures over it and of course Keith had bought it for her. That was before she told him that Alf was coming home.

Keith had been in a terrible temper after that. He'd said he wouldn't give her up and he would come round to the house and tell that damned coward what he could do about it.

'Oh, go to hell,' Sadie had told him. She almost threw the bag with the hat in at him but reconsidered just in time. Anyway, it had given her a good excuse to finish with him altogether. 'I mean,' she said to herself, 'look what Alf did to himself and all for me.'

All this went through her mind as she walked down the

ward, smiling at the patients on either side. And there was Alf, her lovely man. Though he didn't look very lovely at the minute. Pale and wan he looked and there were lines around his eyes that hadn't been there before.

'Eeh, Alf, pet,' she cried and flung herself on him, kissing him over and over and leaving red smudges on his face from her lipstick. 'How are you feeling? I knew you didn't do it on purpose, I knew you didn't!' She took a hankie from her handbag and rubbed at the marks. 'Sorry, pet, you're all lipstick,' she laughed.

In spite of everything that had happened Alf felt a surge of feeling for her, the sexy smell of her, the sight of the top of her breasts as she leaned forward and her blouse fell open showing the white skin.

'Gerroff, man,' he said gruffly and pushed her hand away. 'Don't make a show of me!'

'Aren't you glad to see me, Alf?'

'Yes, of course I am, it's not much fun lying here on your own when all the others have visitors,' he replied. Sadie's big blue eyes filled with tears.

'You don't care any more,' she said.

'Aye I do, just don't take on, like,' said Alf. He patted her hand. 'I'll be coming home next week, the doctor said I could.'

'Will you be going back, Alf?'

Sadie's mood changed quicker than the weather now she had Alf's reassurance.

'Depends on the foot,' said Alf. Now he'd had time to think, he regretted having done what he did. The fact was, he missed the lads of the D.L.I. and now they had landed on Sicily and were advancing he wanted to be part of it. As if to remind him that this wasn't likely now his foot started to throb. 'They likely won't want anything to do with me now any road,' he said glumly. 'Not me marras, like.'

'I don't want you to go, Alf,' said Sadie. 'The bairns miss you an' all.'

'Aw, don't be so soft,' Alf replied. 'Some of me marras

38

have been away for years. How d'you think their women cope? They do, that's all.'

'I know that, Alf,' said Sadie. She cast around in her mind for a good reason why it was worse for her and found one. 'I think I might be expecting another bairn, Alf.' She looked at him sideways through lashes thick with mascara.

'You what?'

'It's true, Alf. I told you to be careful, didn't I?'

'Bloody hell,' said Alf. 'And are you going to get rid of this one? Sell the poor little bugger, will you?'

'No, Alf, I wouldn't!'

'Not if I'm at home you won't,' said Alf and grasped her wrist hard so that she squealed.

'Let go, you're hurting me!'

'I'll hurt you all right,' Alf said savagely. But he let go of her wrist and lay back on his pillows. He had always boasted that he had never hit a woman but by, she brought him close to it, she did.

'Is it mine? Tell us the truth, now.'

'Why aye it's yours, who else's would it be?' Sadie opened her eyes as wide as they would go and gazed at him. 'You know you were there all right, don't you?'

Alf stared back at her. Her expression was open, she looked outraged. Below the line of the bed her fingers were crossed. He couldn't see them but he knew it. He knew her through and through.

An orderly came to the door of the ward and rang a bell.

'Time!' he shouted.

'Oh, Alf,' Sadie whispered, her blue eyes filling with tears. 'I won't see you till next week now.' She leaned over the bed and kissed him on the lips. Her full breasts brushed against his arm and he felt a surge of desire despite the ache in his foot. He glanced around at the other men to see if anyone had noticed her display of affection but they all seemed to be occupied with their own leavetakings.

'I might be home by then,' he said, pulling his arm away from her.

Sadie stood up straight. 'You do believe me, don't you?' she asked. 'This bairn is yours, Alf.'

'Aye well,' said Alf, his tone noncommittal.

After she'd gone he found the packet of Woodbines in his top drawer and took one out. He lit it with the lighter made from a rifle bullet and took such a long drag at it that the cigarette burned half-way down, the tip glowing brightly. He held it with the lighted end turned inward towards the palm of his hand, hiding the glow from any enemy automatically.

Another bairn, he thought. He had to stay now and when his foot healed he would have to go back down the pit. But by heck, Sadie would have to behave herself after all he had been through; she would an' all.

Chapter Five

'I told you not to come back any more.'

Cath was pulling handfuls of the long grass, which grew behind the rackety old shed where Marina's dad kept his hens. At least, he used to keep his hens there before he went off to the Middle East but now old Mr Peart from West Row came up and looked after them. The grass was for the rabbits that her dad kept in the yard. He'd just got the rabbits this week and they were small, with lovely black and white fur and Cath loved to feed them.

She paused now and looked towards the corner of the shed where the voice had come from. Her mam's voice it was and she sounded a bit panicky.

'I had to come, Sadie,' a man's voice said and Cath felt her heart beat rapidly in her chest. It was the Canadian flyer.

Cath glanced over her shoulder at the path that led up at the bottom of the gardens where the old wagon way used to be. Supposing her dad came up that way from the club?

'Well, you can just go back to Darlington,' said Sadie. But she didn't sound angry or anything. Not like she did when Cath went somewhere she wasn't supposed to go. It was very quiet except for the clucking and scratching of the chickens in the wire-enclosed dirt run.

'Sadie, I can't forget you,' said Keith. 'I was on a raid last night and all I could think of was getting back and seeing you again.'

'Don't be daft, Keith' said Sadie. 'I'm married.'

'So you were before,' said Keith. 'Look at him, will you, honey? He's a cripple for God's sake! He'll never amount to anything.'

'Don't you say nowt about my Alf,' said Sadie, her voice sharper now. Cath peeked around the corner. They were standing close together, the man with Canada strips on his shoulders and her mam. She pulled back quickly and held her breath as her mam turned her head and looked towards her. But Mam must not have seen her for she carried on talking.

'You'll have to go, Alf will be coming home,' Sadie said. 'Go on and don't come back.'

'I'll go,' Keith said. 'But I'll be back, I promise you. I'm not going to give up.' Cath shrank against the wall as he strode away along the path to Coundon. After a moment Cath heard the engine of his MG roar into life and then fade into the distance. He must have left it where the path met the top road.

'Now, madam, what are you doing hiding behind there? Waggling your ears again so that you can tell your dad? You sneaky little bitch, you'd better not or I'll swing for you, I will, I'm telling you.'

Cath had been wrong, Mam had seen her; she must have done for she bent over her and grabbed her forearm in a painful grip and pulled her to her feet. Bits of grass floated to the ground as Sadie swung back her arm and fetched Cath a blow across the ear that made her head ring. For a minute the pain was blinding and Cath closed her eyes tight and dug her teeth into her top lip but she didn't cry.

Sadie bent until her face was cose to Cath's. 'You'd best keep your mouth shut, hadn't you, my lass? Never saw a thing, did you?'

Cath shook her head, more to clear it than in answer to Sadie. Opening her eyes, she saw the figure of her father in the distance, walking up the dirt path of the old wagon way.

'Mind what I said now,' Sadie warned. She went up the garden to the house and Cath squatted down with her head bent over. She started to pull at the grass and to stuff in into the sack.

'Is that for the rabbits? You're a good lass,' her father's voice came from just above her and she sat down on her bottom and looked up at him. 'Have you been crying? he asked. 'Your ear looks red.'

'I fell and bumped it on a stone,' said Cath.

'Aye well, no need to weep over it,' he said. 'I've seen many a man in the desert with worse than that and he hasn't blared about it.'

'I'm not blaring,' said Cath. She gazed up at Alf. His foot was out of plaster now and he walked with a stick but she wouldn't have said he was a cripple. 'Is your foot going to get better altogether, Dad?'

'I expect so,' Alf replied. 'I'll be good as new in a week or two. Are you coming back to feed the rabbits now?'

'In a minute. I want to dig up some worms for the hens first.' Cath watched as he limped up the garden path. It wasn't much of a limp, she thought; he *wasn't* a cripple! She went over to the wire netting enclosing the hen run and began digging outside it for worms. The hens clucked exc-itedly and came over to her. She found a few worms and pushed them through the netting and the hens scrambled for them. But then she began to wonder what it was like for the worms and stopped. Might as well go back and feed the rabbits, she thought. She rubbed her ear absent-mindedly as she trailed the sack up the path, around to the end of the row and in the back yard to the rabbits.

'Cath? Howay in, lass, there's news,' Alf called from the back door. He was beaming as he disappeared back into the kitchen. Cath dropped the sack by the rabbit hutch and brushed bits of grass off her dress before following him in.

'Who's a clever clogs then? Winning a scholarship to the grammar school!' Sadie greeted her. The letter was on the table, a page of recycled paper headed DURHAM

COUNTY COUNCIL. It was lying on the American oilcloth among the dirty plates from dinnertime.

She picked it up and read it through. It was true, the council was offering her a scholarship to Bishop Auckland Girls' County School. Elation flooded her, she could hardly wait to get back to school to see who else was going with her.

'Well, don't get too excited,' said Mam.

'What do you mean?' Dad demanded.

'Well, she can't go, can she? We can't afford it for a start. Not with you on the sick, like.'

'Aye, she'll go,' said Dad. 'I'm not going to be on the sick for ever, am I? An' I'll get my discharge from the army and go back down the pit. There's plenty of pit work. Why, they're crying out for hewers. And the pay's not so bad now.'

'They might decide you can go back to the army,' said Mam.

Cath looked from one to the other, they seemed to have forgotten her as they argued.

'If they do you'll get your allowance, won't you?'

'Such as it is,' said Mam, her tone scathing. 'She would have to have a uniform an' all. Where's that coming from?'

Sadie turned to Cath as though the necessity for the uniform was the decisive argument. That was it, she couldn't go to the grammar school. 'Wash the pots up Cath and be quick about it. It's nearly time for our teas.'

Cath gazed at her dad imploringly. He was looking at her mam as though he hated her. But she knew it would be her mam who made the final decision and it looked as though she had already done so. She brought the washing-up bowl and poured a ladle full of water in it from the boiler by the side of the fire and added Rinso and washing soda, swishing it around before washing the plates and cups and putting them on the tin tray which served as a draining board. She dried the pots and put them away and took the dirty water to the sink in the yard and poured it away.

44

'I'll talk to her, Cath,' said her dad. He was squatting on his hunkers by the coal-house wall smoking a Woodbine and watching her.

'It won't do any good,' said Cath dully.

'Yes, it will,' he replied. 'It'll be all right. Any road, at least you know you were good enough to be picked. That's something, isn't it?'

'Dad!'

Alf got to his feet and shrugged before walking to the gate. 'I'm just going for a walk,' he said. 'Tell your mam I won't be long.'

Cath put down the bowl by the sink and walked over to the rabbit hutch. She fed the rabbits with the grass she had pulled earlier and stood watching them eat through the wire grille on the door. They snuffled and their noses twitched as they ate busily. The had nothing to worry about except eating and sleeping, she thought. But they had, of course; they were prisoners. She made sure the catch on the hutch was closed properly then picked up the washing-up bowl and took it back inside. Then she backed to the door again and looked straight at her mam.

'Mam, I am going to the grammar school,' she said. She was poised to run up the yard and away should her mother chase after her or throw the black lead brush she was using to brush up the range at her. Sadie had done that before. Sadie smiled.

'Lady, you're asking for it,' she shouted. 'Don't you dare tell me what you're going to do or not going to do.'

Cath felt sick and she could feel a pulse beating wildly in her throat but she stood her ground. 'If you don't let me go to the grammar school, I will tell Dad all about Keith. And I will tell the bobbie about the other baby, the one before Timmy.'

Before Sadie could erupt in rage she turned and flew out of the yard and ran and ran, past the ends of the rows of pit houses and along the road to the path, which went up past Coundon. She didn't stop until she was at the entrance

45

to Eden Grange Hall. She stopped there because she had such a stitch in her side it bent her double and she could only breathe in retching, painful gasps. She looked into the park. The drive curved in until it was out of sight behind the trees. The house was out of sight too so no one could stare in, she supposed.

The wrought-iron gates had been taken off in 1940 to go to the war effort along with all the other railings in Eden Hope and so she was able to creep just inside the park and collapse down by old, sun-warmed bricks of the high perimeter wall.

The pain in her chest eased slowly and she hugged her knees and put her head down on them. She didn't care if her mam murdered her, she thought. She didn't care if she gave her away like she had done with Timmy. She just didn't care about anything at all, no, she did not. She closed her eyes and the sun dipped behind the trees so that they cast long shadows across the grass.

'Who are you? You can't sleep there, girl, come on, you'll have to go home.'

Cath sprang to her feet and swayed slightly so that she had to put out a hand to the wall to steady herself.

'Are you all right?' The voice became anxious and she looked up at the man. He was outlined against the setting sun, which struck through the trees so that he was hard to see at first, the sun shining like a halo around his head. He was carrying a gun, she saw, but it didn't worry her. After all, the Home Guard all had guns.

'I'm fine,' said Cath then added, 'sir,' as a precaution. Not that the man was dressed at all posh like the toffs she had seen on the pictures but neither was he dressed like a miner. He was wearing corduroy trousers reaching to just below the knee and a tweed jacket with leather patches on the elbows and he had a funny hat on his head. The gun was broken over his arm and had a double barrel. Cath saw all this in the first glance after the dizziness left her.

'You're trespassing, young lady,' he said. She looked up

46

at him. His eyes were a lightish brown, not so dark as her own, and his hair, what she could see of it under the funny hat, was grizzled. He gazed sternly back at her.

'Are you the gamekeeper?' she asked. Cath had heard the off-shift miners talk about the gamekeeper as they sat on their hunkers on the end of the rows. They rolled badly shaped cigarettes with tiny amounts of baccy and smoked and talked. She was interested because she could roll them really well and did so for her dad. Cigarettes weren't on ration but they were short and the store allowed only a few per customer with the weekly rations.

Anyway, the miners had been chased by gamekeepers when they went snaring rabbits to eke out the meat ration. One, Mr Patton from West Row, had been caught by the gamekeeper and was up before the magistrates next week. All this flashed through her mind like lightning as she stood warily before the man with the gun.

'The gamekeeper? What do you know about game-keepers, girl?' He continued to look sternly down at her.

'Nothing, sir,' she replied.

'Where do you live?'

'Eden Hope Colliery, sir.'

He regarded her for a moment then said, 'Come with me and I'll show you a quick way back. It's getting too dark for little girls to be out and with no streetlights because of this damn war—'

'I'm not a little girl, I'm eleven. I'm going to the grammar school in September. And I can manage the road,' said Cath.

'Don't argue with me, girl,' he said and set off up the drive. After a moment's hesitation she followed him.

After about a quarter of a mile the big house loomed up ahead of them.

'We'll go round the back to the kitchen,' the man said. 'Cook will give you a piece of cake and then I'll show you the way home.'

The kitchen was big, as big as the schoolroom at the

Methodist chapel where Cath went on Sundays, dragging Annie with her so that her mam and dad could have a rest. There was a boy sitting at the kitchen table eating cake and drinking tea and Cath was soon sitting beside him and doing the same. She ate every crumb because she had missed her tea and besides, it was sponge cake, which she liked.

'When she is finished you can take her home, Jack,' the gamekeeper said.

'Aw, Dad,' said the boy 'I wanted—'

Whatever he wanted to do rather than take her home, Cath didn't find out. The gamekeeper just gave his son a stern glance and went through a door at the other end of the kitchen. The boy pulled a face.

'Hurry up then, I haven't got all night,' he said to the girl. She was still busy picking up every last crumb of cake with a wet finger but she stopped and lifted her chin.

'I can go myself, you don't have to go,' she said. 'If you just show me the short cut.' The boy was about fifteen, she reckoned, and thought he was the bee's knees, just like the lads in Eden Hope who had just started work in the pit and came out with black rims round their eyes.

'Come on,' he said getting to his feet. 'You heard my father.'

Cath was about to say the man wasn't *her father* but, looking at the boy's face, decided against it. After all, it was quite dark now and she would never find a short cut on her own. Without streetlights she might not even find the road.

'Thank you for the cake,' she said to the woman who had come into the kitchen and was sitting by the fire smiling. She must be the cook the gamekeeper had talked about. The woman nodded.

'Tell the gamekeeper thank you an' all,' said Cath and followed the boy out into the dark so she didn't see the cook's startled glance at Jack. It must be very late, Cath realised, what with double summertime an' all. Mam would clout her round the ear again. At least Dad would be home

48

and Mam wouldn't murder her for what she had said before she ran away.

Jack had a flashlight and he led the way to a path going steeply downhill a few yards from the house. Now and then he turned to make sure she was all right. He didn't speak so she decided to be saying something herself, just to keep out the strange noise coming from the undergrowth.

'I'm going to the grammar school in September,' she said. 'Do you go to King James?' King James was the boy's grammar school in the town.

'No, I don't,' he replied. 'Stop talking and watch where you're going.'

Cath stumbled after him and sure enough, they came to the road just above the rows in less than half the time it would have taken to go round the road.

'Go on, you'll be all right now,' he said and disappeared back up the path.

Chapter Six

'Where the hell have you been?'

Sadie and Alf started towards her from where they had been standing in front of the range. Sadie's hand lifted as she shouted and Cath's hand went up automatically to shield her ear.

'Let the lass speak before you hit her,' Alf warned. And Sadie stayed her hand.

'I went for a walk and got lost in the woods up by Coundon way,' said Cath, lifting her chin.

'Never thinking about us, worried to death about you and me having to see to Annie and everything.' Her fingers clenched into fists by her sides. She glared at Cath and Cath stared levelly back. After a moment Sadie turned away and the girl knew that some understanding had been reached.

'Howay in and get warmed,' said Alf. 'I've missed my pint at the club now, there'll be none left. I might as well stay in. Your mam's saved you some supper.'

Sadie took a plate out of the oven and to Cath's surprise she saw that Mam had made a pie, a Woolton pie filled with vegetables not meat but still, she had bothered to make pastry. There was Oxo gravy but it had dried up around the edges.

'You can eat it all up, spoilt or not,' said Sadie. 'We can't afford to waste food, there's a war on.'

'I won't waste it,' said Cath and picked up her knife and

fork and began to eat.

'Me and your dad, we've decided you can go to the grammar school,' said Sadie. She picked up the poker as she said it and stirred the embers in the grate, not looking at her daughter.

'Thank you, Mam,' said Cath and continued to eat.

'Is that all you have to say?' her father demanded. 'Do you not want to go? You were keen enough this morning.'

'Aye, I do want to go,' said Cath. She tried to show some enthusiasm for his sake but suddenly she was just too tired. 'Where's our Annie?'

'In bed where you should be,' snapped her mother. 'Mind, I hope you know the rest of us will be having to do without things so you can go to your fancy school. You might at least show some appreciation.'

'I'm pleased, Mam, really I am,' said Cath. She cleaned her plate with a bit of bread and then stood up. 'Can I go to bed now?'

'Aw, hadaway now,' said Sadie.

Once in bed, Cath lay by Annie, feeling the small warm body by her side. She could hear the murmur of voices downstairs as her parents talked. After a while the back door opened and closed and her father's footsteps went up the yard. He must have gone to the club any way, hoping there might be a drop of beer left.

'Don't think I'll forget this, our Cath, you ungrateful little bugger,' her mam's voice came from the doorway. Cath closed her eyes tightly, pretending to be asleep. She thought about the gamekeeper and his son. Jack, the man had called him.

Jack was tall with fair hair and hazel eyes like his father. He would have had a pleasant face if he learned to smile, she thought drowsily. As it was he was a right miserable-faced lad. Thought he was something special an' all, better than her, she could tell. Well, he wasn't. He didn't even go to King James Grammar, he must not have been good enough to pass the scholarship. She fell asleep smiling at

51

the thought and slept through the night.

Friday, 3 September 1943 was a very important day for Cath. The war was four years old to the day and, almost as if to celebrate it, the Eighth Army landed on the mainland of Europe; the toe of Italy, to be exact. That was the headline in the *Daily Herald* anyway. Cath read it as she sipped her tea and ate a slice of plum jam and bread for breakfast before they went into Auckland to buy her school shoes. The shoes were what really made it an important day for Cath. She had been thinking she wasn't going to get them in time for school which started on Monday.

Aunty Patsy had a sewing machine and she had made her a tunic in the bottle green that was the school colour and Mam had got her a hat and coat from the second-hand stall in the school when they had gone to the open day. By this time Sadie was quite proud of having a daughter going to the grammar school and took care to let everyone she spoke to know about it.

'By heck, I wish I was there with them,' Alf said wistfully. In his mind he pictured the lads of the D.L.I. racing up the beach in warm and sunny Italy. In the north-east of England, autumn had already begun and it was raining and blustery.

'Don't be so soft, Alf,' snapped Sadie. 'Your place is here, man, look at the size of me.' Her belly was sticking out a bit, thought Cath, looking at her mother. Maybe it was a big baby.

'Many a soldier's wife manages on her own in this war,' Alf reminded her.

'Aye well, I wouldn't have to but for you,' Sadie whined. 'Anyroad, you can mind the bairn.'

'I cannot, man,' Alf protested. 'I have to go to see the manager, haven't I?' He was starting at the pit on Monday. Not Eden Hope or even Winton but the pit at Chilton, seven miles away. The miners had to go where they were told during the present emergency. It meant walking up to

Coundon and getting a bus from there. Alf regretted the incident with the pick bitterly.

'She'll have to come with us then, won't she?' Sadie replied sharply. 'Cath, get our Annie ready.'

They were walking down Newgate Street towards Benton's department store, for Sadie had taken out a five-pound club with them, when Cath saw the boy, Jack again. He was in a large car and sitting beside a woman with a fancy hat on, not a headscarf as most of the women were reduced to wearing. It sailed up Newgate Street towards the station and as it passed Jack stared straight at her, then gravely inclined his head.

'All right for some, isn't it?' Sadie demanded of Cath. 'Some folk can get petrol coupons.'

'They'd be no use to us anyroad,' Cath protested. 'We haven't got a car nor the money to buy petrol if we had.'

'No but Keith—' Sadie stopped and looked sideways at her daughter. Cath hadn't seen or heard anything about Keith since the time she saw him with Sadie on the cinder path. Surely her mam wasn't still meeting him? No, she couldn't be, not when she had got so fat with the baby. Her mam was very proud of her figure normally.

'Look at them, even the lad,' Sadie was saying. 'They think they are bloody royalty, bowing their heads to the peasants.'

She glared venomously after the car as it went on up the street, making slow progress because the shoppers had got into the habit of wandering across the road all the time, since most people's cars were laid up for the duration.

'He's the gamekeeper's son,' said Cath. 'I met him once.'

'Oh aye, where did you meet a lad like him? Don't make up so many stories, our Cath, or them teachers will have you out of that school as soon as look at you. I mean it, no more lies!'

Cath opened her mouth to protest it wasn't a lie but Sadie was turning into the door of Benton's and Cath and Annie had to hurry to follow her. It wasn't very often they got to go in the big shop and especially not to buy anything.

Jack and the lady descended from the high step of the car at the station.

'Wait here, Joseph,' she ordered her driver. 'Master Jack can carry his own case.'

Joseph was an old man. Retired, he had been called back into service when the younger men of the estate had gone to the services. His son, Martin, had been a pilot with the RAF but was missing over Germany.

'Yes m'lady,' he replied. He sat in the chauffeur's seat of the Rolls-Royce and watched as a group of soldiers hurried through to the platform. Steam from the train swirled down and along the cobbles in front of the station before dispersing in the wind. Joseph wished for the thousandth time that the war was over. Then he wouldn't have to go back to an afternoon working in the vegetable patch behind the Hall or drive this dratted car again. Maybe, just maybe, he and his wife, Meg, would hear just what had happened to Martin. The familiar heartache settled on him like a blanket.

Jack was standing at the door of the first-class compartment. 'I shouldn't have to go to school, Mother,' he said. 'Other boys my age are working to help the war effort.'

'Don't be silly, Jack,' said his mother. 'By the time you are old enough for that the war will be over, thank God.'

Jack watched moodily from his corner seat in the first-class carriage as the train picked up speed and hurried towards Shildon Tunnel. That was what he was afraid of, he thought as they chugged into the dark tunnel. That the war would be over before he had a chance to do anything. Joseph's son Martin, now, he was barely three years older than Jack himself and there he was in the RAF. No, he corrected himself and blinked as the train came out into the light. Martin was missing over Germany. But that didn't mean he was dead. He was probably having a great adventure hiding from the Jerries. Briefly he thought of his own brother, Aiden, killed a year ago. Well, there was no use in thinking of it.

A picture popped into his mind of the girl his father had brought into the kitchen that evening. She had been walking down Newgate Street today, towing another, tiny child. They were with a woman, poorly dressed and with a painted face, the sort his mother warned him against. She must have been the girl's mother. Somehow, the girl's face stuck in his mind. She had such big dark eyes and hair, hair that was almost black like a gypsy's, her eyes were bright, vivid, full of interest in everything.

Jack sighed. He didn't know why he was giving her even a moment's thought, she was just a miner's brat. He looked out on to the fields. They were coming into Darlington where he was to change for York. He would have to fight his way off the train for there were soldiers filling the corridors, sitting on their kitbags or leaning out of the windows. The air was thick with cheap tobacco smoke and Jack grimaced.

Cath had forgotten all about Jack and the fancy motor car in her excitement at choosing new shoes. Not that there was a lot to choose from, only two styles in her size were in the shop apart from some with wooden soles like Dutch clogs. No coupons were needed for these and Cath rather fancied them but the school had said brown leather lace-ups. Only one pair of the shoes fitted this description. Still, Cath was delighted with them. She held them, wrapped in plain paper in one hand and held on to Annie with the other while Mam bought some steel studs for dad to hammer into the toes and heels to save cobbler's bills.

They came out into the market place and looked for the bus that went to Shildon. They were to pick up Cath's new school tunic from Aunty Patsy's before they went home.

'Fancy seeing you here!'

55

Cath had been looking at the apples on the fruit and vegetable stall by the bus stop. They were the only fruit on the stall; it was a long time since she had seen oranges or bananas, in fact she could barely remember them. But the apples looked lovely, green with a red blush on one side. There was a queue though. Mam would never stand in a queue, not for apples.

Now Cath looked up at her mother's exclamation. The Canadian flyer stood before them, dressed in muftie. Even in a suit he stood out among the people around him. They were shabby even in their best clothes compared to Keith in his tweed suit.

For Cath it was as though a cloud had suddenly covered the sun. She scowled at him even as he held out two apples he must have bought on the stall.

'Go on, take it,' Mam commanded her. She pushed Cath in the shoulder and Cath took the apple. She gazed down at it. She didn't want it now.

'I'm not hungry,' she said.

'Aw, don't be daft, our Cath. Course you are. Go on, get on the bus, I'm coming in a minute.'

Cath helped Annie climb on to the bus and up the stairs to the top deck. Annie wasn't eating her apple either. She was staring out of the window at her mother and Keith with an anxious expression.

'Mammy come?' she asked Cath fearfully but at that moment the driver started his engine and Sadie stepped on with Keith behind her. They clattered up the stairs and Sadie sank on to the seat behind the children, slightly out of breath.

'You OK, honey?' Keith inquired as he sat down beside her.

'I am now. Though why you had to come up those dratted stairs I don't know, our Cath,' Sadie scolded. Satisfied, Annie began to eat her apple, looking out of the window as she bit into it. Cath sat staring at the one in her hand. Behind her she could hear her mother and Keith whispering together, her mother giggling sometimes, Keith giving a low chuckle.

'Tickets please.' The conductor came up the stairs, puffing a little and limping. He must have a bad leg like her dad, Cath thought dimly. That would be why he wasn't in the army an' all.

'Two to Darlington and a half to Shildon,' said Keith.

'What?' asked Cath, turning round in shock rather than surprise.

'You can take our Annie to Aunty Patsy's, can't you?' Her mother's eyes were challenging. 'Get your tunic then walk down the bank and over to Eden Hope. It's a lovely day for a walk.'

'But—'

'Don't argue with me, our Cath, do as you're told. Your dad's out but the door will be open. I'll be back later. I won't be long. And there's no need to say anything to anybody, is there?' Sadie nodded her head up and down meaningfully. She glanced out of the window. 'Go on now, this is the stop. Watch the bairn going down those steps. I told you you should have stayed downstairs.'

Cath got down from the seat and Annie began to cry, a frightened and bewildered cry. A woman in front turned round and stared. 'Why don't you come?' Cath asked.

'Aw go on, I have something to do. Go on, take the bairn, the bus is stopping now, you'll miss the stop.'

As Cath dragged Annie down the winding steps of the bus she could hear her mother telling the woman to keep her nose out of it, her kids were fine. The children reached the bus platform at last and the conductor lifted Annie off on to the pavement.

'Are you all right now, pet?' he asked Cath and she nodded.

'We're going to Aunty Patsy's', she told him. As they walked along the pavement she looked up at the bus window. Her mother was looking out and she smiled and waved. From a few seats in front of her mother the woman

57

was also staring out at them.

'Where's Mammy gone?' Annie asked. She had stopped crying but her eyes were red and snot was running down her upper lip. Cath found a clean rag in her pocket and wiped it.

'She's coming back,' she said. 'Come on, Aunty Patsy will have made our dinners. You're hungry, aren't you?'

It wasn't a long walk to her aunt's house but it was uphill and round a side alley. There was a sort of tunnel running through to Bell's Building that opened out on to a short street of little houses with privies on the end.

'I want a wee,' Annie suddenly wailed and Cath ran with her but of course they were too late and Annie had wet her pants.

'Oh Annie, I've no clean knickers with me,' said Cath as they went into the house. Patsy peered round the children.

'Where's your mam?'

'She had to go to Darlington,' Cath replied.

'Darlington? What the heck for?'

'She went with the man,' said Annie. 'I wee'd my knickers, Aunty Patsy.'

'A big girl like you, how old are you?' Patsy demanded. 'Four is it? Well, never mind. Howay here and I'll rinse them out and dry them.' She took off Annie's knickers and rinsed them in a bucket under the cold-water tap by the back door then hung them on the short line outside. All the time she was grumbling about her sister.

'Just like her, the little slut!' she said. 'Who's she gone off with now? Is is that Canadian, our Cath? By, that lass doesn't deserve kids. I bet Alf knows nowt about it. He wants to bat her over the ear a few times, bring her to her senses.'

Patsy had no children of her own. Her husband, Jim, worked at the munitions factory at Aycliffe. He was much older than Patsy but nice, Cath thought.

By the time Annie's knickers were dry they had eaten their dinner, corned beef stew and sandwiches filled with

58

golden syrup because Patsy had no butter or margarine to spare from the rations. But the bread was lovely, fresh and homemade and the sandwiches tasted good.

'You'd best go home now,' said Patsy. 'You'll have to walk because the bus doesn't go for another two hours and it will be getting dark by then. You'll be all right, won't you?' She bit her lip as she looked at Cath. By, our Sadie, she thought. The poor kid had had to grow up fast with that one for a mother. But she had to be in for Jim coming home from the factory and then she had to go to work herself. Patsy was an usherette at the Majestic pictures.

Cath and Annie walked down the black path that had been part of the old Stockton and Darlington railway before they built Shildon Tunnel. It was very quiet and Annie tailed behind, tired and out of sorts, so that by the time they finally got to Eden Hope Colliery Cath was carrying her as well as the bag with her tunic. As she went up the back yard it was already dusk. No light showed inside but then the blackout curtains were supposed to stop that anyway. But inside there was no light on to block and the fire was just a pile of grey ash in the grate.

Chapter Seven

June 1944

Cath stood in the bus queue with the other girls, all dressed in bottle-green Burberry coats with pockets bulging where hats had been stuffed in them as soon as the girls came out of the gates. All except Cath's, that is, she had forgotten all about hers, she had forgotten she even had a hat on. She was off in a world of her own.

The United bus came in and the girls pushed and shoved their way on with boys in maroon blazers joining in. These were the boys from King James, laughing and boisterous and showing off to the girls. One of them snatched the hat from her head and threw it over the fence so she had to run round and through the gate to get it. When she got back the queue was gone and everyone was on the buses except the boy who had snatched her hat.

'Sorry,' he said. 'Hurry up get on, I waited for you.'

Cath favoured him with a frozen stare and they got on, crammed together like sardines.

'I said I was sorry,' said the boy. It was Brian Musgrave and he lived in Winton. She looked up at him, having to lift her face they were so close. He was blushing, she saw, and had a funny look in his eyes. Brian was older and taller than she was; his father had come home from Tunisia with only one arm but he held down the job of manger at the Co-operative store.

'You're just stupid,' said Cath as they were pushed even closer together at the stop at South Church when some people squeezed past to get off the bus. Brian's face went an even deeper red, contrasting with his fair hair and blue eyes.

'Will you go for a walk with me after tea?' he blurted out.

Cath stared at him in amazement then put her nose in the air. 'I will not,' she said.

'I could call for you.'

'No. And move away from me, there's plenty of room now they've got off.'

Cath gazed determinedly away from him until he got off the bus at Winton. She found an empty seat and glanced out of the window and there he was, staring at her.

'Brian's soft on you,' Enid Brown, who was sitting beside her, said and giggled.

'It's you that's soft,' Cath replied and stood up ready to alight at Shildon.

It was her mother's birthday, she thought as she walked up Auckland Road to the opening to Bell's Buildings. Her mother's birthday and she couldn't even send her a card because she didn't have her address. The afternoon sun shone warm along the road but Cath hardly noticed the weather. She wished with all her heart she was going up the rows to her mam and dad but she wasn't, she was going to Bell's Buildings and Aunty Patsy and Uncle Jim. And Annie, of course.

Everything had changed when Mam ran off with Keith Armstrong. She remembered that night when she had taken Annie home to the dark house. Her mam hadn't come back like she had promised. She had gone away to the south; there had been a letter on the high mantelshelf. Dad had found it when he came in. He had groped for his brass lighter, made from a bullet case and there it was. Keith was being moved to the south coast and she was going with him.

'Why didn't you tell us she was going?' he had shouted

at Cath. 'You knew didn't you, you little—'

'I didn't, I didn't!' Cath cried as he towered over her. She thought he was going to hit her. But then he had sort of crumpled, that was the only way she could think of it. He sat down on a hard kitchen chair and crumpled. He fingered the cigarette between his lips and tried to light it but his hand was trembling so much he couldn't and Cath had to do it for him.

Upstairs, Annie cried out and then was quiet. She must be having a bad dream, Cath thought dully. Like this one but this one was real.

'It was all for nowt,' he said. 'All for nowt.' He kept on repeating and then 'What about the babby?'

Cath thought of the other babby, Timmy, and she felt as though she was weeping inside but there were no tears. And there were no answers to her dad's question.

Alf stood up suddenly and pulled on his jacket and cap. 'Get yourself to bed, our Cath. If I stay in here much longer I'll go mad. I'm going down the club for a pint. If they have any left, that is.' He laughed mirthlessly.

Cath didn't bother to wash or clean her teeth. She went upstairs and pulled off her clothes and put on her nightie and climbed into bed beside Annie.

Now, as she opened the door of Aunty Patsy's house and went in, dropping her schoolbag in the tiny vestibule, her aunt's voice greeted her. It sounded so much like her mother's voice.

'Where the hell have you been? Daydreaming, I suppose, dawdling along like there was no tomorrow. As you usually do. Did you get the taties from the store like I asked you? No, you bloody well didn't, I can see you didn't. Well, you can just go back for them and be quick about it, Jim will be in for his tea in half an hour.' She aimed a slap across the top of Cath's head but Cath saw it coming and ducked, which enraged Patsy even further. 'Go on!' she yelled.

'Can I go?'

Annie was sitting by the fire, which was lit despite the

heat. A saucepan simmered on the bar.

'You stop here, pet, with your Aunty Patsy.' Patsy's tone had changed completely but then it always did when she spoke to Annie. She adored Annie.

Cath went back out into the sunshine and down the road and up the hill to the Co-operative store at the top. She bought the half-stone of potatoes and lugged them out and down the hill again. By the time she got back to the house her arm felt as though it had pulled out of its socket.

'Hurry up and get some peeled then,' her aunt greeted her, glaring resentfully; why she had no idea. Except that she wasn't welcome here. Aunty Patsy had changed since they came to live with her and Uncle Jim. Not towards Annie though. Annie was her favourite but that was all right. 'By, you're about as much use as a man off, our Cath,' said Patsy. It was a frequent complaint of hers. 'If you don't buck your ideas up I'll put you in the orphanage, I will, I'm telling you.'

Cath was only half listening. She had learned to close off her mind to Aunty Patsy's tirades. She didn't mean them anyway. Cath was too good a worker. She peeled the potatoes in an enamel dish on the table then cut them up and put them in a saucepan and set it to boil beside the other one. She set the table for the meal and filled the coal bucket ready for the night. When Uncle Jim came in they ate and afterwards Cath cleared the table and washed up. At last she was free to do her homework. She usually did this in the bedroom, away from the noise of the wireless. Uncle Jim listened to the news on the Home Service and then whatever was on the Forces network. He was a bit deaf and the volume would be turned up so that she could still hear it through the bare floorboards but not so much.

Cath finished her French for Naggie Aggie, the French mistress, and her algebra. Then Annie came up to bed and that was that. She would have to get up early in the morning to do her English essay. She might as well go to bed now, though it was still light with double summertime.

She lay beside Annie and allowed her thoughts to go back to that awful time after Mam went off with Keith.

'I can't bear to be parted from him,' her mam had written in the letter that her dad had thrust at her.

'Read that,' he had said in a dead sort of voice. 'Go on, read it. See what a whore your mother is, our Cath. Running after that bloody flier like the slut she is.'

Cath didn't know what a whore was except that it must be something bad and to do with going with men.

'The baby isn't yours, it's Keith's,' her mam had written. 'You can get a divorce if you like, I don't care. I couldn't bear letting him go to Kent without me.'

Careless words cost lives, thought Cath dully. There were posters on the buses warning about them. A Fifth Columnist could have got hold of the letter and then they would know where the Canadian airmen had gone. But what was going to happen now, with Mam gone?

Alf had started drinking, beer when he could get it and rum or anything else when he could get that. He'd been sent home from the pit for being drunk and then one day, near Christmas it was, he disappeared. Cath had come home from school and Annie was at Betty Lowe's house.

'Your dad's gone after your mam,' said Betty. Cath looked stricken, Betty thought pityingly, her eyes too big and showing her every feeling in her white face. That blooming Sadie Raine should be strung up from a lamppost, she reckoned. But something had to be done about the bairns.

'You'd best go to your aunty in Shildon with little Annie,' she advised. 'I'll give you the bus fare.' So they had gone back to Shildon after Cath wrote a note for her dad.

Cath turned over in bed as Annie stirred and whimpered. She put an arm around the little girl and murmured soothingly. At least Annie had stopped wetting the bed.

'Please, Jesus,' Cath prayed, closing her eyes tight. 'Please bring Mam and Dad back. Annie misses them too much and so do I.'

Overhead there was a droning of planes and Cath tensed. It was a long while since she had heard an enemy plane but still, you never knew. But no, they were British planes, she could tell by the sound they made. A lot of them too, going down south, she thought. Maybe they were going to invade France, everyone knew they would soon.

Next day the headmistress called a general assembly in the afternoon and they all sat cross-legged in the hall, which had parallel bars at the side and thick ropes hanging from the ceiling for it deputised as a gym.

'Today our troops landed on French beaches,' said Dr Agnew. 'It is a day that will do down in history. His Majesty, the king, has asked for general prayers to be said for the success of our gallant forces and fine weather to aid them.'

Cath sat between Joan and Enid with her hands together as the headmistress prayed but she couldn't help thinking of her dad. Was he in France too? Or was he in Kent with her mam and Keith? No, Keith wouldn't be there, he was probably in France too.

Her dad had sent her a letter saying he was going to join up again. He said his foot was all right now, he hardly limped at all. If he could work down the pit he could fight. But the man from the Ministry of Labour had said that he should not have left the pit, every experienced miner was needed. Coal was necessary to help the war effort.

Today the man from the Ministry of Labour had come to the house even before she set off for school. He was like a kiddy catcher but for grown-ups. He said her dad had been seen in Salisbury. He asked if Alf had been in touch, it would be an offence not to give the ministry his address. But of course they didn't have it anyway. Her dad had just disappeared, like a lot of fathers of girls she knew. 'Missing, believed killed'. Well, maybe not exactly like them but similar.

The other girls were scrambling to their feet. Dr Agnew had finished praying. They filed out to their different form rooms to collect their schoolbags ready for home.

Brian came to stand beside her in the queue for the bus. Cath tried to ignore him, turning away and staring over the boy's football field at the distant trees. Enid giggled and nudged Joan.

'I've made you something,' Brian said and held out a ring made from aeroplane glass. It had obviously started as a small square but he had rubbed off the sharp edges and smoothed it with sandpaper. The hole for her finger was almost a perfect circle and he had carved a fancy C on the top of it.

'Go on, take it, Cath,' said Enid. 'He's sweet on you, isn't he?' Brian was holding it out and the other boys were taking notice so in the end she took the ring and shoved it deep in her pocket.

'You're engaged,' jeered Enid and laughed. 'The soft lad.'

'Shut your mouth,' said Brian.

Really, he was quite handy, Cath thought as they crowded for the bus door. He got behind her and helped her push her way on so that she actually got a seat.

'You'll have to look after Annie today,' said Aunty Patsy. 'I'm going into Auckland for a day out. Your uncle Jim is working a full shift overtime so I might as well meet the girls.'

The girls, Patsy's friends, were middle-aged women but she still saw them as girls for she had gone to school with them. Sometimes they met and went to the pictures and afterwards to the Co-op tearooms for tea and cakes.

It was Saturday and Patsy had on her high-heeled shoes and her new utility costume. It had a short, tight skirt to save cloth and a close-fitting jacket. She also had a little hat tipped over one eye. Patsy had decorated it herself with a scrap of lace and a feather dyed red with cochineal.

'How do I look?' she asked, smiling. She patted her curls before the mirror over the fireplace.

'Very nice,' said Cath dutifully.

'Is that all? Nice?'

'Very smart, lovely,' said Cath for Aunty Patsy was frowning now and Cath didn't want a slap.

'I think so,' said Aunty Patsy as she picked up her handbag and gloves and, as an afterthought, a shopping bag. 'I'll bring something back for Jim's tea.'

An hour later Cath and Annie were walking down the old railway path towards Eden Hope Colliery. Annie was getting bigger now, she was five and had started school. She skipped along happily now, pleased to be out.

There were buttercups growing in the grass at the sides of the line and dandelions and daisies. Annie picked them as she went along. 'We'll put them in water when we get home,' Cath promised.

At Eden Hope they walked up the side of the rows to the ramshackle house just beyond. Cath just had a yearning to have a look, just in case her dad had come home or even her mam. There was somebody there all right but it was a new family. A strange woman was hanging out nappies on the line in the yard.

'What's she doing in our house, Cath?' asked Annie, her pet lip trembling. Cath took her hand and dragged her on, to the end of the row and along the path to the woods.

'It's not our house any more,' she said savagely.

Chapter Eight

The two girls sat down beside the tiny trickle of a stream, which ran into the Gaunless and which itself was a tributary of the Wear. Their backs were against a willow tree and the leaves made a moving, dappled pattern on their brown legs, stretched out before them on the grass.

Annie was unusually quiet. She sat staring at the water, occasionally throwing in a pebble from the pile she had collected on the way. Cath brought out a packet of jam sandwiches from the string bag she had with her and they munched in comparative silence with only the song of a blackbird sounding on the air.

Cath had discovered the entrance to the path that led up to the back of Eden Grange Hall and on impulse had gone a short way along it. This was private land, she knew that now, the gamekeeper and his son had made that clear the year before. But she didn't care. After all, what could they do to her and Annie? Nothing to Annie and if they put her in a girls' borstal she didn't care about that either. After all, it probably wasn't any worse than a children's home and Cath had been threatened with that often enough.

'I don't care,' she said aloud. Annie looked at her, a ring of jam around her mouth.

'I don't care either,' she said and Cath smiled.

'Well, you jolly well should,' a male voice said from the bankside behind them. Cath jumped up and stared at the two youths walking down towards them.

'What are you doing here? Trespassers will be prosecuted. Haven't you heard that term?'

It was the other boy speaking, not the gamekeeper's son, Jack. Jack recognised her about the same time as she did him.

'Oh, it's you. The miner's brat. I thought I told you to stay off our land.' He stared at her with his nose in the air. Annie moved towards her sister and buried her face in Cath's skirt.

The two boys had been walking around the estate, more to get away from the stifling atmosphere in the house than anything. It was almost two years since Jack's older brother, Aiden, had been killed in the war but his mother was still in deep mourning. She was also desperate to stop Jack following in his brother's footsteps.

'You are going to Oxford,' she had said. 'Tell him, Henry.' She had appealed to her husband. 'By that time this dreadful war will be over and you won't have to go.'

Jack had no intention of going to university and what worried him was that the war would be over before he had a chance to go. He had glanced at his father who shook his head slightly, warningly.

'Leave it,' he mouthed.

'Yes, Mother,' Jack had said and as soon as they decently could he and Mark, his friend from school, had escaped to the woods and green fields to talk of how they would go as enlisted men if there was no other way. The Allies were already in France. Soon they would be driving for Berlin and then the war would be at an end.

'We'll go to Newcastle to enlist,' Jack said, warming to the idea as soon as it occurred to him. 'We can alter our identity cards.'

'Newcastle, yes,' said Mark. He and Jack usually agreed about everything. He glanced down at the stream, the water sparkling in the sun. 'Look, there's someone there,' he said. 'Behind that tree.'

'Poachers, I bet,' said Jack. 'Come on, we'll send them packing. The miners around here are a menace, my father says, snaring rabbits and whatever else they can catch.' He was quite ready for a scuffle with the poachers. It wouldn't be a fight, not when the pitmen realised who he was. So he was disappointed when he saw the two girls.

'We're not hurting anything,' said Cath. 'Anyway, my dad says the land should belong to the people.'

'Does he now? And what does an ignorant pitman know about it?' asked Jack. 'Sounds like a Bolshevik to me.'

'He's not a Bolshevik, he's in the army,' Cath replied. She wasn't exactly sure what a Bolshevik was but it sounded like something shameful. 'He's in France.' She put the hand not holding Annie behind her back and crossed her fingers. It wasn't exactly a lie, was it? Her dad was likely to be in France with the army. That was where he'd wanted to go. Annie was crying in earnest now 'Cath, Cath!' and Cath lifted her up and cuddled her.

'You're nowt but big bullies,' said Cath. 'Howay, Annie, let's go home.' She was half-way up the bank-side when she turned.

'Anyway,' she shouted. 'What's so special about you? Your dad's only a gamekeeper, he's a nob's lackey, that's what he is!' She began to run, fleeing along the path as the boys started after her. They didn't go far; after a few yards they collapsed on the grass, giggling helplessly.

Cath didn't know why they were giggling but it was just as well, she reckoned. Little Annie had had enough running and was gasping and crying. And anyway, when she thought about it, she didn't want to go to borstal after all.

They decided to go down the line to Winton and get the bus to Shildon. It only came every two hours, 'for the duration of the war', the bus company said, but one was almost due. Cath made a game of it and they jumped from sleeper to sleeper, counting as they went. They ran faster as they passed the place where the track branched off to Old Pit where there were ghosts. Some people said they were

70

tommy-knockers, the ghosts of miners who were buried in Old Pit but Cath didn't believe it. Well, their marras would have dug them out, wouldn't they? Still, she hurried Annie past, just in case.

They were walking past the rows in Winton when the gang of boys came along, Brian among them.

'Hey, Brian, here's your sweetheart come to see you,' one of them cried and they all laughed. 'Howay, now, give her a kiss, she's come all the way from Shildon to see you.' He guffawed.

'I have not done anything of the sort,' said Cath. 'We've been for a picnic and now we're going to get the bus home.'

The boys surrounded her so that she had to stop walking.

'I thought we were going to the trenches to practise fighting,' said Brian. His face was bright red with embarrassment.

'Get out of my way,' said Cath to the boys. She was more worried about missing the bus than what they might do. What could they do anyway?

'Leave her alone,' said Brian.

'Ooh, leave her alone!' a boy jeered. He was bigger than the other lads, fourteen or fifteen. Cath had seen him before about Winton.

'If you won't kiss her, I will,' he said to Brian, grinning.

'Leave her alone!' Brian said again. But suddenly the lad caught hold of Cath and dragged her on to the field where the Home Guard had dug their trenches and she fell to the ground and he jumped on top of her. She couldn't believe it, he had his hands up her blouse, touching her small breasts, grabbing at them, hurting them. She opened her mouth but his mouth came down on hers stifling the scream.

She could hear Annie wailing in fright. The lads stood around them, egging him on. 'Go on, give her one, Eric,' she heard one shout. Then Brian was there, thrusting his way through the ring of lads, pushing and punching his way

71

to her. He grabbed hold of Eric and pulled him off Cath and punched him in the eye.

Cath scrambled to her feet and pulled her blouse down as a man's voice shouted, 'What's going on here? Leave that lass alone!' He was an old man but he waved his stick at them. The whippet by his side began barking and tried to get off his lead to get to them.

Cath grabbed Annie and ran for the bus, which had just appeared along the top of the rows. She didn't look up at all, she just ran, her head down, the tears spilling from her eyes. Humiliation filled her to overflowing, she couldn't bear to look at anyone or for anyone to look at her. Her mouth felt bruised, she could still feel his teeth against her lips and her chest was sore; she was conscious of her breasts as she had never been in her life before.

Annie ran after her, crying, 'Cath! Cath!' and after a minute the call penetrated Cath's brain. She stopped and waited for Annie to catch up.

The bus was coming along the top of the rows now and she rubbed her eyes dry and caught hold of Annie's hand. The stop was only a matter of feet away and they caught it easily. They stood in the aisle for the seats were full. Cath looked down at her feet for she would not look out of the windows at the scene of her humiliation. In the crush she hadn't noticed that Brian had got on to the bus too until they were alighting at the stop in Shildon. She turned her face away and hurried on, dragging Annie after her.

'Wait, Cathy, wait,' said Brian as he came after her.

'I've brought your bag.'

Cath turned; it was the string bag she used for the sandwiches. Stonily she waited until he caught up with her and took it from his outstretched hand.

'I'm sorry, Cathy,' he said. 'I'm really sorry. I'll pay them back, I will.'

'Don't call me Cathy,' she said coldly. 'And go away, why did you follow me? Get out of my sight.' That had been a favourite expression of her mother's.

'Go away,' said Annie, ranging herself beside Cath. The girls walked down the hill then up the road to Bell's Buildings. There was no one in so Cath got the big enamel dish and took water from the boiler at the side of the fireplace and washed herself, scrubbing at her breasts and making them more sore than ever, though she hardly felt it at the time. Annie sat on the sofa and watched her solemnly.

'If my dad was here he would have gone after those lads, wouldn't he, Cath?' Annie asked her. 'If he knew he would come back and pay them out wouldn't he? Cath?'

'Well, he's not here is he, and neither is Mam. So shut up about it, will you? And don't you say anything to Aunty Patsy or Uncle Jim neither. They'll only say I led them on.'

'I won't, our Cath,' said Annie, looking hurt. 'I wouldn't tell anybody.'

'Well then,' said Cath but she pulled on a clean blouse and went to sit beside Annie and put her arm around her. 'That's all right then.' Only it didn't feel all right, she thought. It didn't feel all right at all. Misery welled up in her. By, she thought, her mam and dad must think nothing of her or Annie or they wouldn't have gone off like that.

After a while she got to her feet and stoked the fire and peeled potatoes and shredded cabbage and put them on to boil. Aunty Patsy would bring home some savoury ducks, not real ducks but minced offal and herbs and stuff and they would have a proper dinner when Uncle Jim got home from the factory.

The door opened but Cath didn't look round, she was drawing the potato pan more on to the bar as it started to boil, carefully holding the handle with both hands.

'By, our Cath, I'm bloody knackered,' her mother's voice said. 'I had to stand all the way from London on the train. It was a good job I had me case to sit on in the corridor. Them soldiers couldn't care less. Not a gentleman among the lot of them. Make us a pot of tea, for goodness sake, will you?'

The shock made Cath lose her hold on the potato pan and

it tipped on the bar, spilling boiling water over the steel fender and splashing it on to her bare legs. She jumped back and stared at Sadie, unable to believe it was really her and hardly feeling the scalding spots on her legs.

'Mummy!' cried Annie and flung herself on her mother.

'Careful, pet, careful,' said Sadie. 'Don't ladder my nylons. There'll be no more where these came from, not now.' But she lifted Annie and hugged her. 'Go on, Cath, put the kettle on like I asked you,' she said over the little girl's shoulder. 'I suppose our Patsy's down Bishop Auckland with her friends, is she?'

Cath nodded and picked up the iron kettle and shook it to check if there was enough water in it, then lifted the pan aside and put the kettle on. Then she went to her mother and kissed her on the cheek.

'Oh, Mam, I'm that pleased to see you,' she said. And she was, in spite of everything.

'Mind me make-up, our Cath,' said Sadie. 'Well, I'm pleased to see you.'

Cath gazed at her as though at an apparition. Sadie looked smart in a red-flowered dress and a red jacket with a tiny, flower-bedecked hat tipped over an eye. She must have had the baby for her waist was as slim as ever. She wore high-heeled, peep-toed shoes and, in spite of her complaining words, she looked as bright as a button.

'Have you seen our dad?' Cath asked. 'Has he come home with you?' Sadie's look of incomprehension told her everything.

'You mean he deserted you?' Sadie demanded. 'Why, the rotten sod! I thought it was funny when I opened the door and saw you. I was just calling on our Patsy.' She saw Cath's stricken expression. 'Then I was coming down to Eden Hope to see you, honest.'

The kettle boiled and Cath made tea and poured some into Aunty Patsy's best cup. She and Annie stood together and watched Sadie add milk and look around for the sugar bowl.

'There's no sugar,' Annie said.

'Why not? You get your rations, don't you?'

'Aunty Patsy locks it in the cupboard so we don't eat it,' said Annie.

'I'll have to have a word with her,' Sadie promised. 'I bet she always has plenty herself. She always did have a sweet tooth, our Patsy.' Sadie nodded her head. 'She'll be wanting your ration as well as her own, I know her.'

'Are you talking about me, our Sadie? Anyway, where the hell have you been?'

Patsy came in and stood, arms akimbo, staring at her sister. 'You've done some funny things, our Sadie,' she said. 'But this one takes the bloody biscuit.'

CHAPTER TWO

Part Two

Chapter Nine

1948

The sun was hot on her back as Cath walked along South Church road on her way home from school. Today she wore no school hat or blazer and this was the last time she would wear the cotton-checked dress, which was regulation wear for the grammar school. Over her shoulder she had the old leather schoolbag she'd carried for five years but this was the last time she would carry it. Today was her last day at school.

At the top of the gentle rise, by Wilson's Forge, she paused and turned to look back. Behind the trees she could just see the roofs and chimneys of the school. She had never thought she would make it to the fifth year so that she could take her School Certificate.

'A great girl like you still going to school,' Mam had grumbled. 'It didn't hurt me leaving at fourteen did it? You're not natural, our Cath. Instead of having your head stuck in a book all the time you should be thinking of getting out and having a good time. You could help your mother out an' all, me being a poor woman on her own.'

Cath forbore to say that if she took the job in the cardboard box factory her mam wanted her to have she wouldn't get out much anyway. Not with having to tip her wages up to Sadie. That was what her mam was really after. Sadie wasn't too often on her own anyway; there was always a man in her life, usually a new one, for they didn't last all that long. So she had resisted her mother's threats and arguments and anyway, Sadie never ever had the five pounds to pay the fine if Cath left the grammar school before she was sixteen so it had made no difference in the end.

Cath sighed and turned to walk on. When she came to a dustbin, which hadn't been put away after the dustcart's visit, she stuffed her hated school hat in it.

'I saw that,' said Enid. She had come up behind without Cath noticing she was so deep in thought. Enid herself had her hat on, but a straw, summer one with a green band and the initials embroidered on the front. Cath had had to wear her winter gabardine hat because she didn't have a summer one. Enid was staying on at school for another two years to take her Highers and Cath was desperately envious of her.

The girls had been friends since the first year and now they lived in the same village of South Church. Cath lived in the pre-fabs on the outskirts but Enid's dad was a builder and they had a new bungalow with a big garden and a lawn with two trees on either side. Enid's mother disapproved of Cath's mother but Enid told her not to take any notice.

'You're not your mother, are you?' she would say.

Now the two girls walked along the road to where the pre-fabs stood behind two crescents of council houses. Then they paused, feeling the occasion.

'I'll miss you at school,' said Enid. 'Are you sure you won't be coming back in September? You've got a Saturday job, that gives you some money, doesn't it? You've the best brain in the form, you would be bound to do well. It's a shame, there's me will have to struggle to do half as well as you could.' Enid had no perception of what it was like for Cath. She was not allowed into the pre-fab that had been Cath's home for four years. Sadie was well aware of Mrs Brown's opinion of her.

'Stuck-up cow,' she had said when reminded of the builder's wife. 'Thinks she's something special 'cause she

80

married that man. He was nowt but a profiteer an' all, making money out of the council after the war. And now you're not good enough to play with their daughter. The day will come, you mark my words.'

What the day was, Cath hadn't an idea. She and Enid remained best friends though not when their parents were there.

'I can't, it's no good,' said Cath. 'I'm starting at Shire Hall a week on Monday, aren't I?' She had got a position in the treasurer's department in the offices of Durham Council Council in Durham. Mam was pleased as punch about that at any rate. 'Not but what you'd make more at the clothing factory,' Mam had said. 'The lasses are on piecework and can bring home as much as a man. You're pretty nimble fingered, an' all.'

Cath turned to walk up to the pre-fabs that made up Laburnham Grove. 'I'll see you around,' she said.

'We could go to the pictures on Saturday night,' said Enid.

'No, I can't, I have to look after Annie,' Cath replied.

'Why do *you* have to do it all the time?'

Cath shrugged and walked on. 'See you,' she said. They had had this discussion quite a few times before and Cath knew that, if she didn't look after Annie, Sadie certainly wouldn't, not on a Saturday night when she liked to go to the dance at the King's Hall. Cath wasn't going to leave Annie on her own in the house, she was only nine and she was still scared of the dark.

She could hear the raised voices as she opened the front gate. Mam had brought a man home again, she thought, her heart sinking. She walked round the side of the house to go in the kitchen way and Annie was leaning on the back wall by the kitchen door, crying soundlessly. Annie cried a lot – she didn't seem able to control it. It got her a lot of grief because other girls called her cry-baby and it maddened Sadie who would shout at her, 'Come here and I'll give you something to cry about, you big babby!' And she would raise a threatening hand. But Cath knew Annie couldn't help it.

'Who's in there?' Cath asked Annie but Annie just shook her head, too full to speak. Cath opened the door and went in. The breakfast pots were still on the table in the kitchen and the fridge door was open. Now she'd have to defrost it and clean it out. She'd been so happy when she discovered the pre-fabs came with a fridge; she'd never ever seen one before, except on the pictures.

She put her schoolbag down on a chair and went through to the living room. Her father was standing there, towering over her mother who was looking up at him. They were both shouting at each other. On the sofa sat a blonde woman in an elegant 'new look' suit that showed off her tiny waist and her face made up like Marlene Dietrich. She had a sort of fixed smile as she looked out of the window, ignoring Alf and Sadie.

'You owe me!' Sadie was shouting. 'You wanted our Cath to stay on at school till she was sixteen, didn't you? Well, you'll just have to pay.'

'But she leaves today, doesn't she? She can earn her own money now. My Gerda's having a bairn, man. It's her I owe.'

'Annie's your bairn. She's still at school.'

'Aye, she's still at school, I know,' said Alf heavily, 'but I'm not made of money, man. I'm only on the datal what with me foot an' all. I'm telling you, I'll give you a pound a week and that's all. So that's the end of it. Why don't you get off your arse and get a job yourself? Why don't you go down one of the factories then?'

'I can't leave our Annie to come in from school on her own,' said Sadie.

Alf laughed. 'You don't mind leaving her at night, do you? You never did.'

'I don't, I—'

'Hallo Dad. Hallo Gerda,' said Cath.

'How are you, my dear?' Gerda asked. 'A new baby

brother you will haf, pet.' She rose gracefully to her feet and kissed Cath on the cheek. Though Gerda had a poor command of English, she had picked up the local intonation and her speech was sprinkled with both Geordie and German words and expressions. She smiled at Cath and nodded her head towards the warring couple and rolled her eyes.

Alf had come back from Germany a few months after the end of the war in Europe. He had, after all, been part of the British force occupying the British sector there. He had met Gerda and brought her home with him, wangling her papers somehow and they had set up house in the old row in Eden Hope before it was demolished. Sadie had got her divorce on the grounds of his adultery and he had married Gerda. Now they lived in a new council house on the outskirts of Bishop Auckland and he was back down the pit. Cath had seen nothing of them for months.

'I'll take our Cath to live with us,' said Alf.

'I'll not have it!' Sadie shouted. 'I've had the expense of her all her life and now when she's going to be earning you want her? Not bloody likely!'

'You were the one who said you still need the maintenance to keep her,' Alf said reasonably. 'You'd like to live with us, wouldn't you, Cath?'

Cath looked from one to the other. She didn't know what to say, about the baby brother (how did Gerda know it was a boy?), or about going to live with her father. But there was Annie to think of.

'I cannot, Dad, what about Annie?'

'Ah, man, she'll be all right, pet.'

'No. I'm staying with Mam,' said Cath. In fact, she was beginning to feel sorry for her mother who was looking stricken and older than her age. Sadie was not used to being rejected by a man and she had certainly expected Alf to stay with her even after all she had done. And he had come back from Germany with a blonde. How could he? Now he wanted to take Cath away from her. Well, he couldn't have her.

'Get yourself away, Alf,' she said. 'And take your fancy piece with you. We don't want you.'

'No, but you want my money,' said Alf, grinning. Oh aye, he had changed all right, she thought bitterly. 'And Gerda is my wife now, now you.'

Sadie lifted her chin. 'Well, I thank God for that then.' After he and Gerda had gone, she brought the bottle of gin out of the cupboard and poured herself a stiff drink.

'Mam,' said Cath. 'You haven't even had your tea. Don't start.'

'I need a drink after that,' snapped Sadie. 'Don't you tell me what to do, our Cath.'

Cath went outside and brought Annie in. 'Come on, we'll make pancakes for tea,' she said to her. 'Everything is going to be fine, you'll see.'

Cath liked working at the County Council offices in Durham. It was a bit of a walk to the market place in Bishop Auckland to get the bus so she had to leave home at half past seven and often she didn't get home until nearly seven o'clock in the evening but she didn't mind. There was always a crowd of people rushing down Old Elvet Bridge to Shire Hall and she enjoyed being part of it. She worked in one of the houses in the old street opposite the hall and her window overlooked the racecourse and River Wear. The racecourse was not used any more for racing but everyone still called it that. In the summer months she could sit on the banks of the Wear and eat her lunchtime sandwiches as she watched the punts on the river and sometimes the university students practising for a boat race, the cox perched precariously at one end and calling instructions through a loud hailer.

Sometimes Brian came and sat beside her. He didn't say much, just ate his sandwiches and offered to buy her orange juice from the shop on the corner of Old and New Elvet. Cath always refused. Brian was a trainee in the Surveyor's Department at Shire Hall.

One sunny October day, when the leaves still left on the trees on the far bank of the Wear glinted gold and bronze, Brian came and sat beside her on the steps leading down to the water.

'Go away, Brian,' she said as she so often did.

'I have as much right as you to sit here,' said Brian as he so often replied. In fact, it was getting to be a small ritual.

'I'll move away then,' said Cath and did so, standing and walking a short way up the path to where there was a bench. Sometimes he reminded her too much of that day when she was twelve, going on thirteen, and one of his gang had jumped on her. She shivered. She could still feel his hands, dirty and grasping, all over her. Oh, it had only been a bit of fun to them, she knew that. Brian had helped her too; it was none of it his fault but still, he had witnessed it and she still couldn't see him without remembering that.

Margaret and Joan, two of the girls she worked with came along and sat beside her and they talked about the boys from Hetton-le-Hole, which was the village on the other side of Durham where they came from. They giggled and told stories of one who looked like Gregory Peck only younger.

'He knows it an' all,' Joan said. 'He's a right bighead, that one.'

'Well, you wouldn't turn him down if he asked you out,' said Margaret and they giggled some more.

'Why don't you give that lad a break, Cath?' Joan asked, looking to where Brian was calmly finishing his sandwiches. 'Anyone can see he's keen on you and he's not half bad looking, is he?'

Cath glanced sideways towards the steps where Brian was just throwing the last of his bread to the ducks, which came clucking and crowding round.

'He's all right,' Cath replied. 'But I'm not interested in lads.'

The other girls hooted. 'What's the matter, you a

lesbian?' Joan asked and they both laughed again. It took Cath's breath away; she barely had an idea of what a lesbian was and they certainly didn't figure in any conversation she had ever heard.

'Joan!' she said, scandalised. 'You want your mouth washed out with soap!' Which only served to make the other girls double up with laughter yet again. She stood up and took the paper bag from her sandwiches to the litterbin, recently put there by the steps. The council was running an anti-litter campaign. A church bell rang a quarter to one and she turned to walk up the incline to Old Elvet.

'They're only having you on,' said Brian, who had fallen into step with her. 'Don't take any notice of them.'

'I know,' Cath replied. 'I'm not.'

Encouraged that she was talking to him, he went on, 'How about coming to the Odeon with me tomorrow night? It's a good picture, *Whisky Galore*.'

'No, I don't think so, thank you. I have to look after Annie.'

'Little Annie can come with us,' he said, 'She'd like it.'

Cath looked at him. What did he know of Annie or what she would like? 'Why don't you leave me alone?' she snapped as she turned into her building. She didn't look round so she didn't see his hurt expression.

Chapter Ten

'There's that girl,' said Mark as he and Jack emerged from the university library into the pale December sunshine on Palace Green. He paused, leaning heavily on his silver-topped cane. Sometimes the cold winds of north-east England affected his thigh where the muscle had been half shot away in the very last stages of the war. He gazed openly at the girl hurrying along the path from the cathedral, her dark hair blowing about and tangling with her bright red scarf. She had her head down against the force of the freshening wind so she wasn't aware of the men as yet.

'What girl?' Jack asked, turning to follow Mark's gaze.

'The miner's brat you called her, can you remember, she was trespassing in the woods? That day before we enlisted?'

'I don't – wait a minute I do—' Whatever else he was going to say was lost as Cath cannoned into him, dropping her bag at the impact. It opened and the contents spilled out over the pavement.

'Oh!' she cried and bent to pick them up, stuffing them in the bag higgledy-piddledy. 'Sorry, I'm so sorry.'

Jack bent down and caught a rolling lipstick on its way to the gutter. 'Why don't you look where you're going?' he asked. At this level all he saw were her shoes. They were a cheap leather and slightly scuffed at the toe and beginning to crack across the instep. But as they rose to their feet and he handed her the lipstick he saw the girl properly and she was lovely, striking in fact. She put up a hand and pushed a hairgrip further into the tangle of her hair in an attempt to control it, futilely it seemed. Her large dark eyes darted from him to Mark and she was blushing, no doubt from embarrassment. Whatever, the rising pink on her white skin enhanced his impression.

'Did you hurt yourself?' he asked.

'No, of course I didn't,' she snapped as her embarrassment turned to anger. She had recognised them all right and she was ready to give back as good as she got this time.

'I know you,' said Jack. 'You're the – girl from the mining village aren't you?' He had almost said the wrong thing there, he thought and oh, she was a very attractive girl. 'You remember my friend, Mark, don't you?'

'Yes indeed, I remember you both,' said Cath. 'You frightened my little sister.' Her dark eyes were accusing.

'Sorry about that,' said Mark. 'We didn't mean to.'

'Let's go into the café here so you can catch your breath,' said Jack. 'You'd like a coffee, wouldn't you?'

Cath had been rushing to catch her bus but as the cathedral bells rang out the hour she realised she had already missed it. She had missed the earlier one too, which was the reason she had been visiting the cathedral. It was out of the wind and she loved to sit in a back pew and just relax. There were few tourists about at this time of the year but the great nave echoed the footsteps of the odd one or two. It was Saturday; a half-day for the workers at Shire Hall and most of them had already left the city.

'I'll give you a lift,' Brian had said. 'Hop in.' He had been waiting for her on the street outside the building where she worked and opened the door of his car invitingly. It was a pre-war car, a Standard circa 1931, but he

88

was proud of it. New cars were almost impossible to get even for those who could afford one. Most went to help the export drive for Britain was in dire straits after the war. The waiting list for the few cars allowed on the home market was long.

'No thank you,' Cath had replied. 'I'll catch the bus.' She edged away for she was late already and would have to run to the bus station to have any chance of catching her usual bus.

'Oh come on, Cath,' said Brian. 'Why not?'

'No, I won't, thank you,' said Cath. 'I want to go somewhere first.' She had scooted away before he could persuade her but those few moments were enough to make her miss the bus. So she had gone up the steep, narrow alley that emerged just below Palace Green and gone into the cathedral. She shouldn't have been so soft, and taken the lift, she told herself crossly. Now she was going to miss the next bus too.

'Come on, a cup of coffee won't hurt you,' said Mark. 'Now, what did you day your name was?' The two of them fell in on either side of her, Mark walking with only a slight limp despite his stick. Cath knew she should have refused but she didn't. She was fascinated and yet repelled by them. It was as though they were from another planet. The office workers from the County Council and the students and others from the university thronged the streets of New and Old Elvet yet never actually took the least bit of notice of each other.

'It's Cath, isn't it? And I'm the gamekeeper's son, Jack, aren't I?' Jack grinned at her as he steered her through the door of the café.

'You acted as though you were lord of the manor and Annie and me peasants,' said Cath and the two men laughed and Cath felt gauche. What was so funny?

Jack saw her blush. 'Don't take any notice of us,' he said. 'I'll order coffee.' He lifted his hand and as if by magic a waiter was there and the coffee appeared on the table in an instant. He wasn't a snob at all; Cath began to realise it. In fact, he couldn't have been nicer to her. He talked to her easily of so many things, occasionally bringing Mark into the conversation. He talked about his time at Oxford after the war, how he just moved to Durham to do his Master's because his mother had died and anyway Mark was studying at Durham.

He asked her about herself and her life and what she was doing and seemed genuinely interested in the Treasurer's Department and what she did there. That was punching holes in cards and sorting them for the tabulator and it bored her to death. Now she began to look at it in a slightly different light herself as she strove to make it interesting.

Jack glanced across at Mark and Mark rose to his feet.

'I must go,' said Mark, 'Things to do.' He nodded to Cath, 'Nice to see you again,' and left.

'I must go too,' said Cath, 'My mother will be worrying where I am.' Sadie would not be worrying at all but Annie might.

'Oh, come on,' said Jack. 'We'll have some lunch and then I'll run you home in no time.'

It was a strange afternoon, Cath felt intoxicated even though she barely touched the wine he ordered. It was a good wine; he wouldn't order a cheap wine but she hadn't ever had wine in her life and it tasted like vinegar. She was drunk with the sound of his voice, the look in his eyes that said she was someone special.

Jack ran her home in his MG sports car and he was right, the journey was fleeting. He parked on South Church Road, below the entrance to Laburnham Grove. He kissed her lightly on the lips and her lips tingled.

'Lovely Cath,' he murmured. 'No, I'm going to call you Catherine.' He got out and walked round to open the door for her; as she got out his hand sort of accidentally brushed against her breast and her nipples hardened instantly and it showed through her blouse. Jack smiled.

Cath hurried up the road to Laburnham Grove and the pre-fabs, with trembling legs. Behind her she heard the car setting off again and roaring away along South Church Road.

As she opened the back door of the house Cath came down to earth with a bump. There was a dirty plate on the table with sauce from a tin of baked beans coagulated on it and a smell of burned toast. There was a cracked cup beside the plate and crumbs on the table.

Annie came through the door from the living room. 'Where've you been, our Cath?' she asked plaintively. 'I've been on my own all day.'

'Where's Mam?'

'I don't know. She went out ages ago,' Annie said. 'I did some beans for my dinner.'

Cath sighed. 'Yes. I see that.'

Jack had said he would call her Catherine and that meant he was going to see her again but he had made no arrangements with her. He had liked her, she was certain he had. But even if he did, she couldn't bring him here; couldn't introduce him to her mother. She'd do well to forget him. He'd probably forgotten her already, anyway. He lived in an altogether different world to the one of pre-fabs and baked beans for dinner, or rather, lunch. What's more, she was beginning to be aware that he had been having her on about being the gamekeeper's son. Though he was a student, albeit a mature one, he owned a car that was miles away from Brian's Standard. How had he got that? No, he must be a Vaughan, one of the family that owned the Hall and the surrounding land. He must have been having a 'bit of fun', as they called it with her. He hadn't even mentioned his full name and now she knew why. Her mood swung from hope to despair.

'Did you get anywhere?' asked Mark when they met later in the evening. He was staying with Jack at the Hall for the weekend and they met in the games room for a pre-dinner game of snooker.

'Paving the way, old boy, paving the way,' said Jack, talking like Gregory Peck as he leaned over the table to line up his cue.

'She's quite a looker,' said Mark. 'I'd have tried myself but I could see she was taken with you.'

Jack grinned at him. 'Sorry, son, no contest,' he said.

'Will you see her again?'

Jack shrugged. 'I might.' But already he was planning something for the following Saturday. 'I wonder what Father is up to? It's not like him to go out in the evenings.'

'Maybe he has a girl in the village too,' said Mark.

'Not him.' Jack was positive about that. Since his mother had died, his father had been a bit of a recluse. He spent most of his time working on the estate, turning his hand to various labouring jobs and even rebuilding a wall that had tumbled down. In the evenings he went into his study after dinner and stayed there until bedtime.

The following Saturday Cath walked up Castle Chare to the cathedral and lingered in Palace Green for a while but she didn't see Jack or his friend Mark. Christmas came and went and still there was no sign of him though she went up there most Saturdays.

'It's nice when the students are on holiday, isn't it?' Joan and Cath were walking along by the Wear, both of them huddled in scarves and mittens and winter coats against the bitter cold. The early January day was already darkening although they were still on their dinner hour. They had eaten in the basement of their building where there was an old-fashioned black range, like the one in the house in Eden Hope Colliery, and had braved the weather to take a quick walk before settling down in the stuffy atmosphere in the punch-card room. The wind got through the holes in Cath's scarf and mittens and she rolled her fingers up tight and tucked her nose down into her collar. Annie had knitted the set for her Christmas box and there were a few dropped stitches.

'What do you mean exactly?' asked Cath as they turned to go back.

'You know, they aren't bumping into you on the bridge or practically knocking you out of the way when the pavement is crowded.'

Cath looked up the deserted street as they reached it. That was true, she hadn't even noticed there were no students at all. They were missing; it wasn't just Jack and Mark. Her heart lightened. What a fool she was, of course they wouldn't be here over Christmas.

'Make the most of it, they'll be back next week,' said Joan. Next week! Cath could barely wait.

She stood by the sorter watching the cards going through, slotting into the holes in order, one or two going into the error section. She would have to punch those again. Her attention wandered to the window by the sorting machine. The afternoon was really darkening now and lights were showing along the river and twinkling through the trees on the opposite bank. The trees no longer looked bare and forlorn but dark and mysterious. And she might see Jack next week.

'Cath! What are you doing? Watch out.' The supervisor was striding up the room and the sorter was making a whirring sound. A card had stuck and others were piling on to it and they were twisting and tearing. Cath hastily stopped the machine.

'This is no good you know, Cath,' said the supervisor, Miss Green. 'You'll have to do this lot over again. And not so many errors this time when you're punching. Keep your mind on the job, will you? Otherwise I'll have to do something about it.' She nodded meaningfully at the door at the end that led to the section manager's room.

'Yes, Miss Green. I'm sorry, Miss Green,' said Cath. This would make her late, she would miss the bus. 'Blooming heck,' she said under her breath. 'Bloody rotten

Chinese pokers.' It was the fashionable swear phrase.

It was after seven by the time Cath got home. It would be all right if Mam were in, Annie would be all right. But if Mam was out Annie would be in a state for she was still frightened of the dark even though she was ten. She would sit in the living room and shiver, frightened to go into the kitchen because the window looked out on to the dark garden and fence at the end and there were no curtains to pull against it. She would not switch on the wireless in case she didn't hear anything sinister and was caught unawares by whatever horror was stalking her. She would be hungry too.

Cath hurried up Laburnham Grove to the house and let herself in the front door. There were voices from the kitchen, everything was fine, her mam was home and there was a lovely smell of panackelty coming from the oven.

'Where've you been, our Cath?' her mother asked. She was looking really smart with her hair in a long bob like Veronica Lake's but held back from her face by a glittery pin. She wore a red skirt and white lacy blouse pulled tight into the skirt so that it showed the outline of her ample breasts and the vee between them. Over this outfit she wore a frilly pinny, new and clean, not with the edging torn and ragged like she usually wore. Annie was sitting at the table with her knife and fork in her hands and smiling happily.

'Em, I missed the bus,' Cath mumbled. She was slightly out of breath from running up the street.

'Well, sit down, we'll eat,' said Sadie. 'I have something to tell you.'

94

Chapter Eleven

'You stupid woman,' said Aunty Patsy. 'It won't be long before he tires of you and then you'll be on the streets with nowhere to go. And don't think I'll take you in again. I vowed never again—'

'Aw, shut up, Patsy,' said Sadie. 'That's not going to happen, Henry promised me. I can have the house for ever if I want it. He's not my fancy man any road.'

'Oh aye?'

Patsy pursed her mouth and stared sourly at her sister. Trust her to fall on her feet; Sadie always came off better off than her.

Patsy had come in to see her sister this Saturday evening to tell her she had got a council house and to crow about it. Bell's Buildings were being knocked down to make way for new housing. Only Sadie didn't care, in fact she had hardly listened.

'I've got a new house an' all. It's on the edge of Eden Grange land. It's got four bedrooms and a bathroom and a cloakroom downstairs with a shower and water closet.'

'You're having me on, our Sadie,' said Patsy.

'No, I'm not. We're going to move in the morrow. So we have to pack up, I'm busy can't you see?'

Sadie gestured at the old straw box that had been packed so often before and the cardboard suitcase alongside it on the sofa. She smiled a complacent sort of smile at her sister.

'You got a council house, then? Isn't that nice. I'm sure it will do very well for you and Jim.' Cath came down the stairs carrying a bundle of her and Annie's clothes. 'Hurry up and put them in the box, Cath. Then put the top on and fasten that belt round it,' said Sadie. 'I'm sorry, Patsy, did you want a cup of tea? I'll make you one though as you can see I'm busy. Henry is coming at ten o'clock tomorrow to take us up there. You can see how it is.'

'Oh, don't bother about me,' said Patsy, moving to the door. 'But like I said, don't come running to me when your fancy man lets you down.' She banged the door after her and stomped off down Laburnham Grove. Cath lifted the curtain and watched her as she passed under the streetlight on the corner, turning once to stare back at the pre-fab, her face shadowed.

There was a noise on the stairs as Annie came down; she was sleepwalking. She came into the room and opened the top drawer of the press, taking out something invisible and folding it on the table with quick, nervous gestures. Her mouth worked all the time.

'Oh, for God's sake, Annie—' Sadie began but Cath had dropped the curtain and gone up to her sister and put her arm around her.

'Ssh!' she said to her mother, then, 'Howay, Annie, let's go back to bed, eh?' She led Annie gently back to the stairs then lifted her and carried her up. Although Annie was thin and small for her age, she was a dead weight and Cath was puffing and blowing by the time she got the little girl back in bed. She felt the sheet but it was dry, thank goodness for that at least. Annie didn't often wet the bed nowadays but when she had a nightmare she sometimes did.

'She's a pain, that kid,' Sadie observed. 'Come on now, let's get finished. I'm tired meself.'

'Who's fault do you reckon it is that Annie's like that?' Cath was stung into saying.

'Don't you be impittant, now,' her mother warned. 'Any road, I've always looked after her, you know I have. I came back from Kent, didn't I? Why would I do that if not for you kids?'

Cath was struck dumb at this. Her mother actually seemed to believe it. But then Sadie had always had the capacity to forget unpleasant facts about herself. She might as well let it go.

'What did you say his name was? This man who is going to let you have the house?'

'Henry, I told you. Henry Vaughan. He's a lovely fella and not a bit stuck up, you'll see. He's right well off an' all. Oh, Cath, it's going to be lovely, it is really.' Sadie was like a kid herself after Santa Claus had been and brought her everything she ever dreamed of.

'He's not doing it for nothing, is he?'

'He likes me, that's all. He says I'm like a breath of fresh air. His wife, you know, she was a lady, thought she was something special 'cause she had a bit of money. Henry now, he came from nothing, worked for all he's got he told me. He talks to me lovely.'

'I bet he does,' Cath muttered and prayed silently, Lord, don't let it be Jack's father, please, God. But she had an awful feeling it was.

'What's that, our Cath?'

'Nothing, I said nothing,' Cath replied.

'You'd better not an' all,' said Sadie but she was in too good a mood to hit out in her usual manner when she thought Cath was cheeking her.

'What about the furniture?' Cath looked around at the old, battered press and the utility table and chairs.

'We're not taking it. It can go on the tip. Henry says I can have the stuff that's there. I saw it, our Cath, it's grand, everything is tickety boo!'

Tickety boo, thought Cath as she sat in the back of the pre-war Bentley with Annie and stared at the house. It was at the end of a quarter-mile drive in from the road and looked quite isolated, standing as it did on the edge of a beech wood. The trees rising behind it were bare of leaves and a thin winter sun shone through them, showing a faint sheen of green on the slates of the Teesdale stone roof. The house was built of stone, grey and solid, and the windows were tall and small paned. By the side of the house was a sort of lean-to except that it was stone too and the roof was quarry-tiled. The door was like a stable door with a top half that could be opened separately.

'How do you like it, Cath?' Mr Vaughan asked, turning and smiling at the two girls.

'It's lonely,' said Cath. He looked older than when he had caught her trespassing and taken her into the kitchen for cake. He didn't seem to recognise her as that girl but then she had been only eleven.

'It's great, Henry,' Sadie said quickly and frowned a warning at Cath. 'And lovely of you to let us have it at such a low rent. Come on, let's go in, I can't wait.'

Annie clung to Cath's hand as Mr Vaughan opened the door with a large key then put the key in Sadie's hand. 'There you are,' he said. 'Your new home.'

Sadie squealed and Cath looked at her in disgust. Her mother was acting like a love-struck schoolgirl, it was revolting. She followed them into the hall, almost dragging a reluctant Annie and looked around. The hall was narrow and at the far end a staircase rose up to a large window, like the window of a church, and then turned and went up the other way, like the staircase in Shire Hall but smaller. There was a strip of red-patterned carpet on a stone slab floor and a picture of old Hartlepool with a sailing ship being unloaded at a dock, faded to a sepia colour with age. Doors opened on either side of the hall.

'Your new house is not so new,' Cath commented and Henry Vaughan glanced sharply at her. His eyes could have been Jack's eyes. Oh yes, they were father and son, she thought bitterly.

'Come into the sitting room,' he said, opening a door on the left. 'You'll get a better idea of the place. It's not new, no, but it has been renovated. The plumbing is fairly new and it has electricity.'

The room was large, as large as the whole of the pre-fab. The tall window let in the morning sunlight and showed the furniture, not new but comfortable. There were deep armchairs and a sofa and a low table beside it. There was a light wallpaper with a leaf pattern and a real painting – a portrait of a man with a beard and the same blue eyes – over the marble fireplace where a wood fire burned. The view through the window was of a garden and beyond that the wood and rising above the wood the distant view of Shildon Bank. To Cath it looked like a film set.

Mr Vaughan brought in the tatty straw box bound with an imitation leather belt. 'That's the lot,' he said as he stood and wiped his hands together. 'I'll leave you to get settled in. There's a box of groceries in the kitchen to welcome you.' He looked at Sadie. 'Walk me to the car?'

Cath was still holding Annie's hand. The little girl was looking around apprehensively.

'It's big, isn't it, Cath?' she whispered, afraid to speak any louder.

'It is but it's nice, isn't it?' Cath said brightly. 'And warm an' all. We'll sit by the fire a bit, eh? Then we'll go and explore.' She could hear the murmur of voices outside. Mam must have left the door open for a cold draught was coming into the room.

The kitchen was a typical farmhouse kitchen with a scrubbed wooden table in the middle of the floor and a range not too unlike the one they had had at Eden Hope Colliery. Cath gasped when she saw the basket of food. There were eggs and fresh milk; fresh bread and cold cuts of meat.

'He's a black marketeer!' she gasped to her mother. Food was still rationed. This had to be under-the-counter stuff and illegal.

99

'Don't be soft, our Cath,' said Sadie. 'He has a farm, hasn't he? More than one, I bet. Come on, get the kettle on and we'll have a bite of dinner before we do anything else. We can have an egg each day.' She couldn't stop smiling. Like the cat that got the cream, thought Cath.

They had a room each of course. Cath's was almost as large as the sitting room and was furnished in old-fashioned but good furniture, beech, like the trees outside. Annie had a bedroom too but hers was smaller and there was an old rocking horse in the corner. She gazed at it – the mane was stringy and its painted eyes faded. She gave it a push and it rocked with a squeak of protest.

'I'm too old for a rocking horse, our Cath,' she said.

'Well, look, there's a feather eiderdown on the bed, that'll be cosy, won't it?'

Annie regarded the bed and the wash table and dressing table and went to stand by the window without comment. The trees were closer here than at the front of the house and there was some sort of creeper on the wall outside; its tendrils waved in the freshening wind.

'I'll lend you my flashlight, eh?' Cath told Annie. 'Then, when the light's out, you can switch it on if you wake during the night so that you can see the light switch.'

About eleven o'clock that night, just as Cath was dropping off to sleep, the door opened and a beam of light preceded Annie as she ran in and hurled herself on the bed. She burrowed under the eiderdown and clung to Cath.

'What's the matter?' Cath asked.

'I like to sleep in your bed,' said Annie. Her eyes were already closing. Cath took the flashlight and put it on the bedside table then turned to cuddle her sister.

'It's all right, Annie,' she said. 'Everything will be fine.'

*

The house was called Half Hidden Cottage, though it was not so isolated as it had seemed at first. The drive curved away so that it couldn't be seen from the road but it was only a few minutes' walk and there was a bus stop a few yards from the gates. The bus ran between Durham and Bishop Auckland too, which was handy for Cath going to work. She wondered why it had been built in the first place. Had some ancestor of the Vaughans' built it as a love nest for *his* mistress? If so, it was well enough hidden. She hadn't even known of its existence until they came to live in it.

The following Saturday, Cath walked up Castle Chare to Palace Green once again. Not on the off chance that she would meet Jack again, oh no, she just had a yearning to sit in the quiet back pews of the cathedral again and think things out. She looked up at the exquisite fretted stone screen erected by some long ago Lord Neville in thanksgiving for the English defeating the Scots at Durham when they had marched into England.

It was quiet in the nave and her thoughts ranged over the last few weeks of living in Half Hidden Cottage. Her mam was happy most of the time, Mr Vaughan visited her regularly in the evenings and Cath and Annie would disappear upstairs out of the way. But it was when he wasn't there that Sadie would become restless and Cath knew she hated the quiet and the loneliness. They had always lived in amongst people. Sadie had fought more with her neighbours than become friends with them but still, she missed them. And Annie was frightened. She was frightened of going into the large, empty rooms by herself, she was frightened of being upstairs on her own, she was frightened of ghosts.

'There's no such thing,' said Cath. 'It's just shadows. Put the lights on, it's OK.'

'You great soft baby, our Annie,' Sadie jeered and crooned. 'Cry baby, cry baby, put your finger in your eye, baby.' And Annie's eyes would be swimming once again.

She had to catch the bus into Eden Hope Colliery to go to school on her own. Everything was a nightmare to her.

'Oh shut up, our Annie,' Sadie would say. 'By, I should have given you away.'

Cath had come in one day as she said this and it made her remember Timmy, her little brother. 'Don't say that!' she had shouted at her mother.

'I'll say what the hell I like,' Sadie shouted back. 'I'm sick to death of her snivelling, I am, I'm telling you! I might give her away an' all, I can still do it, you know.'

It had taken Cath all evening to pacify Annie who, in the end had fallen asleep still murmuring, 'She won't will she, Cath? You won't let her, will you, Cath?'

Cath was remembering Timmy as she sat in the cathedral. Where was he? And the other one? The one her mam had been expecting when she went to Kent, chasing after the Canadian flyer, where was he? And the one before? It would have been a he, Cath thought, as she sat on the hard wooden seat in the great cathedral and pondered on her life. There was a hassock hung on a hook on the back of the seat in front and she took it down and knelt on it; bending her head and folding her hands together as she had been taught in Sunday School. But her thoughts were too much of a jumble so God couldn't be listening. Or else there was no one there. She sat up.

'Hello, Cath,' a man's voice said and for one insane moment she thought God had really spoken and her heart beat fast. Then she relaxed. It wasn't God and no, it wasn't Jack who sat down beside her.

'Brian,' she said. 'What are you doing here?'

'The same as you, it looks like,' he replied. 'I come in here sometimes.'

'Well, I'm going now, I have to catch my bus,' said Cath, rising to her feet.

'Me too,' said Brian. 'Would you like a lift?'

'I don't live in Auckland now,' she replied. 'Thanks all the same.'

'I know where you live,' said Brian. 'It would be no bother to take you there.'

'No thanks, I'll get the bus. It's due anyway.' Cath walked down the aisle and out into a day of wintry sleet, which pricked at her cheeks like needles. Behind her Brian stood in the doorway by the brass sanctuary knocker and watched her go.

It was probably all over Winton and Eden Hope Colliery villages by now, Cath thought, as she pulled her scarf up over her nose against the sleet. Sadie Raine was living in sin with a nob. But still, they had always known she was no better than she should be, hadn't they?

Chapter Twelve

Jack gazed out of the window of the guest room. He was staying with Mark and his parents for the weekend.

'Come to Staindrop, old lad,' Mark had said. 'It'll please the old folk no end to have you. They'll kill the fatted calf for you. On Saturday night we can go into Darlington and try out the local talent.'

Nigel and Daphne Drummond had only recently come back up north, buying an imposing old stone house set back from the green at Staindrop. Nigel had made a fortune during the war running a factory making some sort of army supplies. Now they were trying to cultivate the local gentry. Having Jack to stay was an achievement for Daphne.

Jack was already regretting accepting the invitation. He gazed out of the window and wished himself back in Durham or even at Eden Grange Hall with his father mooching around being miserable. Though he hadn't been so bad lately ... He'd seen that girl last Saturday, hurrying along from the cathedral and disappearing down an alley. He should have followed that up; she was probably quite amusing and she was definitely worth looking at with her great dark eyes and hair and white skin. It probably wouldn't do though; she was too close to home, living at Bishop Auckland.

Outside, the green beyond the hedge was ruffled by the

wind and sleet ran down the windowpane. Jack pulled the curtain to one side and watched a couple of girls walk along the path bordering the green, their heads bent against the wind. One of them glanced up at the window and saw him standing there and smiled. Her mouth was a pillar-box slash in her white face. He dropped the curtain and turned back into the room, feeling exposed. Why did they live in a place where anyone could look in?

Mark knocked and put his head around the door. 'Ready to go?'

'Indeed,' Jack replied. They ran down the stairs together and opened the front door whereupon Mrs Drummond, coming out of the drawing room, stopped them.

'You'll be in for dinner, boys?' she stated rather than asked.

'Yes, of course, Mrs Drummond,' said Jack, 'Wouldn't miss it, looking forward to it. You know what university food can be like.' He smiled at her.

'We'll see, Mother,' said Mark. 'We might be held up.'

'Mark! I have dinner guests and they wish to meet you both.'

'Don't worry, Mrs Drummond, I'll bring him back,' said Jack.

'You'll do nothing of the sort,' said Mark as they climbed into the car and took the road for Piercebridge and Darlington. 'The old woman just wants to show you off to her friends. It would bore us both to death.'

'We'll see,' said Jack. He glanced across at his friend. He had met Mark at school and they had been friends ever since. But for some reason he had not met Mark's parents before; it had always been Mark who visited him. Now he was struck by how unlike Mark was to his parents. In colouring especially – Mark was dark while both his parents were fair. He was tall and slim whereas his father was of medium height and stockily built. In fact, Mark had the same colour hair as that girl ... Why on earth was he still thinking of the miner's brat, the girl with the mundane name of Cath?

They sped along the road to Darlington where Mark roared into the centre and parked outside the Majestic ballroom.

'The local hop, is it?' Jack asked as they followed a group of chattering girls in the queue for tickets. But he was feeling happier already as the strains of 'Peg of My Heart', could be heard from the dance band inside.

It wasn't until after eleven and Jack was crooning softly in a girl's ear, 'Walking My Baby Back Home', as they walked, arms wrapped round one another along Houndgate, that he remembered about the dinner. And that was because he suddenly felt hungry as they passed the fish and chip shop.

'We'll be in trouble,' he said to Mark later as they retrieved the car and set off for Staindrop. It was one o'clock in the morning and the streets were practically deserted as they roared out of Darlington on the Barnard Castle road.

'No, I don't think so,' said Mark. 'Don't you know you belong to the landed gentry, you can do no wrong in my mother's eyes.'

'Rubbish, the Edens were the landed gentry round here. My great-grandfather made his money in trade in the last century. Railways mostly.'

'Three generations are enough for my mother. Besides, the Edens took off for the south. Never mind that though, how did you get on with yours?'

Jack's father was sitting on the sofa with an arm around Sadie. He was comfortable; there was a good fire in the grate and the curtains were drawn against the weather. Henry was disinclined to go home and why should he, after all? This was his house and Sadie was soft and compliant and he was very fond of her. Jack was away somewhere, staying with a friend. There would be no one at home; even the cook went back to her cottage every evening. Servants were hard to find nowadays.

Henry slipped his hand down the low front of Sadie's dress, selected and paid for by him. His thumb rubbed the nipple and he felt in harden.

'The girl's in bed, is she? Will she come down?'

'No, she won't, not when you're here,' said Sadie. Her eyes were glazing and she licked her lips. 'Oh, Henry, don't stop, it's lovely.'

'Let's go to bed,' he said. 'I'm getting too old for this rolling on the sofa business.' The excitement was building in him.

'Quiet then,' whispered Sadie. They crept up the stairs and past the door of Cath's room, to hers, closing the door softly behind them. He undressed her, pausing once or twice to touch and kiss and feel particular places, and she undressed him, holding and caressing him until his half-hardened manhood was erect. They fell into bed and the springs squeaked slightly and Sadie moaned.

Along the corridor, Cath closed her eyes and tried to close her ears too. One of these days she would leave, she told herself. One of these days. But always, it came back to the question of Annie. There was no way she could leave Annie. She put her arm around the little girl whom she had found in her bed fast asleep, with her thumb firmly in her mouth when she came up. Would Annie ever grow up?

Even now, well over four years after the end of the war, Cath liked to see the lights of the city come on from the window above the sorter in the machine room. Though the days were getting longer, still it was dark before the end of the working day and the lights twinkled between the trees and on the bank that rose on the opposite side of the Wear.

The large, cumbersome tabulator in the middle of the room clanked for the final time that day and Cath pulled the cover over her punch-card machine and picked up her bag. The other girls were talking and laughing now but Cath had to get home; she couldn't be sure that her mother would be

there for Annie. She grabbed her coat from the cloakroom
and ran down the stairs. If she hurried she would get to the
bus stop in New Elvet in time to catch the bus at five. As
she emerged into the street, she didn't notice the car parked
a short distance along or the man leaning against it with his
legs crossed.

'Hey, Cath!' he called.

Cath stopped and turned and there he was. 'Jack?' She
was surprised and delighted and mixed up. She took a hesi-
tant step towards him.

'Hello there, long time no see,' he said. 'Would you like
a lift home?'

'Hello Jack,' she said. Oh, Lord, she looked a mess, she
knew she did. She wished she'd taken the time to renew her
lipstick in the cloakroom, wished she had put on her new
skirt that morning, wished she had had her hair cut and
styled at that new salon in Silver Street. The car was parked
right under a streetlight too. She put up a hand to push back
a strand of hair from her brow.

'I ... I don't live in Bishop Auckland now,' she said.

'Don't you? Well, it doesn't matter. Where do you live?
Eden Hope Colliery?'

'No. Nearer to Coundon,' she replied.

'That's all right then, I'll take you there,' said Jack.
'You want a ride, don't you?'

'Yes. Thank you.'

He opened the door and she slid into the seat. A couple
of the girls from the punch-card room stopped and looked
as he got into the driver's seat and set off, roaring up New
Elvet. He said nothing until he was on the A1, then he
glanced at her.

'You're looking lovely this evening,' he said. 'What do
you say, shall we stop somewhere for dinner? Would you
like that?'

Cath cleared her throat nervously. 'I'm not dressed for
it. Besides, I must get home. My sister will be on her own.'

'Why do you have to be there? How old is she? Where

are your parents?'

'She's ten. I don't know, she will be expecting me,' Cath answered. 'We live in a pretty isolated place. She's nervous.'

'Oh come on, we'll have an early dinner. She's not your responsibility. Besides, I'll see you get home quite early. Nothing is going to happen to her.'

Perhaps nothing would. Sadie had been home more often lately too. Jack was slowing and turning into the forecourt of the Bridge Hotel at Croxdale.

'Jack,' Cath said weakly. She looked at the front of the hotel. It was lit up and exciting and she had never eaten a meal out in anything other than a café before. 'Will I be home before half past seven?' she asked.

Jack grinned. 'Of course you will. I'll have a word at the desk. They won't be serving dinner yet but I'm sure they'll rustle up something.' He parked the car and they went into the hotel.

'Wait here,' he said. 'I won't be long.' Cath hovered a few yards behind him, very conscious of her shabby coat and plain lace-up shoes. Her bag was leather but the saddler at the pit, who made them in his spare time to make extra money for Christmas, had made it. Jack came back.

'Come on,' he said. 'We can go into the residents' bar. They can serve us there.' He took her arm and led her along the corridor to a small room with a bar at one end. A man in a white coat was polishing a glass behind the bar.

'Good evening, sir, madam,' he said politely. 'What can I get you?'

Jack ordered pink gins and they took them across to deep leather armchairs by the fire. Cath drank hers too fast and the fire of it burnt her throat and she coughed. Suddenly everything seemed slightly hazy. She had forgotten about Annie, or rather, getting back to Annie no longer seemed important.

They ate omelettes and salad and slices of chicken in a lemony sauce and Jack ordered a bottle of white wine. Cath took a sip but no more. She didn't like it.

'It's not a bad wine, is it?' Jack asked. 'Not the best, but drinkable.'

'No,' said Cath. She took another tiny sip. It was awful, she would never be able to finish it. But the food was lovely and she was hungry. Jack watched as she cleared her plate.

'You liked that anyway,' he said and she blushed. Had she eaten it too enthusiastically?

'I have to go,' she said. 'Thank you for the meal.' She got to her feet and Jack looked surprised.

'Already?' he queried. 'But we could stay, we could—' He stopped. He had been about to say they could take a room but something told him that would not go down well with her. Still, he had made a start.

They went out into the cold of the night and Cath stumbled against him, feeling a little dizzy. He put his arm around her and laughed.

'Whoops! Lean on me, you'll be fine,' he said softly.

Safely in the car, he leaned over to her and kissed her softly on the lips and her mouth opened a little. His hand was on her breast and suddenly it was under her jumper, pushing her bra up to free her breast to his touch. For a minute she was swept along with him. She closed her eyes and let the exciting sensations sweep over her. He nibbled her ear.

'I think I love you,' he whispered softly. 'You're so sweet. Let's go back in, I can get a room, please darling. It will be OK, I'll look after you.'

'No, no, I can't, Jack, no.' She could smell the wine on his breath. What was she doing? Dear God, she had almost let him. She struggled and he resisted. 'Let me go,' she whispered, for a car had pulled up beside them and a man was getting out. He looked at them curiously. 'Let me go,' she said again. 'I have to go home.'

'Oh, all right,' said Jack, frustrated. 'You bloody virgins make me sick.' He sat up and started the car and drove out on to the road. They drove through Spennymoor in silence

110

and took the road for Bishop Auckland. Cath sat beside him quietly. He was annoyed with her she could tell. Now he would finish with her, he wouldn't come back. But Jack seemed to recover his spirits by the time they had driven through Spennymoor and were heading for Coundon.

'I'm sorry,' he said and smiled at her and her heart lifted. He wasn't going to finish with her. 'Where to now?'

'Turn off here,' she said as they approached the opening to the drive leading to Half Hidden Cottage.

'Here? Are you sure?' he asked.

'Yes, of course I am,' she replied with a small laugh. 'Mr Vaughan rented this place to my mother.'

'My father keeps your mother in Half Hidden Cottage?' Jack was incredulous. But then, hadn't he known there was something going on with his father? Of course he had. He had speculated to himself whether his father was seeing a woman but he never for a minute thought that it had gone this far.

Cath watched the changing expressions on his face; the incredulity was turning to anger. He hadn't known about his father and her mother; she could see he had not and he didn't like it.

'Get out of the car,' he said eventually. 'Go on, get out!'

'Jack,' she protested. 'It's black dark out there and it is a long walk.'

Jack leaned over her and opened the car door then pushed her. She couldn't believe he meant it. She resisted for a moment and he got out of the car and walked round to her side. He took hold of her arm and pulled her out roughly so that she stumbled, catching her foot in the strap of her bag which she had placed at her feet when she got in. She didn't fall because he had such a tight grip on her arm, so tight it hurt.

'Jack, please Jack,' she gasped. Finding her feet she grasped her bag.

'Don't you speak to me, you're a little whore, that's what you are, just as your mother must be. Leading a man on, teasing him until you get what you want.'

Cath gasped anew at the injustice of it. He thrust her away and went back round the car to the driver's side. He opened the door but before he got in he shouted at her again.

'Go on, get away before I give you a hiding you won't forget. Tell your mother to get her claws out of my father, do you hear? Oh, I'll see about this I will, you'll be out on your ears in the morning so you might as well pack your bags now. I ought to have known what you were, nothing but a miner's brat, why did I ever have anything to do with you?'

The anger was rising in Cath too now; her arm hurt where he had gasped it so tightly and his words so full of contempt and scorn rang in her ears.

'Why? Why?' she shouted at him. 'Because you thought you could get what you wanted from me, that's why. Because you had an itch and I could scratch it, that's what. You thought it would be easy with a miner's brat, didn't you? Well, let me tell you—'

But what she had to tell him he didn't hear because he was in the car and roaring away down the road, his lights disappearing over the slight rise in the road and the noise of his car engine fading in the distance.

It was very dark under the trees as she set off up the drive towards Half Hidden Cottage. She stumbled over the ruts for the drive was not asphalted, it was really more like a cart track. She fell on one knee as she slipped over the edge into soft mud as the track curved away then straightened again. She had no flashlight because she had lent it to Annie so she could find her way in the house in the middle of the night. The wind soughed in the treetops, unearthly somehow. Don't be stupid, she told herself, she was thinking like Annie.

Annie, oh Annie, why hadn't she just come home to Annie instead of being tempted by that man. Well, he had shown what he really thought of her, he had. Miner's brat, the insult burned into her brain. Not the fact that she was a pitman's daughter but that he should make it a term of abuse. Oh God, she hated him, how she hated him.

She rounded the last bend in the drive and there was the house, looming even blacker than the black trees around. There was not a light in the place.

Chapter Thirteen

'Annie? Annie, where are you?'

Cath ran through the house from the front door to the kitchen, switching on the lights as she did so. She ran upstairs and through the bedrooms and the bathroom but there was no sign of Annie. Where was she? Annie wouldn't be out in the dark; she hated the dark. Oh, she should have come home as she had intended to before she saw Jack in Old Elvet. Why had she let that man talk her into going with him? She admitted to herself that she had known he wouldn't like her and her mother living in Half Hidden Cottage, but why had she thought he must already know? He was an arrogant snob, the worst kind there was.

The thoughts ran through her mind as she searched for Annie. She picked up her flashlight, which Annie had left on her dressing table, climbed into the attic to look for her, shining it all around and into the corners where the large, old roof trees met the walls. Tiny eyes shone in the light, birds twittered nervously. There were nests in crannies in the walls. Downstairs Cath dithered in the hall, unsure what to do next. Annie might have gone out with her mother. She might have done but it wasn't likely. Sadie rarely took Annie anywhere. 'She cries at the drop of a hat,' she would complain to Cath. 'I can't be bothered with her. You take her.' Annie's eyes would fill up.

Cath gazed at the telephone on the hall table. It was

newly installed and paid for by Mr Vaughan for his own convenience more than anything. But whom could she ring? Dad had no phone. She couldn't ring the police, what could she tell them? She was saved by the sound of a car coming up the drive and stopping before the house. She flung open the front door and ran towards it. Sadie was just getting out.

'Where've you been? Have you got Annie with you?'

'No, of course I haven't, why would I? I've been out all afternoon; we've been shopping in Newcastle.'

'Newcastle? You've been to Newcastle?'

'I just said so, didn't I? For goodness sake Cath, stop making a fool of yourself in front of Mr Vaughan. And give me a hand with these bags, will you?'

Henry Vaughan was taking bags out of the boot of the car; bags with names on them like Bainbridge and Fenwick. He carried them round to Cath.

'I have to go, I have a dinner engagement and I'm late as it is. Sorry,' he said. 'What did you say about the little girl? Well, she's not so little, is she, surely she will be all right?' He smiled at her, unconcerned.

'She's nervous, she wouldn't be out in the dark on her own,' said Cath.

'Well, she's not with us,' he said easily. 'I have to go, I'll call you tomorrow, Sadie.' He climbed into his car.

'Wait, you can help us – give us a lift to my father's place at Eden Hope Colliery,' said Cath.

'I'm afraid I haven't time now,' he replied as he got into his car. 'Don't worry, she'll be all right. Probably playing at a friend's house I should think. Bye, now.'

Cath couldn't believe it when he drove away. She turned to her mother. 'Why didn't you stop him?' she cried. 'We have to find Annie. She might be anywhere.'

'For goodness sake, she'll be all right, didn't Henry just say so? If she is lost, it will do her good. She has to get over being such a little coward about everything.' Sadie was beginning to sound angry. 'Give me a hand with this lot, will you?'

Cath ignored her. She wondered whether to ring for a taxi, there was one in Winton Colliery. A returning soldier had started a service after the war.

'Cath! Pick those bags up when you're told.'

Cath picked them up and ran into the hall where she threw them down and picked up the telephone.

'What are you doing? I'm not made of money you know, or are you going to pay the bill?' Sadie asked.

'I'm getting a taxi to go into Eden Hope. I'll pay for the call,' said Cath. 'I asked you not to leave her alone, I asked you not to.' Cath was repeating herself in her anxiety.

'Don't be stupid. I told you, she'll be somewhere near, she's too much of a baby to go far.' Sadie was half-way up the stairs with her bags. 'Come up and see what I've bought,' she said. She was unconcerned; happy after her day's shopping spree.

Cath was irresolute; she stood with the telephone in her hand for a moment then she put it down again. It might be quicker to walk up towards the Hall and then cut down the path leading to Eden Hope Colliery. She had left the flash-light on the table by the telephone, now she picked it up, pulled on her coat and went to the front door.

'Get yourself back here! Where are you going?' Sadie shrieked, her mood changing. 'Annie will be fine, I'm telling you, get back here!'

Sadie was shouting at no one, Cath was gone. She cut across the fields to the Hall and skirted round it to the path going down into the valley. She swept her light in broad swathes to either side and called as she went, stumbling once or twice on the uneven ground.

'Annie, Annie where are you?' There was no answer. Annie might have caught a bus. It would be still daylight when she got home and she might have just turned round and gone back to the main road when her mother was out. She was probably sitting in her dad's kitchen having supper with his new German wife.

116

At last Cath saw the lights of Eden Hope through the trees. First the lights in the pit yard, showing the tall chimney beside the engine winding house and the billow of smoke coming from it, the turning wheel. Then the rows of colliery houses and the new ones, some of them prefabricated and built where the older rows had been cleared. Alf lived in one of these now. He was used to living near his work. She ran down the road to his house and banged on the door.

'Cath? What's up?' Gerda opened the door and stood aside for Cath to enter.

'Is Annie here?' Cath was breathless. She walked past Gerda to the door to the kitchen and stared around. 'Where is she? I thought she would be here,' she said.

'No, she is not,' said Gerda. 'Why would she be here? She is not at home?'

'No, she isn't,' said Cath. She sank down on a chair. 'I was so sure she would have come here.'

'I have not seen her,' said Gerda. Her English was improving, Cath noted dimly, though her accent was not.

'Where's my dad?' she asked. 'I'll have to tell him.'

'He's at work, of course,' Gerda replied. 'It is the night shift. Extra money, we need it for the baby, it's due very soon.' She patted her now very large stomach.

'When poor Alfie has to pay money to your mother,' she added plaintively.

'I'll go to the police,' said Cath and rose to her feet.

'No, there is no need. Annie is not a baby, Cath. She will be with a friend, no? You worry too much. Sit down, I will make tea. It's so nice to see you. I am lonely here when Alf is on the night shift.'

Cath stared. What was the matter with her? She was as bad as her own mother. Nobody cared about Annie except her. When she thought about it, Annie had no friends, no real friends at all. She was usually on her own unless she was with Cath or her mother. And she played truant from school quite often. Sadie had had more than one letter about it, letters she usually threw into the fire.

'No, I'll go.'

Cath hurried along the street and up one of the colliery rows to where the police station stood. The small office was closed and dark but there was a light in the house where Sergeant Duffy lived. Cath knocked on the door and the sergeant himself opened it. He was in his shirtsleeves with his braces hanging down by his side.

'What do you want? I'm off duty – do you know what time it is?'

'My little sister had disappeared, Sergeant Duffy.'

'Disappeared? You'd best come in. Wait, I'll open the office.' He closed the door on her and after a moment the light went on in the office. Inside he was taking a form from a drawer. He looked up when she came up to the counter.

'Oh yes, I know you. You're Sadie Raine's girl, aren't you? Surely your sister is ten or eleven now, isn't she? I thought you were talking about a little lass. Do you think I've nothing better to do than run after young lasses? She's likely playing chasey with the lads if she's owt like her m—' He coughed as he saw Cath's expression. 'Any road, how long has she been missing?'

'I don't know, she was gone when I came in from work tonight.'

Sergeant Duffy put the form back in the drawer. 'Tonight? She's likely gone to the pictures with her mates, man. Do you think I've nowt better to do with my time?' he repeated. 'I was going to have my supper. Get along home before I charge you with wasting police time. You'll likely find her there any road.'

Cath found herself out on the road outside once again. She hadn't even had time to explain but what could she have said? Nobody took her seriously. She would walk back by the main road, she decided, perhaps she would find Annie there. Maybe it was that she was making a fuss about nothing.

It took her an hour and an half to walk back to Half Hidden Cottage and when she got there the house was in darkness. As she let herself in, Sadie called from upstairs.

'Is that you, Cath?'

'Yes, is Annie back?'

'I don't know, I was so tired I went straight to sleep. Go on to bed yourself, I told you she would be all right.'

Cath was desperately tired but she ran up the stairs and switched the light on in her room. Annie was not curled up in the bed. Nor was she in her own room. She wasn't in the house. The only sound was a faint snoring from her mother's room. Cath felt defeated. She took off her coat and sat down on the bed then lay back against the pillow. Her feet ached and she kicked off her shoes.

When Cath woke light was filtering through the sides of the curtains. Outside a bird twittered and was answered by another. She could feel a dead weight of worry on her but for a moment couldn't think what it was. Then she remembered. She sat up so swiftly her head spun. She stood and went into Annie's room but the covers on Annie's bed were smooth and unruffled.

'Mam,' she cried, standing at the door of her mother's room, 'Mam, Annie didn't come home. Something must have happened to her, I told you didn't I?'

'By, I'll kill the little brat when I get hold of her,' Sadie grumbled. 'Worrying me like this.' She sat up in bed and yawned hugely. Her make-up from the day before was smeared on her face, black eyebrow pencil was down one side of her left eye where she had rubbed it, giving her a clownish look which was enhanced by her rouge, which had spread to her nose.

'Isn't it time you went to work?' she asked as she pushed back the bedclothes and got out of bed. The room smelled stale with body odour and cheap scent.

'Work? How can I go to work?' asked Cath, astonished that her mother should suggest it. 'I'm going out to look for

119

her – she could have fallen in the dark and broken her leg or many a thing, couldn't she?'

'Good God, our Cath,' said Sadie scornfully, 'you're always making a big thing out of nowt. Well, hadaway down and make us a pot of tea and we'll talk about it.'

Cath was about to protest but decided that if she got her mother into a better frame of mind she might listen to her. She went down to the kitchen and lit the fire, propping the tin blazer on the bar to blaze it up so she could boil the kettle. There was no gas ring fuelled by coal gas from the pit here, as it was too far out.

Eventually the kettle boiled and she brewed tea in the old brown teapot they had carried form Eden Hope. She wasn't hungry and she was fairly sure her mother wouldn't be either for Sadie rarely ate breakfast.

'When Annie comes home we will have to see about getting her help, Mam,' she said as Sadie came into the kitchen yawning hugely and running her hands through her tousled hair. She sat down at the table and took the cup Cath handed to her.

'What do you mean?' she demanded 'What help? There's nowt the matter with her.'

'There is,' Cath insisted. 'You know there is. We could go and ask Dr Short, couldn't we? You can go to see a specialist for free now with the National Health.'

'What specialist? Do you mean a mind doctor? You think our Annie's not right in the head, don't you? You think she should be in Winterton, don't you? Why don't you say what you mean?'

'Mam,' said Cath. Her heart sank. This wasn't going the way she had planned.

'I'm not having a lass of mine going in the loony bin, our Cath,' Sadie declared. 'I'd never be able to hold my head up again, not round here I wouldn't. Anyway, there's nothing wrong with her. She just needs to grow up, that's all. A good hiding I'll give her when I get her back, I can tell you, causing all this carry-on.' She drained her cup and poured herself another, adding milk and sugar. All the time she chuntered on. 'I'm not going looking for the little slut neither. She's just making a bid for sympathy, that's what she's doing. I'll give her sympathy when I get hold of her, I'm telling you.'

Cath couldn't stand any more. 'Mam, I'm going to look for her. She might have fallen going down the path and rolled off to the side. She might have broken her leg or many a thing.' If she didn't get away from her mother she might do her some damage, she thought. She felt like throwing the teapot at her – that would shut her up. For a moment she imagined the hot tea running down her mother's face, making channels in the Max Factor pancake she still had on from yesterday. Cath ran from the kitchen and grabbed her coat before she could actually do it.

She went to the Hall first. Not to the front door but to the kitchen door. The cook or Joseph, the chauffeur-handyman, might have seen her. It was worth taking the chance of encountering Jack or even Mr Vaughan though she curled up inside at the thought. She had to find Annie and it was possible she had come across the fields and hidden in one of the outbuildings when the darkness came.

The kitchen door was open for it was an unusually pleasant day for early spring. Cook was making pastry at the scrubbed wooden table in the kitchen. She looked up as Cath stood in the doorway.

'You're trespassing,' she said and carried on rolling out.

'Good morning,' said Cath, 'I'm looking for my sister.'

'Well, you're not likely to find her here, are you?' It was Joseph, the chauffeur-handyman who spoke this time. 'I've seen nobody around this morning. But if I catch her I'll send her home with a flea in her ear. Creeping around on private property, the very idea.'

'We live here,' said Cath with dignity. 'In Half Hidden Cottage.'

'Aye, I know where you live. Did you think we wouldn't? Your mother's that one battening on poor Mr Vaughan. You can't keep anything like that from the staff, you know. We get to know everything. And it doesn't give you the right to wander about the place especially not around the house. So get yourself away.'

'There's nothing poor about him,' Cath was stung into replying. 'But it's my little sister I'm worried about. I asked a civil question and I'd be glad of a civil answer.'

'Aye well, we haven't seen her,' said Cook. She went to the oven and the smell of new-baked pies filled the room, making Cath dizzy. She hadn't eaten since the evening before when she had a meal with Jack Vaughan in the Bridge Hotel. Now wouldn't that little titbit give them something to think about.

'Are you sure? I mean, what about the outhouses?'

'By, you don't give up, do you? Get away with you. I've been round them all this morning, all but the ones that are locked up. I'm telling you, there's nobody there.'

Cath would have persevered, maybe insisted on looking herself, but at that moment she heard a man's step approaching the door leading into the rest of the house and Jack's voice calling out.

'Joseph? Are you there, Joseph?'

Cath turned and fled for the path leading down to Eden Hope. The ground was wet but beginning to dry up as the sun and wind got to it so it was not quite so slippery as it had been the night before. There were footprints in the patches of mud but more than one person had made them and she couldn't be sure if Annie had come this way. There was smaller ones and some made by a man's heavy boots, water standing in the holes made by the studs of the soles. In any case she went slowly, looking about to either side. She found a dead branch and broke off a stick that was manageable enough for her to beat around the patches of tall sere grass and dead undergrowth and that was how she saw that the smaller prints had left the path. There were slip marks and one larger one where someone must have fallen. Further down the bank she noticed a cut in the bankside and below that she could hear water running – some small stream or beck, or just extra water running off after the rain of the week before. Cath followed it down to a miniature ravine and there, in the bottom, was what looked like a bundle of rags.

Chapter Fourteen

'Gran,' Ronnie moaned but without much hope. He was cold and his ankle throbbed and throbbed and he knew his gran wasn't going to find him and neither would anyone else. He was lost in the wilderness, just like in a story his cousin Eric had told him. Only he knew a bear wouldn't get him, not in these woods. Hadn't he been all over them and not seen a single bear. He knew where there was a badger sett and a foxhole with cubs an' all. He knew where the rabbit warren began on the edge of the woods but he hadn't seen a bear.

'You're a soft lad, Ronnie Robson,' his gran had said to him when he came in all upset because Eric had shouted after him, 'Loony! Loony!'

'Why didn't you give him a clout around the ear? You're bigger than he is any road. He's nowt but a bully that lad, he'll come to no good, I can tell you. By, I'll have a word with his mother I will an' all.'

Ronnie knew he was a soft lad, he was told it often enough. But he wasn't a loony, no he was not. He had gone into the woods up beyond Eden Hope and listened to the birds. They were busy building nests and they twittered and sang and flew about busily and he calmed down and sat very still, just watching and listening. He liked it in the woods. He liked to be with the other lads too but if Eric was there they chased him away.

He'd been in the woods all night though and he didn't like that. It was when he had seen the girl coming along the path. She had seen him and run away crying and he forgot his own troubles altogether and ran after her. He had slipped on the path and went tumbling head over heels down the bankside and landed up in a heap on the bottom. He tried to stand but he couldn't.

Cath was now picking her way down to the heap of old clothes. For one horrible minute she had thought it might be Annie but it wasn't, she could see that as she got near. Annie wouldn't be wearing an army surplus greatcoat and corduroy trousers. The coat was the same colour as Annie's, a sort of dark cream colour and, from the top of the bank, she had been fooled but now she could see it wasn't Annie's.

'Please, God,' she prayed as she stood still by a patch of old nettle stalks with a few new green shoots just coming through, 'Please God, don't let him be dead.'

'Gran? Gran? I'm frightened. Take me home, Gran.' He sounded like a little lad.

He wasn't dead, he was moving. He turned his head to look at her and his face was bruised and scratched from where he had fallen through the undergrowth. He had taken off his boot and his foot was blue and white and swollen.

'Ronnie!' She hadn't seen him for years, not since they had moved to the pre-fabs but Ronnie was unmistakable. His skin was normally yellowish though now a pallor was showing through and he was shivering violently. His clothes were wet from the tiny stream.

'What happened?' Cath asked. 'Come on, let me help you get out of the water. Can you walk?' But of course he couldn't walk, she told herself crossly. Not even Ronnie would have stayed in the water if he could have walked.

'I can't move, lass,' he moaned. 'It hurts and I want my gran.'

Cath took hold of his shoulder and tried to pull him clear but he shouted with pain. 'Come on, you have to help me,' said Cath. 'Put your weight on your good foot and push.'

She managed to move him only a few inches but at least he was out of the water. He was sweating now, she could smell the rank odour of him and his nose was running.

'Have you seen my sister? A little girl? She hasn't come home either.'

Ronnie moaned but didn't answer and Cath shook his shoulder until he focused on her.

'A little girl? Do you know Annie? A girl about ten? Ronnie!'

'Aye, a little lass, I did see a little lass. Before it was dark though. She was running along the path. I ran after her and she fell down and then I fell down and she went away. I was only going to tell her about the badgers.'

Cath stared at him. Had he really seen Annie? It was hard to tell. Maybe he was just repeating what she said. It was best to get help for him now. She could ask him about Annie later.

It took only fifteen minutes for her to run into the village to old Mrs Robson's house in the rows and soon she was on her way back with a couple of off-shift miners. They made a chair with their hands and carried Ronnie down to the rows with Cath trailing behind.

'You don't have to stay, I can manage,' Mrs Robson said to her. 'The doctor's on his way and I have neighbours, you know.' She must have realised she sounded short and, as an afterthought, she added, 'Thanks for what you did. Don't think I'm not grateful, I am. And I'm sure our Ronnie will be an' all.'

Cath was reminded once again that most of the folk in Eden Hope disapproved of her and her mother, even her little sister. She had to speak to Ronnie.

'I wanted to ask him about my sister,' she protested. 'It will only take a minute; she's been missing since last night. Ronnie said he had seen her.'

Mrs Robson bridled. 'You're not saying my Ronnie had anything to do with her going missing, are you? By, he

126

wouldn't hurt a fly.'

'No, I'm not saying that but he did say he'd seen her,' Cath insisted.

'Well, you cannot be bothering him now, you can see how he's held,' Mrs Robson said firmly.

'But—'

'Look, here's Dr Short an' all. Go on, I'll ask Ronnie if he's seen her. He'll likely talk better to me,' said Mrs Robson. She had edged Cath to the door and was standing in the opening, blocking it as though she was defending her young. The doctor had walked up the yard and was standing waiting to get in and Cath had perforce to move away.

'He'd seen our Annie, Mam,' Cath said when she got back to Half Hidden Cottage. 'He'd seen her, he said so; he ran after her.'

'The loony ran after her? Did he say that? By, I'm away down to Eden Hope and I'll get to know what he's done with my little lass, I will. I'll have the truth out of him, see if I don't!'

Cath was taken aback by this change in Sadie's attitude. Suddenly her mother was concerned for Annie, as concerned as Cath could wish for. But she hadn't wished it to be like this.

'Mam, don't, the lad's not well, he's broken his ankle and I think he's got a fever. I—'

Sadie interrupted, her voice rising ready to do battle. 'I'll give him fever if he's hurt my lass,' she said grimly. 'And that gran of his an' all. He shouldn't have been living in the village any road; he should have been in the mental hospital in Winterton. That's the only place for such as him; he's not fit to be living among decent folk.'

Sadie was pulling on her coat as she spoke. She went to the mirror on the wall and fluffed out her hair and applied lipstick to her already red lips. Cath watched, dumbstruck. Her mother never ceased to amaze her. Only yesterday she had been saying that Annie would end up in Winterton. She didn't care about her daughter but she was ready for a

127

fight, especially one that might get the village up in arms and on her side for a change.

'Mam, don't,' Cath said at last.

'Don't what? I have to find the bairn, don't I? You were on at me to find her long enough. But I never thought she was in danger, no I didn't, especially not from a loony. Well, now I know she is I'm going to find out what he's done with her and if he's done anything, anything at all, the dirty bugger, I'll flay him alive, I will, I'm telling you.'

'Mam, we don't know that he's done anything. In fact, I don't think he has. He's not a bad lad, you know he isn't.'

'He's not all there, is he? How do we know what he thinks or does? Sometimes he looks at me with a very funny look, he does an' all.'

'He doesn't mean anything,' said Cath. Sometimes Ronnie did gaze blankly at people it was true. But it was just as a baby or a young child would. 'He's trying to understand, that's all, poor lad.'

'Aye, well, I'll make him understand, see if I don't,' said Sadie and rushed out of the front door. She hadn't got far before she was back; she'd forgotten what a walk it was to Eden Hope. 'I'll call Henry,' she said. 'He'll help me. He'll give me a ride to the village anyway.'

Cath stood by; she had to stop her mother from shouting accusations at Ronnie Robson without proof that he had done anything. Suddenly she remembered a day long ago when she and Annie had been for a walk and they had seen Ronnie in a gap in the hedge. She had been about to greet him but then she realised that he had his fly open and his penis in his hand. She had thought he was simply about to urinate but maybe he wasn't, maybe he was playing with himself. She had rushed Annie away in any case, before she saw anything. But surely this was different, Ronnie wouldn't do anything to a little girl, she told herself. Of course he would not. But a tiny doubt was sown.

'I'm going to catch the bus into Eden Hope and go and see my dad again. He'll be in this morning; he's on night shift. And Annie might be there too by now.'

Sadie was sobbing into the receiver, telling Henry, Cath presumed. 'Give me a lift into Eden Hope, please, Henry,' she pleaded. She listened to the reply then raised her voice. 'Why not? Who cares if anyone sees us together? Everybody knows, any road. Henry!' She was still talking when Cath went out and ran down the drive, in time to catch the United bus to Eden Hope just as Sadie could have done. But Sadie liked to ride in style nowadays, she thought bitterly.

Once in the village, Cath skirted the rows and made for the new houses. Alf was in by himself for Gerda had gone to the shops. He answered the door with his braces hanging down by the sides of his trousers, his shirt with no collar and the top button open.

'Cath!' he said in surprise and smiled broadly. 'Howay in, I'm just mashing the tea.'

'Have you seen our Annie?' Cath asked without preamble. 'We've lost our Annie, Dad, did Gerda say?'

'Gerda? No, she said nowt. When did you see her?'

'I came last night.' Cath felt bitter that Gerda hadn't thought to say anything to her father.

'Last night? Do you mean the bairn's been missing since yesterday?' Alf was the first person to respond to Annie's disappearance with alarm and Cath was grateful. She felt a rush of affection for him.

'Oh, Dad,' she said her voice breaking. 'I've looked everywhere for her and nobody cares. But now Mam thinks it might have been Ronnie Robson—'

'Ronnie Robson? The lad that's not all there, do you mean? Why? Why would she think that?'

So Cath told him all that had happened since the day before.

'I'll get me jacket,' said Alf. 'We'll look for her. Me and me marras.'

'But Alf, you have not sleep!' wailed Gerda, who had come in while Cath was talking. 'How you go to work

129

tonight? We need the money for the baby.'

'Is that all you think about woman?' Alf said savagely. 'Annie is my bairn an' all, you know. You wait here, don't go out in case Annie comes here.'

It didn't take long for Alf to rouse his marras. In the event there was a crowd of them searching in the woods and fields round about Eden Hope and Winton and even up the opposite side of the valley, spreading out into wide circles but they didn't find her. The police had been alerted and were taking it seriously now. Sergeant Duffy, back in the tiny police station at Eden Hope, was defensive when Cath confronted him.

'Many a lass stays out late,' he said in self-defence because he hadn't bothered the night before. 'If we looked for all of them we would be doing nowt else. You yourself said your sister had only been gone a couple of hours. It was too soon. But we are looking for her now, aren't we?'

Alf and his marras couldn't find any clue out in the woods or fields.

'She might have gone home, we wouldn't know, out here on the bankside,' Jack Lowe said at last. 'Me and you could go and see, Alf. Any road, we're knackered, we could do with a break.'

Alf demurred but the men were ready to go back, he could see that. After all, they had worked the night shift and had very little sleep since. In the end he agreed and the men trudged back home while Alf and Jack headed off for Half Hidden Cottage. The place was deserted so their journey was fruitless. They too went back to Eden Hope, lucky enough to catch the bus.

There was a crowd in the back street outside Mrs Robson's house; all trying to get into the back yard at least. Sergeant Duffy was there and a policeman from the town, standing in front of the gate.

'Go away or you'll all find yourselves in the lockup for

the night,' the sergeant was shouting. 'The lad's not here, I'm telling you, there's only old Mrs Robson. You should think shame to be frightening her like this, you should an' all.' He folded his arms and stood with his feet apart, his bulk blocking the gateway.

'Where is he then? Where's the loony? He's done something to my little lass and we'll have him for it. We'll cut his bloody balls off when we get hold of him, I promise you that, Sergeant Duffy. An' nobody will blame us for it, will they?'

It was Sadie who was shouting, her voice shrill and venomous. Alf fought his way through the crowd to her side.

'Oh, so you've come have you? I didn't think you could spare the time from your fancy piece to look for our Annie,' said Sadie. Her eyes sparkled and there was a high colour in her cheeks. She is enjoying herself, Cath thought bitterly.

'Gerda's my wife!' Alf shouted back at her. 'She's more of a wife than you ever were an' all.'

'And Annie's your bairn, or had you forgotten that?'

'You should have looked after her,' said Alf. 'I heard you were gadding about in your fancy man's car.'

'Stop it, please,' begged Cath. 'It's no good playing war now, it's our Annie we have to think about.'

'Aye, you're right,' said Alf. 'Does anyone know where Ronnie Robson is? I'm not saying he did anything mind, but if he says he saw the lass—'

'He was taken to the cottage hospital, Lady Eden's, you know,' the sergeant said quietly in Alf's ear but Sadie heard him.

'Lady Eden's!' she cried. 'The sod's in Lady Eden's, that's where he is. Getting his poor little foot attended to, I suppose.' The last was spoken in a parody of sympathy. 'Did you hear that, you lot? Let's away into Bishop, we'll haul him out of there. By, he'll tell me the truth or I'll know the reason why, I will, I swear I will!'

'Howay, missus!' cried a new voice, a young man's voice. Everyone turned to him, it was John Robson, one of Ronnie's cousins and with him were a few other lads from Winton. 'Let's away,' he went on. 'Let's show him what we think of beasts that molest little lasses!'

It was like a rallying cry and the crowd turned round and surged down the row and along the top on the road to the town. Some of them walked, some ran and the lucky few who happened to be at the bus stop when the bus pulled in, climbed aboard, Sadie among them.

'We'll have you all for this!' Sergeant Duffy yelled. 'Causing an affray, public disorder—' He was spluttering to the backs of most of them for they were caught up in the excitement, women as well as men. Only a few remained behind, among them Cath, Alf and Jack Lowe and the two policemen.

'We'll take the taxi,' said Alf then looked at Sergeant Duffy. 'Not that I'm going to do anything to the lad but I have to know what's happening. You never know, he might know where she is. You come with us, Cath.'

Sergeant Duffy looked stunned at what had happened. After all, most of the families in his area were law-abiding, chapel-going folk and for a near riot to develop so quickly – well, he couldn't believe it. He collected himself and turned to the policeman from the town. 'You stay here and keep folk out of the old woman's house. I'll have to go back to the station and ring the inspector in the town, warn him, like.'

The crowd walking along the public footpath through the fields to South Church, and then along the road past the ancient St Andrew's Church and up to Cockton Hill, were angry and voluble with it. Everyone who saw them could see that and a lot of people did see it for the noise brought people out of their houses to gape and then to ask what the commotion was all about and then some of the onlookers joined them. By the time they arrived at the cottage hospital there were a few hundred of them and the police were calling for reinforcements. Nothing like it had been seen since the thirties and the hunger marches. But the hunger marches had been orderly while this was a rabble.

Chapter Fifteen

About the time that Cath was sitting in the Bridge Hotel
with Jack, Annie was standing in the hall of Half Hidden
Cottage staring fearfully up the stairs. Was there someone
up there? She was sure she had heard a noise as she crossed
over from the sitting room to the kitchen. Cath always said
it was nothing, just the old timbers of the house settling but
Annie wasn't sure. Anyway, she thought, she wasn't going
to go upstairs and look. Suppose it was a ghost?

She looked through the open door leading to the kitchen.
The window was bigger in there but it had good strong
curtains with a blackout lining left over from the war years
and if she closed them no one could look in and see that she
was on her own.

Why didn't Cath come home? Where was Mam? The
questions ran round and round in her mind and her eyes
filled with the hated tears. Mam thought she was a cry baby
because she cried so easily but she couldn't help it. No
matter how hard she tried to control them the tears still
came and at the least thing they overflowed. Mam had no
patience with her and sometimes Cath didn't have much.

The sun was sinking; shadows were creeping in from the
corners. The best thing to do was go, she thought, though
Mam would be annoyed with her. She would leave a note,
she thought. Quickly she tore a piece of paper from her
exercise book and wrote on it, 'Gone to Dad's house.

Annie.' She put it on the hall table then took her coat from the hook. There was a bus at half-six; if she ran she could catch it.

Annie rushed out of the house, banging the door closed behind her and ran down the drive to the road. The tears came in earnest when she saw the bus disappearing towards Eden Hope.

'Wait for me!' she shouted after it and waved her arms but the bus only gathered speed and went on its way. Oh, where was Cath? Desperately she caught hold of her fear. There was nothing, nothing at all to be frightened of, hadn't Cath always said so? She would go down the path through the woods, it was a short cut and she had walked it many a time with her sister, hadn't she?

She hurried along the road to the gap where a track led through a field and joined the footpath going to the colliery at Eden Hope. It would be properly dark by the time she got to the bottom of the path but the lights of the colliery would be on, wouldn't they? If she got to the colliery it was easy to get from there to her dad's house on the new site.

Once she was in the woods it was darker because the trees grew tall on either side and there was a lot of under-growth. Some of it was rank and damp, left over from last year and it smelled of mould. It was cold too; Annie shivered and hastened her pace.

She was well into the woods when she realised someone was following her. She looked back and saw it was Ronnie Robson. He was waving and shouting something she couldn't understand.

'Go away!' she called and began to run, stumbling and picking herself up. Then round a bend she saw a grassy bit to the side. It was trodden down and there were wet patches but she thought, if she got off the main footpath and hid in the bushes, Ronnie would go past her and she would be all right if she just waited until he had gone.

He didn't go on though, he turned off after her and she was terror-stricken as he crashed about, stumbling and slipping on the mud. She crouched down behind a gorse bush, pressing into it and it prickled and scratched at her face and hands as though it was pushing her off. But Ronnie was past her; she could smell the male smell of him lingering behind him.

He cried out as he fell heavily; she heard the slurp of him slipping and the squishy sound as his bulk hit the mud. He cried out and this time she heard him plainly. 'Gran! Gran!'

Annie stood up and looked down the bankside. Ronnie was right at the bottom in the little stream that ran there, he was wailing now. She didn't wait to see if he was badly hurt, she just ran. Back up the bank to the footpath and along it and down towards the lights of Eden Hope Colliery, shining in the distance. She was almost through the trees and then it was an easy walk from there to the new houses. She stopped running for she was panting for breath and had a stitch in her side. She bent over, taking great breaths of air, the pain tearing through her chest before slowly subsiding.

Her vision cleared and she realised there was someone before before her, she could see his feet astride the narrrow path. Slowly she straightened and looked him in the face.

'Come away, Mam, come away, leave the lad alone,' said Cath, tugging at her mother's jacket. Sadie pushed her violently away.

'Come away? I most certainly will not, my girl, why should I? It's my bairn that's gone, God only knows what's happened to her. I want the truth out of him, the loony. I want the whole bloody truth and I want my bairn back.'

'This isn't going to help though, Mam,' said Cath, rubbing her shoulder where Sadie had pushed her. Turning, she saw her father pushing his way through the crowd to them. 'Dad, please, tell her, we have to go home. Annie might be there and we don't know that Ronnie has done anything to her, do we?'

Alf was himself startled that things had got so out of

hand. He had been carried along with the others, it was a kind of madness that had seized them. But still, if the girl was all right, where the hell was she? And Ronnie was in there somewhere, wasn't he? Ronnie knew what had happened and he was going to tell them if he, Alf Raine, had to beat it out of him.

'I don't know, Cath, he's done something to our Annie, he must have done. Everybody says so. We have to find out. Don't you care what has happened to your little sister? If he's done nowt why then, she'll be all right, won't she? Who else could have done it but the loony?'

'Move along there! Get away to your homes, you scum, or I'll have the lot of you!'

A mounted policeman was urging his horse through the crowd to stand before the main door of the hospital and he was thunderously angry. 'Ignorant, bloody pitmen!' he said not quite under his breath and those closest to him heard him. They surged forward again and he held up his baton ready to brain the first one of them to touch his horse or him. Their attention was diverted as a curtain was pulled aside for only a minute but it was enough for the crowd had seen it and they had seen who was inside.

'It's him! Look, it's him, it's Ronnie Robson, the dirty sod,' a man shouted. He was still in his black from the pit and his eyes shone bright with excitement. They rushed forward and flung themselves at the window and there was the ominous sound of broken glass. Inside people were screaming.

Next day the pit village of Eden Hope was very quiet and Winton Colliery was also very subdued. There were few people on the streets except for those who ventured out to buy a newspaper. Most people had the *Northern Echo* delivered to the door but the whole stock of national newspapers was sold out at Hetherington's the newsagents on the corner of Main Street. It wasn't often that the nationals took much notice of what happened in the mining villages

137

or the town either, come to that. Unless there was a disaster in one of the pits, that is.

'Aye well, I'd rather we hadn't been in the papers over something like what happened yesterday,' said Betty Lowe. 'I don't know what possessed you lot but I think it must have been the devil, I do indeed.'

Jack didn't reply. He simply picked up his knife and fork and began eating the dinner she had plumped down in front of him.

He had a copy of the *Daily Herald* beside his plate and he kept glancing at it and doing his best to ignore his wife. For the truth was, he was embarrassed and ashamed by what had happened the day before. Some of his marras had broken into a hospital, for pity's sake! They must have been mad. Indeed, yes, indeed they had been mad, him and Alf an' all the rest. They had even laid hands on a patient. Ronnie Robson was in a chair with his foot up on a stool and the plaster of Paris was still wet on his leg. He was whimpering and shrinking back into the chair when two men, who were not from Eden Hope but South Church, had taken hold of him and dragged him out. Jack could hear him now; he had heard it every time he fell into an exhausted sleep.

'Gran,' Ronnie had cried, 'Gran, I didn't do anything!'

His cry was almost drowned out by the shout from outside. The police had arrived in force.

There was the devil to pay. Alf and half a dozen others, the ones the police had said were the ringleaders, were in the lockup on Fore Bondgate and due to go before the magistrates the morn. In fact, when the police had got there in force the main of the crowd had wind of their coming and had disappeared like snow off the oven top. All those left had been hauled down to the police station and had been given times when they were to be summoned before the magistrates. His turn was Friday morning, ten o'clock, and it meant he had to take a shift off work and explain that to the gaffer an' all. The gaffers were all the same even though the pits had just been nationalised. You couldn't tell them nowt. His thoughts were interrupted by his wife.

'I don't know why you're sitting there in a sulk,' she said tartly.

'I'm not sulking.'

'Well, I don't know what you're doing 'cause you're not listening to me,' she said. 'That poor old Mrs Robson—'

Jack exploded to his feet. 'Never mind her, what about the little lass? Where is she, can you tell me that?'

'No, I cannot. But that was no reason to make a riot, this isn't the wild west,' said Betty who spent every Friday night at the picture house over the Workingmen's Club in Eldon Lane and knew what she was talking about. 'This is England, this is, and we're nowt if we're not law abiding.'

'I'm off,' said Jack. 'We have to find little Annie and with Alf in the lockup I have to do all I can.'

'Well, watch what you're doing, man,' said Betty.

Jack went out and strode up to the colliery yard. He still had an hour or two before he had to go on shift and he felt in need of fresh air. There was a breeze laden with the smell of coal and tainted with sulphur but he didn't notice it, having known it all his life.

In his mind's eye he could see the headlines in the papers. MINERS RUN RIOT OVER MISSING CHILD. And worse, MENTALLY HANDICAPPED BOY ATTACKED IN HOSPITAL. Jack shook his head to try to get rid of the images. He walked along the old wagon way past the old workings towards Winton then turned back and cut through the woods towards Half Hidden Cottage.

Cath had drunk so many cups of tea her stomach felt sour and empty but she couldn't eat anything. She had spent two hours in the police station and at the magistrates' court with her mother but the magistrate had allowed them to go home.

'You have a missing child and are worried about her, I

139

can understand that,' the magistrate had said. 'So I am allowing you to go home on condition you don't try to speak or get in touch with Ronald Robson or his family. Do you understand that?'

'We do, sir,' said Cath. She was scarlet with embarrassment and shame and her voice was very low so that the magistrate asked her to repeat it.

'We understand, sir,' said Cath, too loudly this time, so that he looked at her over his spectacles.

'It's not fair though,' said Sadie. Her face was red too but with anger. 'What about my bairn? That daftie has done something—'

'That's enough!' the magistrate roared. 'Another word and I will put you in the cells, missing child or not.'

Cath had taken her mother's arm and pulled her from the court into Fore Bondgate.

'Let go of me,' Sadie said grimly. 'I'm going to ring Henry and tell him to come and pick us up. I have to look for Annie myself since no one else is bothering.'

Cath gasped. All her mam had thought about before now was getting to Ronnie. But there was no point in remonstrating with her. For herself, Cath had a deep dread sitting on her chest like a dead weight. Something awful must have happened to Annie and it was all her fault. She should have been home and instead she was enjoying herself in that hotel with Jack Vaughan, who had then shown how he despised and hated her family only too clearly when he found out exactly who she was.

Henry had not come to pick them up in Auckland in spite of Sadie's telephone call. Cath didn't know what he had said to her mother but she had some out of the telephone box with a grim expression.

'Howay,' Sadie said. 'We'll get the bus, I'm dependent on nobody, me.'

Annie had been missing two nights now. Where was she? The question ran round and round in Cath's tired brain.

140

They were too far from the shops to buy a newspaper. Cath decided to walk up to the Hall and see if she could have a look round the outbuildings. If she approached it from the back perhaps it wouldn't matter if Joseph saw her, so long as she avoided Henry and Jack. Joseph would tell her if there was anything in the newspaper too.

Her mother was still in bed. 'I haven't slept a wink all night, thinking of our Annie,' she said. I'm worried out of my mind, I am, worried out of my mind. Fetch us a cup of tea, will you?'

So Cath had made the tea and taken a cup up to her mother and then slipped out of the house. As she did so she could hear her mother's soft snoring from upstairs.

Getting close to the Hall she saw a police car standing on the drive. She hid behind a tree as the front door of the house opened and two men came out and stood talking at the bottom of the imposing flight of steps. One was Henry Vaughan and the other looked like Sergeant Duffy. There were two other policemen in the car.

Of course the police would have searched the surrounding buildings of the Hall, she thought. But still she would look for herself, satisfy herself. There were some old farm buildings with odd nooks and crannies. Cath began to circle round the Hall, making for the back.

She was in a clump of rhododendron bushes fairly close to the police car when she heard Henry's voice clearly.

'I didn't know the family had something of a reputation when I let them have the cottage, Sergeant,' he was saying, his voice booming loudly. 'I would never have chanced it if I had. Up here we just don't hear anything from the pit villages you know. We were troubled with the miners poaching during the war but there is less of that now. Princely wages they get, or so I hear. After nationalisation that it.'

The sergeant murmured something Cath couldn't catch and turned towards the car.

'Well, you've done your duty and looked for the child,'

said Henry. 'Though as I said, she's not so much of a child is she? Nearly eleven, isn't it? If the lad did do anything she probably led him on. Those miners' girls grow up quickly I've noticed. Well, goodbye, Sergeant. Let me know if you find anything.'

Cath thought of Annie, little Annie who was frightened of her own shadow ... She had to restrain herself from jumping up and yelling at Mr high and mighty Vaughan. Instead, she clenched her teeth and continued to skirt round the Hall to the back and the stables and, behind them, the other outbuildings. Not that she expected to find anything but she had to see for herself that Annie wasn't and hadn't been there.

The sound of the police car going back down the drive faded into the distance.

142

Chapter Sixteen

Cath sat down on a large stone that had fallen from a dry-stone wall leading out and up the hill behind the older outhouses. She was fairly well hidden from the house and the stables for there was an old earth closet on one side and some sort of grain store on the other.

She stared at the door of the closet. It had an ancient brass sneck latch, which was green with verdigris and slightly bent so the door didn't close properly, though there was an old padlock hanging open on the handle. Inside there were two wooden seats over the hole, one adult size and one for a child. There was even a string hanging on a nail on the wall and a couple of small pieces of newspaper on the string, where people had pulled off squares. The old people in the rows called this sort of closet a netty; tiredly, she wondered why. When she had seen it she had thought Annie might have sheltered there if she couldn't find her way home. But there were no signs that she had.

Cath was light-headed and her stomach was empty too. She hadn't eaten since yesterday and very little then. Her head drooped until she heard a sound close by. She jerked up and hurried inside the closet, closing the door until whoever it was went by. Light came in a beam through the heart-shaped hole cut in the door and she put an eye to it. She jumped as a small dog stuck his nose through the opening at the bottom of the door and barked in excitement.

'Come away from there, Tuppence!'

It was Jack, walking up by the hay barn and coming towards where she was. Cath held her breath. The last person she wanted to meet now was Jack. His contemptuous words to her rang again in her ears and she just didn't feel up to it, oh no, she couldn't face him, she really couldn't.

'Tuppence! Come away,' Jack said again and the dog withdrew its nose. But it had been enough for Jack to stop. He pushed against the door and she moved behind it, hugging the wall. He lifted the sneck and glanced in and she held her breath. After a moment he closed the door and whistled for the dog. Cath breathed a sigh of relief. She waited for a few minutes then cautiously opened the door, stepped out and peered round the corner of the netty. There was no sign of Jack, thank goodness. She walked on towards another shed a few yards away. Only he was lying in wait for her at the back of the netty, holding the terrier in his arms to keep it quiet. He stepped out and faced her.

'Oh! You're here,' she said.

'I am, yes. But then, this is our land. What are you doing here?' He spoke quietly enough, his tone neutral but his eyes were as cold as the North Sea.

Cath lifted her chin. 'I am looking for my little sister,' she said.

'You won't find her here. These outbuildings have been searched by my men and the police.'

'I know but I thought I might see something, anything that might tell me she had been here.'

'There is nothing. Go home, she's not here. No doubt she will turn up when she's ready. She'll be like the rest of you, off with someone—'

'She's only ten! How dare you say that!'

He had the grace to look a little ashamed. 'Well, maybe I shouldn't have but you make me angry. Now do as I say and get off this land.'

'I want to look in the shed, it's the last one. She might have been there and dropped something.' Cath looked up into his face. How had she not noticed before how hard he could look, how his lips went into such a thin line? She stood her ground though her heart pounded in her chest.

He had put the dog down and it was nosing about in the grass following some animal scent. Now he grabbed her arm and pulled her towards him.

'Don't touch me,' she said and again through clenched teeth, 'Do *not* touch me or I'll scream the place down.'

Jack grinned. 'Go ahead, scream,' he invited her. 'There's no one about. Who do you think will hear you?' Cath tried to pull away but his grasp only became tighter. He pulled her towards the shed with one hand and opened the door with the other and thrust her inside.

Cath was furious rather than frightened. She struggled violently against his grip and pulled herself loose, but he easily caught her by the wrists and held her against him.

But Cath was not finished yet. The time when Eric held her down when she was nothing but a child flashed into her mind and she was filled with hate. She slumped against Jack and he laughed softly.

'Just playing hard to get, weren't you?' he asked, laughing 'Well, I've had enough. I'm not going to hurt—'

Whatever he was going to say or do he was stopped by Cath who, taking advantage of his slight relaxation, had turned her head and bitten deeply into his lip. Jack exclaimed and let her go. Stepping back, he tripped and fell to the ground. His legs were across her feet but she managed to kick them off, stepping over them to get out. As an afterthought, she pulled the door to and with a great effort managed to slide the padlock over the sneck and force it closed. She stood for a few brief seconds listening to him swearing softly but, when she heard him begin to move about, she ran up the field towards the road. Her breath was coming in great painful gulps but she didn't stop until she was within sight of the village. She might have scarred him for life, she thought.

*

Patsy hadn't seen a newspaper or listened to the news on the radio for a while. Both she and Jim had been busy cleaning out the new council house they had been allotted.

'By, Jim,' she said as she scrubbed at the bits of cement still clinging to the front doorstep where some careless workman had dropped it. 'This stuff is hard to get off.'

'Aw, get out of the way, woman, I'll scrape it off with a knife,' Jim replied. He knelt down and scraped away at the bits. 'Bloody council workmen,' he grumbled. 'Wouldn't get a job with a decent builder, they wouldn't.'

'Still,' said Patsy, 'It's lovely isn't it? And everything's so nice and new, I love it here, Jim.'

Jim sat back on his heels, job done and smiled. 'Aye, I know you do. Better than Bell's Buildings, isn't it?'

They had slept in the house last night though most of their furniture from the old house was still to come. But Patsy wanted it all clean for the furniture van coming today and they already had a new carpet laid in the living room and the surrounding floorboards varnished and shining. They smelled a bit strongly but Jim had opened all the windows and fresh air blew through the house. It was a novelty to be able to open the windows because the ones in the house at Bell's Buildings were stuck tight with years of over painting.

It had been a bit strange sleeping in the new bed from the Co-op store in the room right next to the lovely bathroom that had hot and cold water and a washbasin and lavvy and a shining white bath with gleaming taps. But it was lovely, all the same. Patsy didn't envy Sadie her house miles from anywhere no matter how big it was. Any road, it was old even if it did have some modern conveniences. Jim interrupted her thoughts.

'Howay then, let's get back to the old place. The removal men will be coming in an hour or so. You want to be there when they pick up the stuff, don't you? I have to go to work this afternoon an' all.'

'I'm coming.'

Patsy hurriedly removed her apron and the scarf she had wound into a turban round her head, folding them and putting them on the windowsill for want of anywhere else. Then she put on her coat and hat and followed him out of the house. It wasn't a long walk to Auckland Road though it took them about three-quarters of an hour for Patsy kept meeting women she knew and, of course, she had to tell them all about her new house, even if they had heard it before. It was the first time she had felt really happy since little Annie left and went back to her slut of a mother.

'You shouldn't say that about your own sister,' Jim had remonstrated with her when she had said so.

'No, mebbe not, but that's what she is,' Patsy replied tartly. 'That poor bairn is left to God and providence and has been since she was a babby.'

'Forget about her today, Patsy,' said Jim. 'I thought you said you were happy?'

'Oh, I am.'

They turned off Auckland Road and went under the arch to Bell's Buildings. By, it looked like something out of *Oliver Twist*, she thought. Come tonight she would never ever come back here.

'Look, you must have left the door open,' said Jim and pushed at it so that it clattered against the wall of the passage. The living room looked strange with all the ornaments packed up in cardboard boxes waiting for the removal men.

'I'll go upstairs and bring down everything I can,' said Jim. 'It'll save time later.' He bounded up the stairs, his steps sounding loud and hollow on the bare boards, for the floor covering was already rolled up and tied with string at the bottom. Patsy was just checking everything was out of a cupboard when she was shocked out of her mind by loud screams. Was there an animal up there that had somehow got in? No, it was a child. Annie? How could it be Annie?

'Jim? What is it?' Patsy called up the stairs. The screams had dulled to a low whimpering. She ran up the stairs.

147

'Look at this,' said Jim. The door of the tiny closet in the corner of the bedroom was open and Annie was crouched in the corner.

'Annie! What's the matter, pet?' Jim stooped and attempted to lift the girl up but she struggled free from his hands and ran past both him and Patsy heading for the stairs. She caught her foot in a crack in the old wood on the tiny landing and went head first with a sickening series of bumps and fell in a huddle at the bottom. Patsy ran down after her and picked her up. Thank God she had fallen on the rolled up stair covering and it had cushioned her fall so at least she hadn't knocked her head on the concrete floor at the bottom.

Patsy sat on the stairs cradling Annie. The girl's body was stiff and unyielding and after a moment she struggled wildly to be free before she realised it was Patsy who held her, then she relaxed against her aunt.

'I'll take her and lay her on the sofa,' said Jim, who had come down behind Patsy. But when he put his hands on the child she screamed and clung to her aunt.

'Just give me a pull up and I'll manage,' said Patsy. Soon they had Annie on the sofa with Patsy perched precariously on the edge, for Annie was still clinging to her. After a few minutes the girl quietened and gazed at her aunt.

'You weren't here,' she whispered. 'I came for you and you weren't here.'

'No, we were at the new house,' said Patsy. 'But why, pet? What happened?'

'You didn't come back and I waited all night,' said Annie. She sounded like a three-year-old.

'I'm sorry. But I didn't know you were here, did I?'

'Tell Aunty Patsy what happened,' said Jim. 'What's the matter, hinny?' Annie didn't answer him. She shrank away from him and against Patsy.

'Leave her be,' said Patsy.

Jim shrugged. 'I'll go and get a paper then.'

148

Annie had stopped sobbing and was lying quietly when he ran back into the house carrying a *Northern Echo*.

'Look here,' he cried. 'She's on the front page!'

'Who is?'

'Annie! Annie is on the front page. She's lost, it says. It says that daftie did something to her!'

Patsy couldn't make head nor tail of what he was talking about so she grabbed the paper from him. Sure enough there was a school picture of Annie and a story about her and Ronnie Robson and how he admitted meeting her in the woods and running after her and God knows what else he had done to her.

'Eeh, Jim, no wonder the lass is in such a state,' Patsy cried. 'By, if I get hold of that lad I'll murder him, I will, I'll crucify him, the dirty bugger!'

'I think you had best have a proper look at her, see what he has done to her like,' said Jim. 'Shall I go for the polis?'

'No, no, don't do that. The poor lass is in a worse state than Russia, now, she doesn't want the polis asking questions, no, not yet. I wish I had her to the new house. I'm sure she would be better if she had a nice bath and something to eat inside her.'

'Wouldn't it just happen when we're moving? But I tell you, I think we should tell the polis. I'll walk up to the station now.'

Annie was shivering and crying as she clung to Patsy. Damp was seeping through to her aunt's skirt and stockings. 'Put the kettle on the gas ring then. I'll have to clean her up a bit before anyone sees her and besides, she'll catch her death like this if she hasn't already.'

Patsy lit the fire she had sworn she would never light again and filled a washbasin with warm soapy water. Annie was drooping now, her eyes beginning to close and she had almost stopped shivering. Gently, Patsy took off her clothes and gasped at the bruises on the girl's thin thighs and stomach and arms; all over her in fact. It was obvious she had put up a fight with him, Ronnie Robson or whoever it was. She was just slipping an old dress of her own on Annie to cover her nakedness before anyone came in when the door opened and the removal men came, and the police, and shortly afterwards an ambulance man.

Annie started to scream and shake. She tore herself away from Patsy and ran for the stairs and the cupboard in the corner of the bedroom. The look of terror and betrayal she flung over her shoulder at Patsy, her aunt would remember all her life.

Chapter Seventeen

'When she gets out of that place Annie can come and live with us,' said Patsy. 'At least she'll get looked after properly.'

'What the hell do you mean?' Sadie squared up to her sister. 'You'd best watch your mouth our Patsy or I'll give you a hiding you won't forget.' Sadie looked ready to carry out her threat, her hands were bunched into fists and her face was red with fury. 'I looked after her all right and anyroad, she's ten for God's sake, it's not like she's a baby.'

'Aye well, she's always been a bit femmer,' said Patsy. 'Poor little lass cannot stick up for herself, she's frightened of everything.'

'That was no reason to put her in Winterton,' said Sadie, conveniently ignoring the times she had told Annie that Winterton was the best place for her. 'Well, she's coming home now.'

'She wants to live with me,' said Patsy stubbornly. 'And it's no good going for me neither, I can give as good as I get now, I'm not a kid. You can't beat me up like you did when I was smaller than you, not now.'

'Aw, you were as soft as our Annie is now. A bloody cry baby, that's what.' Nevertheless, Sadie stepped back.

'It was me she came looking for when she was attacked, wasn't it? Not you, she knew she'd get no sympathy from you. She's coming to live with me and Jim, I'm telling you.'

Sadie glanced at the clock on the mantelshelf. 'Aye well,' she said. 'You can have her. I get next to nowt off her dad for her. Mind, I'm not paying a ha'penny towards her keep.' She was fed up with the argument and besides, it was almost one and Henry was calling for her. They were going out for the afternoon and later, dinner at the Grange. Besides, she thought, as she closed the door behind her sister, Henry didn't want Annie about the place. He would rather forget all about her. It had taken her a long time and a lot of cajoling to get round Henry and she wasn't going to upset him again, not while there was a chance of getting him to marry her.

'Annie's going to live with Aunt Patsy?' Cath was taken aback when her mother told her the following day. It was Sunday so Cath was home all day. She was planning to go to the hospital to visit Annie in the afternoon.

'Aye, she is,' Sadie replied. She was sitting at the kitchen table drinking strong tea. Her hair was wound up in tin curlers and covered by a turban made from an old woollen headscarf and there were remnants of last night's make-up still smeared around her eyes. She took the dangling cigarette from her mouth to take a sip of tea. 'It's for the best, anyroad,' she said. 'You dad's not interested since the new bairn came and our Patsy always had a soft spot for Annie.'

'I'll miss her,' said Cath sadly. Annie had been in Winterton for a month but she was getting out next week. The doctors said she was all right but Cath knew she wasn't. If Annie had been like a scared rabbit before she was worse now.

'Do you want to live with Aunt Patsy in Shildon?' Cath asked as she sat in a corner of the visitors' room with her sister.

Annie didn't speak, simply nodded her head. She rarely

spoke these days. In any case, Cath knew Annie hadn't forgiven her for not coming home the night it happened.

'If you're sure,' said Cath. 'I'll come and see you as often as I can, you know that.'

Just then Patsy and Jim came into the room and Annie's face showed a little animation for the first time as she turned to them. Patsy had brought a bag of liquorice allsorts and an Enid Blyton book, a new one, not a library book but one for Annie to keep. She didn't say anything to Cath, simply nodded hello and gave Annie all her attention. Jim had a copy of the *Empire News* with him and he settled down on a chair and began to read.

'I'll go now,' said Cath. 'See you soon.' Annie nodded. In the doorway, Cath turned to wave but neither Annie nor Aunty Patsy was watching.

Oh well, Cath thought as she sat on the bus for Bishop Auckland, it was better all round. But she would miss her little sister. Just as she had missed Timmy and still did even though it was all those years ago that Mam had given him away.

The bus ran down Durham Road and up past the bishop's castle to the market place. The town hall clock struck four as Cath alighted from the bus. Brian was waiting for her; a tall figure leaning against the bus stop, his dark hair that was cut in the new longer fashion in a vee at the back, lifting in the slight breeze. They had been dating lately, something Cath had drifted into rather than planned.

'All right then?' he asked, smiling down at her and suddenly she did feel happier. Happy enough to smile back at him and allow him to take her hand and walk down Newgate Street with him. They passed other couples and sometimes groups of lads, eyeing up the groups of girls walking by on the other side, giggling when a boy wolf-whistled. The girl being whistled at would walk by with a deadpan face and her nose in the air but her cheeks would be pink. Newgate Street might be the main shopping street in the town but on Sundays it belonged to the young, those now called teenagers.

Afterwards they would meet up in Rossi's ice-cream parlour and this was where Brian and Cath headed for now. They found an empty booth at the back and Brian ordered coffee. They sat opposite each other, oblivious of the others now piling in to the shop.

'How was Annie?' asked Brian.

'She's fine, she's coming out next week. She's going to live with Aunty Patsy in Shildon.'

Brian nodded. It was for the best. Some people in the two mining villages blamed the Raines for what had happened. There was poor simple Ronnie in a locked ward at Winterton and not likely to get out for years, if at all. And if he did, where would he go? Who would look after him? Granny Robson was dead. The villagers whispered she had died of a broken heart, though Brian knew it was really a seizure. She had been old but still active and she had cared for Ronnie. Some of the villagers reckoned Annie must have led him on. The whole Raine family was no better than they should be. In fact, that Sadie Raine was a right tart. Look at the way she had carried on during the war when her man, poor fella, was away fighting the Germans. And look at her now, a disgrace she was. No doubt the lasses were the same an' all.

Look what had happened to Alf, he'd brought a German woman back with him, a hoity-toity piece an' all. He wouldn't have done that if it hadn't been for Sadie carrying on.

Brian looked at Cath and knew it wasn't true that she was the same as her mother. Cath was his love; she would always be his love, no matter what. He couldn't believe his luck on the day he had got up the courage to ask her out again and she had agreed.

'Will you come back to our house for your tea, Cath? We have time before the pictures.'

Cath looked at him doubtfully. 'I don't know, Brian, what about your mam?' Going back to the house for tea was

154

practically a declaration of intent to marry. At least it meant they were seriously courting. And Cath wasn't sure if that was what she wanted. She had somehow drifted into going out with him from sheer loneliness. Yet she was fond of Brian, she was.

'Oh, come on, Cath. Mam will be fine. Anyroad, I mentioned to her you might come. The car's just on South Church Road.'

How could she refuse, even if it did mean going into the village and even though she had avoided both Winton and Eden Hope since it happened. So she nodded agreement and walked with him along South Church Road to where the Standard was parked outside King James Grammar School and they drove out to Winton Colliery.

The Musgraves didn't live in the rows, of course, Brian's father being the Co-op manager. They had a bay-windowed house in the old village. It wasn't detached or anything but it was on the end of a row of four set back with front and back gardens. There was a small dining room between the kitchen and the front room and the table was laid with matching china cups and saucers with a floral pattern around the edges. There were home-baked pies and cakes and egg and tomato sandwiches cut diagonally into quarters.

Brian introduced her to his mother and Mrs Musgrave smiled, but distantly, and murmured something inaudible.

'I'll just mash the tea,' she said. 'Brian, will you call your father?' Then she disappeared into the kitchen. Cath, left on her own for a moment as Brian went into the garden, looked around the room. It was very tidy and very, very clean; the windows sparkled and the table linen was snowy white. There were photos of Brian as a boy in silver frames on the mantelpiece and framed prints of Durham Cathedral and Lumley Castle on the walls. But it was chilly, the sun didn't reach this inner room and there was no fire in the grate. Cath shivered.

'You're not cold, are you?' Mrs Musgrave had come

back in with the teapot which she put down at one end of the table. 'We don't usually have a fire after May, but of course if you're cold—' She broke off and looked at Cath inquiringly.

'No, no I'm quite warm enough,' Cath assured her.

Altogether the teas went off quite well, Cath thought. Mr Musgrave, whom she knew well from seeing him in the shop, was cheery and Brian tried to fill any gaps in the conversation. At least no one mentioned Annie or Mrs Robson or Ronnie. But Cath was very glad when Brian said they had to be going.

'There'll be a queue at the Odeon,' he explained. Cath was relieved and Mrs Musgrave looked as though she was too for a minute. It was lovely to be out on the street again, where the air was cold and smelling faintly of coal dust and smoke from the distant colliery chimney.

'I told you Mam would be all right, didn't I?' Brian smiled down at her as they walked to the car. 'She likes you, I'm sure.'

Cath wasn't so sure but she smiled back anyway. Maybe Mrs Musgrave was always quiet and cold and distant. She wondered if she was discussing the girl from the scandalous and notorious Raine family now she was alone with Brian's father. Cath shrugged as she got into the car. What the heck, she told herself, she didn't care what the woman's true feelings were. Anyway, she might be completely wrong about her.

It was the end of July when Cath met Mark again, in Silver Street, the narrow medieval lane leading up to the market place in Durham. He was with a boy of about six or seven who looked so much like him Cath knew it must be his brother.

'Well, look who it is,' Mark said and smiled a lazy sort of smile. 'How nice to see you, er, Catherine, isn't it?'

'Cath,' she replied and tried to edge past him but it was midday on a Friday and the narrow footpath was thronged with shoppers. It was practically impossible to step out into the road for traffic although it was being controlled by a policeman in a television booth in the market place.

'Cath then. Toby, this is a friend of mine, Cath, my little brother.'

Cath smiled at the young boy before saying, 'I have to go, I'm on my dinner hour and I have to get back.'

'Of course. We'll walk with you.'

'No, I need to go into Marks & Spencers,' said Cath. 'And I haven't eaten yet.'

'Excellent! Then we can buy something and eat by the river.' Mark was insistent; he seemed to take her over, grasping her arm above the elbow and steering her towards the shop. In no time at all she found herself sitting beside him on a bench by the river while all three of them ate chicken salad sandwiches from Marks & Spencers café bar.

The boy finished his sandwich and went to stand by the river, staring into its depths. There was something about the white skin of the nape of his neck against his dark hair that made him look vulnerable somehow. He began picking up stones and skimming them over the flowing water. She glanced from him to Mark, sitting beside her. They weren't so alike, she thought, Mark's hair was lighter.

'I'll have to go now, thanks for the sandwiches,' she said. She scrunched up the packet and dropped it in the waste bin by the end of the bench as she got to her feet.

'What's the hurry?' Mark asked.

'Work, I'm due back.'

'Well, we'll walk along with you to Old Elvet.'

They walked along the tow path with Toby trailing behind. Mark watched Cath out of the corner of his eye. He would ask her out, he thought. He remembered that Jack had professed indifference to her the last time they had spotted her on Elvet Bridge so he wouldn't be poaching, would he? And it would be great to win out where his friend had failed.

'There you are, Cath!'

The voice startled him as they came up to the road. It belonged to a man in grey trousers, such as his father sometimes wore and a tweed jacket and tie.

'Hello Brian,' said Cath. 'I had to go to Silver Street – sorry I forgot to tell you.'

The fellow had taken her hand and Mark's hackles rose. He stared Brian up and down haughtily.

'Mark, this is Brian Musgrave, he works in the architect's department. Brian, this is Mark, he's at the university.'

The men did not shake hands. They simply nodded to each other coolly. A group of Italian tourists pushed past them chattering incomprehensibly and they moved back to the wall of the bridge. The antagonism between the two men was unspoken but tangible nevertheless.

'We have to go, Cath,' said Brian, taking hold of her arm. 'We'll be late for work.'

They moved away and Mark called after her. 'See you soon, Cath.'

'What's he to you?' demanded Brian as they walked up Old Elvet.

'He's a friend, that's all. What business is it of yours?' Cath felt like she was a bone between two dogs and that was ridiculous, wasn't it? She came to the door leading to the accounting machine rooms and went in, throwing a goodbye over her shoulder.

'See you tonight?' Brian called after her.

She thought about Mark as she stood by the sorter checking the punch cards showing the salaries of the county's teachers. The machine was running smoothly and she gazed out of the window to the old racecourse and the riverbanks beyond. She realised she was attracted to him and felt a moment of panic. What was she doing going out with Brian?

The sorter stopped and she gathered the cards and redid the couple with mistakes before taking them to the tabulator. Her thoughts wandered to the boy, Toby. He reminded her of someone but of course it could just be that he resembled his brother.

'You're wanted in Mr Tutin's office, Miss Raine,' Miss Green interrupted her thoughts. 'Go along now.'

Cath had forgotten all about her irritation with Brian when she met him at five past five that evening. 'I've been promoted to the tabulator,' she said as she climbed into the car. 'It's more money and it means I'm on my way. Promising management material, Mr Tutin called me. And it means I can look for a place of my own. I can afford a room in Durham now, after all, I won't have any bus fares—'

'You haven't any fares now,' said Brian. 'And when we're married you will be leaving anyway. I'm not having my wife working; people will say I can't keep you.'

Chapter Eighteen

'I'll write as often as I can,' said Brian. He was going away to do his National Service, which had been deferred until he took his final examinations as a draughtsman. Now he was off to Padgate to begin his two years in the Royal Air Force.

They stood close together on Darlington Station along with quite a few other young men and their girlfriends. It was a bright sunny day in September but the north wind whistled down the line heralding autumn and Cath shivered.

'You're cold,' said Brian and put his arms around her. She looked up at the ornate ironwork of the roof and across to where Stephenson's Locomotion No.1 stood, looking frail and small compared with today's engines.

'I'll write too, of course,' she said. Thankfully, she heard the announcement of the imminent arrival of the train for King's Cross and all stations between. Brian would be changing at York for Manchester. The train steamed into the station and Cath wondered why she wasn't distraught. A girl close by was crying and clinging to a skinny youth in a suit too large for him. Bought for him to grow into by the time he had done his time, she thought.

Brian caught her by surprise by kissing her hard on the lips. 'I'll write tonight,' he said and climbed on the train.

She waited until the doors closed and the guard sounded his whistle and the train moved out. Brian was standing at a window waving and she waved back.

'It's a blooming disgrace, they shouldn't have to go away,' the girl who had been crying said to her. 'It's five years since the war ended, why do they want soldiers any road?'

'I don't know, I'm sure,' Cath murmured. 'I have to go now, catch a bus.' As she walked down Victoria Road she realised that what she mostly felt was a sense of relief. In fact, she was suddenly aware of the sunny day and her heart lifted. Oh, she was fond of Brian but he was a bit controlling, wasn't he? She had got into the habit of considering his wishes first. Now she could do what she liked.

Well, it wasn't as if Brian was going to war, was it? He wouldn't be anyway; he would probably be doing a desk job just as he did at home. His eyes were not up to scratch; he had to wear glasses for close work.

Tonight she might go to the dance at the rink in Spennymoor. Joan went there every Saturday.

'Why don't you come too?' Joan had asked her at work yesterday. 'You don't have to stay in just because your boyfriend has gone in the forces.' Well, she would go, she could catch a bus easily from Half Hidden Cottage. That was where she was going this afternoon, to see her mam. Sadie was always complaining that she was neglected now she was on her own in the cottage. Even Henry Vaughan didn't visit her very often but at least she still had the cottage. Henry had never got over the publicity over Annie and Ronnie Robson.

Cath was sitting on the bus gazing out of the window at the sun-dappled fields where already corn was being harvested when someone sat down heavily beside her. She turned to see who it was and was shaken to discover it was Eric Bowron, Eric from Winton, Ronnie Robson's cousin. Eric the lad she remembered so vividly pawing at her body and thrusting his leg between hers when she was just a kid.

Instinctively, she shrank from him.

'Hello there,' he drawled and grinned. He looked her over and licked his lips, his light blue eyes seeming to be able to see right through her clothes. 'Fancy seeing you here.'

'There are plenty of empty seats on the bus, go and sit somewhere else,' she said.

'No, I want to sit here.'

'Let me out then and I'll sit somewhere else.'

'Have you missed me? I've been in the army,' he said. 'But I'm out now, National Service finished. Now I can attend to a few things that need attending to. You for one.'

'Me? You've got no business to do with me!'

'Aye, but I have. With you and your sister.'

He was leaning in close to her now, pressing against her side and squashing her against the side of the bus. Cath looked round for the conductress but she was nowhere to be seen. This was the top of a double-decker bus and the conductress must be downstairs. There was no bell close and only one other person aboard and she was making her way down the stairs.

'What do you think you're doing?'

Cath was scared; seized with an unreasoning panic, which she was struggling to control. It was fuelled by the memory of that day long ago when he had held her down in the grass. And touched her body.

'Nothing to what I will do, I promise you. You and your family had my cousin put in the loony bin and killed my gran. I will make you pay for it.'

'It wasn't any of our fault!' Cath said. She was beginning to get really scared. She looked ahead to see how far they were from a bus stop. It was just around the bend in the road ahead, she realised thankfully. She stood up, ready to push past him but just at that moment the bus swerved into the stop and she stumbled across him and he put a hand on her back.

'By, I didn't know you were that keen, we can get off

162

here and go behind that hedge if you like,' said Eric. His hand slid down to her bottom and he squeezed hard.

'Get off me! Get off me!' Cath pushed and shoved her way past him into the aisle and ran to the stairs. His laughter followed her.

'I'll be seeing you,' he said and started to whistle the tune of the old song. The bus was moving as she jumped off and the conductress shouted something after her. She didn't look back so she didn't see Eric staring fixedly at her – his expression had changed, now it was vindictive.

She was about a mile from Half Hidden Cottage. Well, she would just have to walk it. When she came to a stile in the hedge she hesitated, it would cut half a mile from her walk but the path went across Vaughan land in places.

Still the wind had freshened and there were dark clouds gathering, it would probably rain soon and she wasn't dressed for it. She would take a chance, she decided, it was unlikely that Jack Vaughan was home anyway and even if he was he probably wouldn't be out in the grounds. And what did she care anyway? Cath asked herself as she set out on the path across the fields. She was more worried about the threat from Eric. It wasn't just to her but to her mother and Annie. She shivered. She could still feel his hand on her.

'I haven't got much time, Cath,' said Sadie. She was looking smarter than Cath had seen her for a long time, quite like the old Sadie in fact. 'I'm sorry but Henry rang and he wants to come over. I'm hoping we'll be going out to dinner tonight, maybe the George or somewhere like that.'

'Mam, I told you I was coming,' said Cath. 'Why didn't you tell him? I've come this way from Darlington and I might as well have just gone straight back to Durham.' She sat down on the bed. They were in Sadie's bedroom and her mother was sitting at the dressing table putting on her make-up. She didn't reply for a minute for she was applying eyebrow pencil to her plucked eyebrows, carefully shaping a sort of half moon that gave her a permanently surprised look. She put down the pencil and turned to look at her daughter.

'I'm sorry, lass, but I had to say yes to him. After all, he lets me have this place and helps me out when I need it.'

'I thought you didn't like it here on your own,' said Cath. 'Anyway, maybe you should move. That Eric Bowron is threatening us about his cousin. And he says his gran died because of us. You shouldn't be on your own.'

'Eric Bowron? .Oh aye, I know who you mean. Where did you see him?'

'He was on the bus. He's just come out of the army. He's a nasty piece of work, Mam.'

'I'm not frightened of him. Henry will protect me.'

'He's not here for much of the time,' Cath reminded her.

'No, but he'll see to it I dare bet. In fact it might be just the thing to get Henry more interested. He'll frighten him off, you see, lads like that are all wind and water.'

Sadie thought for a minute then began to apply a post-box red lipstick to pouting lips. She smoothed them together then went on, 'I might just get our Annie back an' all. Tell our Patsy I need her.'

'No! Don't do that. He threatened her besides us and you know she's not up to it.'

Sadie considered. 'Aye well, we'll see. Mebbe our Annie is better off in Shildon. Aw, stop worrying, our Cath, and tell me which costume to wear. Or will I wear a dress? It's not too cold is it? If we go out and it is cold I can get him to buy me a new coat.'

Cath despaired of her. Sadie was hanging on to Henry for dear life and she wouldn't do or say anything to make him give her up altogether. She didn't want to lose the house for one thing. She didn't like the mutterings against her that she had heard in Eden Hope or Winton and she couldn't go back there – they would only rejoice if she got her comeuppance.

'You'd best be going before Henry comes,' said Sadie. 'Go on, lass, don't spoil it for me. You know I like to see you but it's awkward today. Can you come back next week?'

As Cath walked down the drive towards the bus stop she smiled wryly to herself. Her mam would never change. She reached the end of the drive and turned left for the stop. She had decided to give the rink a miss for tonight and go back to her room in Durham. She might go to the dance at the County Hotel or she might not. It wasn't much fun on your own but it was a long bus ride to Spennymoor.

In the end, Cath decided to go to the County. There would be sure to be girls from work there and she definitely didn't want to be on her own. The encounter with Eric had upset her even though she told herself he wouldn't follow her to Durham. Annie was safe enough for she didn't go anywhere without Aunt Patsy and Sadie would be all right for she was going out with Henry Vaughan. It was probably all talk on Eric's part anyway, he liked to scare girls. Still, she would go to the County and get a taxi home even it if was costly.

The ballroom in the County Hotel was thronged. A five-piece dance band was playing a modern waltz when Cath went in. She saw one of the girls from work, Rosemary Carr, who had taken over her job on the punch-card machines and went over to her. The band played 'Moon River', the trumpet lead soaring over the dancers as they whirled and weaved around the floor.

'Hello Rosemary, on your own are you?'

'Waiting for my boyfriend. You know, Jimmy from the Licensing Department.'

'I'm by myself. Brian's gone in the Air Force.'

'Jimmy won't be long, he—'

Whatever Rosemary had been going to say was interrupted by a man's voice. She automatically stepped forward and he put an arm around her and swung her into the crowd of dancers. It was the Progressive Barn Dance and Cath was soon snapped up too and they went into the preliminary quickstep. It was considered bad form to refuse to dance with anyone.

It was at the half-way stage of the dance that Cath came face to face with someone she knew only too well.

'Nice to see you, Cath,' said Jack. 'What have you been doing with yourself?'

The music had stopped and the band were turning over music sheets ready to start again while the couples made small talk or flirted with their partners. Cath made to walk off the floor. Jack grasped her round the waist and drew her with him out of the circle and into the middle of the floor where a few couples who didn't want to progress were just beginning to dance as the band started again.

'Let me go, please,' Cath said through gritted teeth.

'Not until you hear me out,' said Jack. 'I want to apologise for my behaviour that day in the outbuildings.' She looked up at him in surprise and he smiled down at her, a genuine smile that gave her a melting feeling inside. 'Though you must admit you punished me for it enough on the day. I was bruised for weeks – did you know that?'

'You deserved it.'

No she was not going to let him get to her, she was not, Cath told herself. He was only after sex, another scalp to his belt, oh yes; she knew what he was like. She hated him; she remembered everything he had said about her and her family, every nasty disparaging word.

Suddenly she managed to pull herself free of him and turned on her heel and walked towards the circle of dancers.

'Excuse me, excuse me,' she said and managed to get out. She walked to the door of the ballroom, hesitating as to what to do next.

'Why don't we have a drink and talk things over properly?' Jack asked her. He startled her for he was immediately behind her, taking hold of her elbow and steered her towards the bar.

'No, I'm going home,' she said. She was furious at herself, at her body's response on seeing him; his touching her. She loved Brian; she would marry him when he came out of the Air Force, she would. But deep down she knew she had not felt like this with Brian, ever.

'A drink won't hurt you. Look, I'm sorry for the way I behaved last time, I really am. And the time I pushed you out of the car. I'm ashamed of myself. I was angry and I know none of it was your fault.'

Cath looked at him. He seemed so earnest. Surely he wasn't pretending. 'One drink,' she conceded. She was thirsty in any case, she told herself. 'Just an orange juice please.'

They sat down at a table in the corner of the bar and Jack signed to the waiter. He ordered the drinks and then turned back to her.

'What are you thinking?'

'I'm thinking you might still be angry when you discover that your father and my mother have been together today, probably still are together.' Cath waited for him to either explode or walk out but he did neither.

Jack looked across at the bar before replying, watching the waiter draw his pint of beer and then take a small bottle of orange juice from the shelf behind and pour that into a wine glass and bring them over.

'Well, I'm older now and my mother has been dead for a long time. My father has the right to be with whomever he likes.' Jack grinned. 'You look flabbergasted.'

'Oh, I am, I'm amazed.'

Cath took a sip of her juice, unsure what to make of this turn around.

'Come on, Cath, let's be friends,' Jack said softly and put his hand on her wrist. 'Let's finish our drinks and go back on to the dance floor. They're playing a quickstep, I love to quickstep, especially with you.'

Strains of the 'Twelfth Street Rag' came through as someone opened the door of the ballroom.

Chapter Nineteen

'Aren't you going to ask me in for a coffee?' Jack lifted an eyebrow quizzically almost as though he expected to be refused.

'Jack, it's late, I don't know,' Cath replied weakly. He had driven her home to the house in Gilesgate where she had had a room for nearly a year. It was a nice house, double-fronted and three storeys high and in a respectable street.

Cath rented the room from an elderly couple, Pete and Hilda Wearmouth and at the moment she was the only tenant they had for the students had gone home for the long summer recess. Pete and Hilda were on holiday too, in Devon for a fortnight staying with their daughter and her husband.

'You sure you'll be all right on your own?' Hilda had asked before agreeing to go. 'Only it's the grandbairn, you see, we don't get to see little Peter very often.'

'Of course I will,' Cath had replied. 'In any case I might be spending some time at my mother's.'

'Well? Am I allowed in or not?' Jack persisted. 'It's a fair drive home and a cup of coffee would be very welcome.'

Cath looked at him and couldn't help smiling. The moon shone through the window and highlighted his face: he was so good-looking and he smiled so engagingly. She looked at the house with its dark windows and thought about there being no one in and no one to call if things got out of hand and she was about to say no, he couldn't come in. For a brief moment she remembered that time in the old outhouse.

'Yes,' she said. 'Yes, of course you can come in.' They ran up the steps and she opened the door and switched on the light and led the way up to her room. It was only one room but it was fairly large, with a big bay window, an armchair, a double bed, which she couldn't keep her eyes from, and a partitioned-off alcove in the corner that had been rigged out as a kitchen. The window looked out over part of the city with the cathedral looming large at one end.

'Nice view,' he said as he followed her to the window where she was drawing the curtains. She glanced over her shoulder at him and saw he was looking at her, not the view from the window.

'I'll make the coffee,' she said.

'Later,' Jack replied and drew her down on to the bed. 'I've been wanting to kiss you all evening.'

'Jack—'

'Don't worry so much,' Jack murmured into her hair. 'It will be all right. You're so beautiful. When I saw you in the County tonight I realised what an idiot I'd been. I promise you I won't do anything you don't want me to, I promise.'

All the time he was punctuating his words with tiny kisses, on her eyelids, lips, the nape of her neck, her collarbone and the top of her breasts.

This time Cath didn't stop him. She was carried away on the tide of feeling that engulfed them both. His touch on her body was electrifying, irresistible, but she didn't want to resist anyway. The heat of her own emotions, her response to him, overwhelmed her; she was drowning in it. Carried away with it until she thought she would die until release came and she couldn't believe the intensity of it.

Jack collapsed on top of her with his head on her shoulder

and she could feel his heart beating very fast in unison with her own.

The ringing of church bells awakened her. For a moment she was disorientated for she had been dreaming she was in the woods behind Eden Hope, on the grassy bank by the small tributary of the Wear. She was sitting with Annie and they were laughing and throwing pebbles into the water and tiddlers were darting about like bits of quicksilver, shining in the sunlight. She was squinting against the sun shining in her eyes and suddenly Jack was there with Mark.

'What are you doing here?' one of them asked and Annie clung to her for protection. Then the bells rang and it wasn't Annie's arm around her neck it was Jack's. The sun was in her eyes all right but it was streaming in through the side of the curtains where she hadn't finished drawing them properly the night before. She turned her head to look at him – he was still asleep, his mouth curved into a half-smile. His fair hair was dishevelled on the pillow and glinting in the sunbeam. As she moved he instinctively tightened his hold on her.

Dear God, she thought what was she doing with him? How could she trust him after what had happened before? He had tried to force her, yes, he had. Looking at him now she wondered though, he had such a pleasant face relaxed in sleep as it was now. And she loved him. It was an alien thought to her, a new thought that she felt so strongly about anyone. But she did. And she wasn't sorry for what had happened though all conventions told her she should be. Was she really like her mother? Was she wanton? She didn't care, she was not sorry, she loved him. Heck, she sounded like Katharine Hepburn in that film, what was it? She couldn't remember. She wouldn't do it again though, this was not the pictures, this was real and she must be sensible, she had to be.

Suddenly his eyes were open and he was looking straight at her. He gazed at her for a few moments then moved his arm to her waist and pulled her even closer so that they

171

were touching for almost the length of their bodies.

'Good morning, my love,' he said and her heart melted even more than it already had.

'I'll get up and make some breakfast,' she said weakly, feeling suddenly shy which was plainly ridiculous she told herself.

'In a minute or two,' he murmured and kissed her.

It was a couple of hours later that she woke again. There was no sign of Jack, his side of the bed was empty. For a moment she panicked, he had gone, he had fooled her, she wouldn't see him again, not now she wouldn't. She felt hot and sticky and as she swung her legs on to the floor she winced, as muscles she hadn't known she had protested. She took her old robe from a hook behind the door and put it on over her nakedness. She wanted a bath, she was desperate for one but the water would be cold and the old geyser took an age to heat up. Never mind she would have a cold bath and scrub herself clean.

The bathroom was along the corridor but, as she touched the handle, it opened from the inside and there he was, bathed and shaved and with a towel tied round his middle.

'I lit the geyser, you don't mind, do you?' he asked. 'I was just coming to wake you. I thought we could go out and have something to eat.' His words were prosaic but as he spoke he touched her cheek tenderly and his eyes sparkled with something. Affection? Love? She didn't care.

'I have food in the landlady's larder downstairs. I'll do it,' she said. 'Bacon and eggs all right?'

They ate breakfast in the large, old-fashioned kitchen and afterwards he helped her clear away and wash up and they went for a walk along the riverbank in the afternoon sun. As it grew cooler they walked back hand in hand and went to bed again, waking up ravenously hungry about seven and driving out to a country inn for dinner. Everything seemed magical to Cath; she was intoxicated with the whole weekend. She didn't come down to earth until they were parked once again outside the house and there was a light

172

showing through the curtains of the sitting room. It was a great disappointment for she hadn't been expecting Pete and Hilda back for another week.

'I won't come in,' said Jack and looked up at the lighted window. He touched her chin gently with his forefinger. 'I'll see you tomorrow, evening, I'll pick you up from work. The same place is it? Along Old Elvet?'

'Yes.'

Cath could hardly speak; she was filled with sadness and uncertain foreboding. It had been a magical weekend but perhaps that was all it was, a weekend, an episode in his life and if it was she couldn't bear it.

Jack smiled and kissed her lips and she got out of the car and walked up the steps without looking back. She heard the car roar off towards the A1 as she put her key in the lock. She popped her head round the sitting-room door. Hilda was knitting something small and white and Pete was reading the *Sunday Post*: both sitting on either side of the gas fire in comfortable armchairs.

'Would you like a cup of tea, dear?' Hilda asked. 'We're just going to have one.' She put her needles together and stuck them into the ball of white, fluffy wool.

'Not for me, thanks,' Cath replied. 'You're back early, aren't you?'

'Well, you know how we are. We like home the best,' said Hilda. 'Devon's all right, and it was nice seeing the family. Little Peter is lovely, but we like to get home.'

'I'll just go up then,' said Cath. 'Goodnight.'

She went upstairs and stood with her back to her closed bedroom door. When she closed her eyes she could smell Jack's cologne. She would see him tomorrow after work – he would be waiting for her on the street in Old Elvet. Of course he would, he had said so, hadn't he?

Still, as she combed her hair and renewed her make-up at five o'clock on Monday afternoon, she still had doubts about him. She was usually last out of the Powers-Samas accounting machine room for she was supervisor now and

173

liked to make sure everything was in order and papers tidied away before the cleaners came in. Today she was even later than usual. By the time she went down the stairs and opened the front door there were only a few stragglers hurrying along Old Elvet towards the bridge that led into the city and the bus and train stations. There were no cars apart from one heading down from the Licensing Department and turning at the bottom for New Elvet. No cars parked, none at all.

'Well, I knew it,' she said aloud. She stood for a few minutes outside the door then turned and walked off towards Elvet Bridge.

'I thought you were going out tonight,' said Hilda as Cath came in the door.

'I got stood up,' Cath replied and went on up the stairs to her room.

'Cath's in a bit of a mood; she has been let down,' Hilda reported to Pete as she went back into the sitting room. 'I'll take her a cup of tea up later when she's calmed down a bit.'

What a fool she was, Cath thought, as she flung herself down on the bed. What's more, she had known what he was like, she had had doubts about him all along. It served her right, oh, it did indeed. It was humiliating but it wasn't the humiliation that hurt most, it was the fact that she loved him and for a short while she had thought he loved her and he did not.

Chapter Twenty

'Henry has turned over the running of the estate to his son,' said Sadie. 'He was telling me about it last night. Jack's home now you know.'

'Is he?' Cath turned to look out of the window. 'Well, that's their business, isn't it?'

'I was just saying,' said Sadie looking slightly hurt. Sadie loved it when Henry made her his confidante. It made her think that she might yet become the next Mrs Vaughan. She had begun trying to adopt a more refined accent but it was hard, very hard.

I'm just like my mother, thought Cath bitterly, with ideas above my station. But not any more. At least I know where I stand with Jack now, nowhere.

'I'm going up to Shildon to see Annie,' she said. 'I'll get the bus into Auckland and go on from there.' It was the Saturday following the weekend with Jack and she had decided against staying in Durham. Aunt Patsy had recently acquired a telephone and she had rung to tell her she was coming to Shildon after seeing her mother.

'Annie's not well,' Patsy had said sharply. 'I hope you don't upset her.'

'Why should I do that?' Cath had asked. 'We're close, Annie and me. What's wrong with her, anyway?'

'It's her nerves,' said Patsy. 'The doctor's put her on tablets again.'

'Well, tell Annie I'll see her Saturday afternoon.'

Cath had reported this conversation to her mother and asked her if she wanted to go to Shildon too.

'Annie is going to have to pull herself together sometime,' Sadie had answered. 'I have no patience with her at all. She gets enough sympathy from our Patsy. I don't hold with pampering her, most folk just have to get on with it. Anyway, I can't go. I'm expecting Henry.'

She was always expecting Henry, Cath said to herself as she waited in Bishop Auckland market place for the number one bus that ran to Shildon and Darlington. The market place was thronged for the market was on and the queue for the bus stretched between a shoe stall and a fruit and vegetable stall. She was jostled by shoppers and people trying to get past to the other bus stands and there was a great bustle and noise from the stallholders shouting their wares to that of buses revving up to go. So at first she didn't hear Mark addressing her from behind.

'Hello, Cath,' he said again. 'How are you?'

She turned in surprise then smiled. 'What are you doing here?' she asked him. 'I haven't see you in the town before.' She thought of the last time she had seen him and how nice he had been to her as they walked by the Wear in Durham.

'I was just visiting a friend,' he replied, interrupting her thoughts. 'Where are you off to?'

'Shildon. I'm visiting my sister.'

'No boyfriend today?'

'He's in the Air Force doing his national service. But he's not my boyfriend.'

Mark smiled. 'Does that mean you're free this evening? Only I'm at a loose end myself. We could have dinner and go on somewhere afterwards. The Majestic ballroom in Darlington, if you like, or the pictures. Only if it's the pictures it will have to be an early dinner.'

'I don't think so, thanks anyway.'

The bus had come in and the queue was moving forward.

There was something about Mark; he was attractive to her but she wasn't going to go out with him or anyone else, not for a long time, if ever. He wouldn't want her anyway if he knew what had happened with Jack. No one would want her.

'Oh, come on. Can't we be friends? Nothing else, I promise you.'

Mark smiled again, lifting one eyebrow quizzically. She had reached the door of the bus. She was about to refuse once more then thought again. Why not? She had nothing against Mark and why should she let Jack Vaughan spoil her life?

'Righto,' she said. 'I'll meet you in Rossi's coffee shop at seven.'

She climbed on to the bus and took a seat on the roadside of the vehicle. So she didn't see him as he walked back to his car, which was parked by Barclays Bank behind the market stalls. As he went he took an envelope out of his pocket and looked at it before putting it back. 'Sorry Jack,' he murmured as he got into the car. 'All's fair in love and war and all that.'

How inconsistent she was, thought Cath, as she gazed out of the window at the shops as the bus moved slowly up Newgate Street to Cockton Hill. Why couldn't she make a decision and stick to it? Thoughts of Jack and his love-making clouded her thoughts. But she would get over him, yes, she would. She wouldn't be such a stupid fool as to be taken in by him again. Meanwhile, she had Annie to think about. She got off the bus at the Hippodrome in Shildon and walked to the house.

The wind had freshened and a few early, fallen leaves scurried across the pavements. It was autumn already.

The front door was locked so Cath walked round the house to the back. Aunt Patsy and Annie were there, sitting in deckchairs watching Uncle Jim dig over the vegetable patch. In the shelter of the house it was quite warm and something of a suntrap.

'Cath!' Annie stood up and went to her sister, kissing her

on the cheek. Annie looked well, considering, Cath thought, as she gazed at her.

'How are you, pet?' she asked. 'I've missed you.'

'Me too,' said Annie. 'Thanks for coming.'

'She's fine with us,' said Patsy. She had not risen from her chair. Uncle Jim paused in his digging and nodded a greeting.

'Yes, of course she is,' Cath agreed. In spite of Annie's greeting she felt decidedly unwelcome. But after a few minutes Patsy offered her a cup of tea and went into the kitchen. Uncle Jim brought out a couple of kitchen chairs and they sat down together.

'Don't worry about your auntie,' he leaned close to Cath to whisper. 'She's just afraid you'll take Annie away.'

'I won't do that, I couldn't,' Cath replied.

'What are you two whispering about?' Patsy had come out again with the tea tray.

'Nothing,' said Jim. 'By, I'm gasping for a cup of tea, Patsy.'

Cath came away feeling thoroughly depressed. Annie was so quiet and so obviously dependent on Patsy. She watched her aunt anxiously all the time. It was the drugs she was still taking, oh, Cath knew that's what it was that made Annie so dull but it saddened her to see her sister like this. It was all the fault of Ronnie Robson, she told herself savagely.

'Walk with me to the bus, Annie?' she asked. 'A walk will be good for you.'

'She'd better not,' said Patsy but Annie surprised them both.

'I will,' she said. 'It's not far to walk home by myself from the bus stop, is it?'

Patsy demurred but Annie had made up her mind. 'I'll follow you down then,' said her aunt. 'I'll meet you coming back. Don't say anything to upset her, now, Cath.'

The two girls walked down the road, Annie's hand tucked in Cath's arm.

'Don't worry about me, Cath,' Annie said suddenly. 'I'm

happy here, no one will hurt me here. See, I'm not frightened of walking back on my own.'

'Hurt you?' asked Cath. 'Of course they won't.' But they didn't get to say much else for the bus was trundling down Redworth Road to the Hippodrome and there was no time left. Cath kissed Annie goodbye and jumped aboard. Poor Annie, she thought, as she waved out of the window. She was just a kid and she had no life, no life at all. Cath turned to face the front so she didn't see the man coming around the corner from Main Street.

Walking into Rossi's at a couple of minutes after seven o'clock that evening, Cath saw Mark straight away, sitting in the first booth with a cup of coffee before him. He jumped to his feet with a smile.

'There you are,' he said. 'I was wondering where you were.'

'Hello Mark. I'm not late, am I?'

'No, not really, I was early though. I've been to Staindrop to see the parents.' He paused for a moment before going on, 'You don't want a coffee do you? Only I booked a table at the Bridge for seven-thirty. It's half-way to Durham and I'll give you a lift back to Durham. I'm going anyway.'

'Great, only I'm not really dressed for it.'

Mark glazed at her blue tweed suit with the fitted jacket and full skirt that showed off her slim figure. She wore it with a white blouse with a mandarin collar and a small blue hat, which fitted over her dark hair with the aid of a plastic hairband concealed in it, and blue court shoes to match. She had renewed her lipstick before leaving Aunt Patsy's house and the wind had whipped colour into her cheeks.

'You look beautiful,' he pronounced. 'Stop fishing for compliments.' Taking her arm, he led her outside. 'I've parked in South Church Road,' he went on, smiling down at her.

'Watch where you're going, can't you?'

Cath looked up startled as a woman bumped into them. 'Sorry,' she said then gasped, for of all people it was Mrs Musgrave, Brian's mother. The woman drew herself up and her eyes gleamed but she said no more, simply brushed past and on.

'Do you know her?' asked Mark, as they walked on to where his Armstrong Siddley car was parked.

'It's Brian's mother,' said Cath. 'You know, you met Brian on Elvet Bridge one day.'

'The ex-boyfriend?'

'That's right.'

She would write to Brian as soon as she got home and tell him it was over between them, Cath decided. Before his mother did.

The film was *Mr Blandings Builds His Dream House*, with Cary Grant. Cath and Mark sat in the darkness and he didn't put his arm around her nor did he hold her hand. He didn't touch her at all except when Cary Grant said something funny in his clipped accent and Myrna Loy smiled up at him with that 'All men are boys at heart,' look and then he squeezed her arm. It was a light-hearted film, not exciting really but they came out of the cinema happy and comfortable in each other's company somehow.

Mark drove back to Durham and dropped her at the door and it wasn't at all like the time Jack came. Mark didn't even kiss her goodnight.

'Thank you for tonight,' he said. 'I'll be seeing you soon.'

She ran up the steps to the front door and he drove off into the city. As she opened the door and went in the tele-phone was ringing.

'Get that, will you, Cath?' asked Pete who was just emerging from the sitting room. 'It'll be for you anyway. The ruddy thing has been going mad all evening.'

Cath's heart leapt, for a wild moment she thought it was Jack ringing to say he was sorry he hadn't got in touch sooner, he'd had to go to Timbuktu or somewhere. But it was her mother's voice that came from the receiver.

'Cath? Cath, where the hell have you been? What did you say to our Annie this afternoon? I've had your Aunty Patsy on the telephone and she's frantic. Annie's only gone and tried to kill herself, she has. Taken a load of her tablets, the selfish little pig, doing this to us!'

The telephone table was by the side of the staircase and Cath sat down heavily on the stairs, as her legs suddenly seemed to give way.

'Tried to kill herself? What do you mean?'

'What the bloody hell do you think I mean? She's tried to do herself in! She's in hospital, the General at Auckland. Well, I tell you, if she gets over this they'll have her in the loony bin again and they won't let her out in a hurry, indeed they will not. Our Patsy's having a fit! You'd best get yourself home tomorrow and explain yourself, do you hear me?'

'I hear you, of course I do.'

'Well then, do as I tell you. By, I dare say Henry won't have me now. I—'

Whatever else Sadie had been going to say Cath didn't wait to hear. She put the telephone down. She was seething with rage at her mother's selfishness. Sadie seemed more bothered about Henry's reaction than she was about poor Annie.

'Would you like a cup of tea, pet?' Hilda was standing at the sitting-room door, her face showing her concern. 'Is there something wrong at home?'

'It's my sister—' Cath was saved from having to explain further by the telephone ringing again. This time it was Patsy.

'What did you say to Annie?' Patsy shrieked down the line. 'I've had to go to the hospital with her she's in such a state, poor lass. By, I cannot trust any of you Raines with her, I just cannot! I wasn't five minutes behind you and when I got there she was sitting on the Hippodrome steps shaking and crying and I couldn't get a word out of her—'

'I didn't do anything, she was all right when I got on the bus,' said Cath. She felt sick.

'Well, she's not all right now, she's knocked back as far as she ever was. You must have said something to upset her!'

'No, I tell you I didn't. Oh, I would come back tonight but I can't get a bus or a train, not now.'

'They wouldn't let you see her any road. She's in a coma or something, she's out of it anyway.'

'But how did she try to kill herself? I mean, if she was on the steps when you found her, how could she?'

'I took her home and put her to bed and then ...' Patsy choked over her words before she went on. 'I thought she was just asleep when I first went up but then after a couple of hours I went up and she looked funny somehow and she wouldn't wake up and she'd taken the whole bottle of her tablets, the ones that make her sleep. I tried to wake her up; me and your Uncle Jim tried. We walked her up and down but I had to send him for the doctor in the end.'

'I'm sure you did everything you could, Aunty Patsy,' said Cath dully. She leaned against the banister as she tried to think. 'I'll come tomorrow morning. We'll have to get to the bottom of this.'

'Aye well, I'd best go,' said Patsy. 'They wouldn't let me stay at the hospital, you know. I'm not her mother, that's why. Next of kin only, they said. It makes you sick, I've done more for her than her blooming mother ever did.' She was beginning to sound bitter and her tone had changed to a whine.

'It's true, you have,' Cath said sympathetically. 'Look, why don't you go to bed and try to get some sleep. I'm sure everything will look better in the morning.'

'Aw, how can it?' asked Patsy but after a moment she said goodbye and Cath put down the receiver.

'I'll just go straight up, Hilda, goodnight. Goodnight Pete.'

'Oh, I've made some tea,' Hilda protested. 'Aren't you going to tell us what is wrong?'

'My sister's in hospital. I'll be going first thing in the morning,' Cath replied and ran up the stairs and closed her bedroom door behind her. She couldn't face any more questions even if Hilda and Pete did take offence.

Chapter Twenty-one

Cath was up early on the Sunday morning. She had a bath and washed her hair before seven so that it would be dry before she went out. She had hardly slept and when she did she dreamed of Annie: her sister was upset and crying and she blamed Cath for whatever it was that had caused her trouble.

'I didn't do anything,' Cath was insisting when she woke up suddenly in a sweat and the church bells were ringing, the chimes loud through the open window. So she had got up and tidied the room and kept herself busy until it was a reasonable hour to go out for the bus to Bishop Auckland. Usually on Sunday mornings she had breakfast with Pete and Hilda so at nine o'clock she went downstairs and into the dining room.

'Are you all right, pet?' asked Hilda as she brought in plates of bacon and egg and fried bread. The smell of the food made Cath suddenly ravenous. 'Did you sleep well?'

'Not really. I was too worked up about Annie' said Cath.

'Eeh, poor lass. What's the matter with her exactly?'

Cath hesitated, but after all, it was probably best to tell Hilda now. If Annie were sent to Winterton again it would be hard to cover the fact up. Hilda was a kind-hearted woman but she was inquisitive and would have it out of her eventually. And Hilda knew her sister had had trouble with

184

her nerves before. So she told her landlady what had happened.

Hilda shook her head. 'Well, I don't know, she must be in a bad way,' Hilda commented. 'But come on, sit down and eat your breakfast. You'll need fortifying. By, I do hope she's all right. How are you getting to Bishop?'

'On the bus.'

'It doesn't start running until one o'clock, not on a Sunday, did you forget? It's Sunday service.'

Cath had forgotten; she could kick herself for it. She sat down heavily by the table. If only she knew where Mark lived she would ask him to take her but really she had no idea. It would be all right, she knew it would.

'Your breakfast is getting cold,' said Hilda. Cath picked up her knife and fork and began to eat mechanically. She had finished her meal and was going through the hall when it occurred to her that she would probably find his number in the telephone directory. Of course! It was just that such things were fairly new to her so it hadn't occurred to her.

There it was; Durham 426. Mark Drummond, Claypath it was. She had a few misgivings about ringing him but ring him she would. She thought she would die if she waited until afternoon and then had to spend an hour on a bus ambling through the countryside.

'Well, hello. I was just thinking of you,' said Mark. 'What can I do for you?'

'I need to get to Bishop Auckland and there aren't any buses until this afternoon,' said Cath. 'My sister has been taken to hospital.' She was about to explain further but Mark butted in.

'OK, I'll take you,' he said. 'I'll be over pick you up in fifteen minutes.'

Cath was waiting outside the house when Mark drew up and soon they were on road out of the city and making for the south-west of the county. There was little traffic and Mark relaxed and glanced over at her. She looked strained

185

and anxious with dark smudges under her eyes as though she hadn't slept.

'What's it all about, Cath?' he asked.

She hesitated but in the end she told him about Annie and how her sister had been affected by what had happened to her.

'She was all right when I left her yesterday, I swear. Something else must have happened to her in the few minutes after I caught the bus.' Cath looked at him, wondering what he was thinking. 'She took all her tablets at once, Aunty Patsy says. She's in hospital in a coma.' Cath's voice broke and for a minute she couldn't go on. Then she told him about the bad feeling in Winton Colliery and Eden Hope, about the retarded boy, Ronnie and his grandmother. By the time she finished Mark was driving up Durham Road and turning into the market place at Auckland. He had said nothing until he had driven up Newgate Street and Cockton Hill to the hospital and parked by the gates. Thoughtfully, he switched off the engine then turned to face her and for one awful minute she thought he was going to say he didn't want to get involved but she was wrong.

'Do you think she must have met someone from the villages? Someone who frightened her perhaps? She couldn't have seen the boy, could she?'

'Not Ronnie, no, he's in a locked ward at Winterton. I don't think anyone else would say anything to her, no one would be so cruel, seeing how she is.'

They got out of the car and went in to Reception, which was in one of the old workhouse blocks. Annie, they found, was in H Ward, one of the prefabricated huts built as a hospital for ill and injured prisoners of war.

'Close family only,' the receptionist said. 'Visiting hours are not until two.'

Cath explained she was Annie's sister and proved it by showing her Identity Card but Mark was not allowed in. 'I'll wait in the car,' he said. 'I don't mind.'

186

Annie was first on the left in the long cheerless ward with its high windows and dark brown composite flooring buffed to a high shine. The bed was hidden behind drab, fawn-coloured screens.

'She has come round,' said Sister coldly. 'I hope you don't upset her.' She stared at Cath with hard blue eyes through thick glasses as she pulled the screen aside a little so Cath could pass through.

All Cath had eyes for was the small figure in the bed, her face as white as the pillowcase her head rested on. A policewoman sat at the side looking very, very bored. Annie's dark hair straggled over the pillow in stark contrast to the white pillowcase and her eyes seemed sunken and glazed. She opened her mouth to speak but nothing came out but the barest whisper. Even that seemed to tax her strength.

'You came then.'

Cath jumped as the voice came from behind her. Aunt Patsy was there. 'I expect you haven't said anything else to upset her,' Patsy went on. She approached the bed and patted Annie on the forehead before sitting down in the chair that was by the bed. 'Are you feeling better, pet?'

Annie looked at her, her dark eyes large and so despairing somehow that Cath had to steel herself not to cry.

The policewoman stood up and they looked at her. She nodded to Patsy.

'I'll take my break now, as you are here,' she said. 'I could do with a breath of fresh air.'

'What is she doing here?' Cath asked.

'What do you think? It's a crime to try to take your own life, didn't you know that?' Patsy spoke in an undertone for she didn't want Annie to hear her. 'They think she might do it again.'

Outside they could hear the policewoman talking to Sister. 'I have better things to do with my time,' she was saying. 'Better than sitting here watching someone who wants to die. I'd let her if it was up to me.'

Cath flushed a bright red, she felt like storming out from behind the screen and screaming at her that Annie could hear every word, the screen wasn't a wall, it was just a bit of cloth on a metal frame. In fact she stood up to do so but glancing at Annie she realised the girl hadn't heard at all, she had her eyes closed and seemed asleep.

'Hard-faced cow,' said Patsy. She put her hand over Annie's and held it gently. 'They won't let her have a water jug and glass, you know. In case she breaks them and uses the glass to slash her wrists.'

'Oh,' said Cath. She sat down again. She hadn't thought of the law getting involved, not with Annie and the way she was. It was just so ridiculous.

'You might as well go, Cath. At least she's out of danger now. Though God alone knows what will happen next. I suppose a psychiatrist will be coming to see her. I doubt it's Winterton again for her and if not it'll be reform school.' Patsy's eyes were wet; she leaned her elbow on the bed and rested her head on her hand. 'I'll stay until I'm chucked out. Your mam might turn up any road.'

Cath could see her aunt was very upset; she loved Annie, oh, she did indeed.

'I'll go then,' she said. 'I'll come back tomorrow.'

'Not until half past seven, mind. Annie's off the danger list now. Visiting 7.30 until 8.15. Ta ra then.'

Cath went out of the ward and down the corridor in a daze. There was nothing she could do for Annie, nothing at all. She felt guilty, she had failed her sister, Annie thought it and so did Aunt Patsy. Just outside the door the police-woman was smoking a surreptitious cigarette and leaning against the painted corrugated iron of the hut cladding.

'You want to think before you speak in there,' Cath said to her. 'Just because a patient is behind a screen, doesn't mean they can't hear, you know.'

The policewoman shrugged. 'I said nowt but the truth,' she replied as she threw the stub of the cigarette on the ground and pressed it out with the sole of her shoe. 'A

188

waste of our time it is minding folk that want to kill themselves. Let them, that's what I say.' She turned and pushed open the ward door and allowed it to swing to with a bang behind her.

Cath was seething but she walked up the ramp and across to the car park. Mark saw her coming and sprang out of the car to open her door for her.

'Get in.' He waited until she was settled before going on. 'How was she, your sister?'

'Coming round, I think. Still very quiet and sleepy.' She turned her head and gazed at him, judging his reactions.

'The psychiatrist is coming to see her. And the police are there. I'd forgotten it is an offence to try to commit suicide.'

Mark nodded. 'Barbaric, isn't it?'

'I hadn't thought of it much before but this has brought it home to me.' She thought with bitterness of the policewoman.

Mark put his hand over hers and squeezed it. 'Don't think of that – nothing will come of it. It rarely does in such cases.'

'Annie's not a case, she's my sister,' said Cath. Still, she was glad of his sympathy and comforting presence. It was funny, she felt a closeness to him at odds with her first view of him when she had met him with Jack in the woods near Eden Hope.

'Where do you want to go now?' Mark asked. 'Back to Durham?'

'No, I'd rather stay near for a while. I'll go to my mother's.'

'Oh yes, Half Hidden Cottage.'

Cath glanced quickly at him but his face was expressionless. Of course he knew where her mother lived, he was friendly with the Vaughans, wasn't he? He would have heard of her mother all right.

'Look, we could go out for lunch. Or we could go to my parents in Staindrop. My mother wouldn't mind us dropping in at all.'

189

'I don't know . . .'

'Oh come on, you don't want to be on your own. Too much time to think.'

Mark started the car and drove out of the hospital grounds and turned right on to the Barnard Castle road. Cath lay back against the leather seat and closed her eyes for a few minutes for she felt very tired suddenly and willing to leave everything to him. It was as they drove through West Auckland and were climbing the hill leading to Staindrop that the thought of Eric popped into her mind. Eric had threatened her and her family on the bus that day. Had he followed her to Shildon and seen Annie and threatened her? He could have done. Though surely she would have known if he were about. But why hadn't she thought of Eric before? He had been so vindictive when he cornered her on the bus.

'What is it?' Mark slowed down at the top of Raby Bank and looked at her. Cath had sat up and gasped and now she was clutching at the end of the seat convulsively. He pulled into the side by the castle wall.

Cath forced herself to relax. 'I just thought of something.' She told him about Eric and how he had threatened her on the bus. She had to explain further about what had happened to Annie but was surprised that he didn't know all of it anyway.

Mark was angry, she could see it in the way his mouth set in a thin line. 'It seems to me that this man is dangerous,' he said.

'Oh no, I don't think so, not really. A bully perhaps and that would be enough to frighten Annie.' He had frightened her too, but no, he wouldn't actually hurt them. Of course he wouldn't. He was just angry for his cousin and his grandmother, poor soul; none of it had been her fault.

Mark studied her for a moment then restarted the car. 'Well,' he said. 'We will have to see. For now I think we should just go to Staindrop and have a nice meal with my family. Try to put it out of your mind for a while.' He would not forget it though, he told himself. He would check out this lad from the mining village and see what he was about. For Mark was beginning to realise he felt more for this girl than he had for anyone. He didn't care that Jack was mooning after her, in a situation like this it was every man for himself.

'Mum, this is Cath. You don't mind that I brought her along, do you?'

'Of course not. How nice to meet you, Cath,' Daphne Drummond said and looked Cath up and down. Cath was in her blue tweed suit and a fresh white blouse so she felt reasonably sure she would pass muster. After all, the suit had cost her half a month's salary. Daphne frowned slightly then covered it up with a smile.

'Do come and sit down. What would you like to drink?' She indicated the drinks stand, which was in the shape of a globe though now the top half was turned back revealing an array of bottles and glasses.

'Just water, please,' said Cath. The table was set lavishly with salads and patés and cold meats despite the fact that rationing was still in force.

'Nonsense, you must have a glass of white wine at least,' said Daphne. 'Nigel?' Her husband handed Cath a glass of wine. She took a sip and found it acidic on her tongue but still, refreshing.

Cath couldn't help comparing the meal with the one at Brian's house. Both Brian's mother and Mark's had the same attitude to her, she realised, as she took another sip of wine. The wine definitely made her feel better, perked her up a bit. She took another drink. Annie was going to be fine, she told herself. Even if she had to go into Winterton she would get out again surely and Aunt Patsy would look after her.

Cath began to relax. What did it matter if Mrs Drummond sat at the table regarding her with the air of unassailable superiority she had noticed in other middle-class women?

191

She smiled at the older woman tolerantly and took another sip of wine. Mr Drummond refilled her glass.

'Do have a little of the smoked salmon,' Daphne Drummond said. 'What about you, Mark?'

Mark helped Cath to a couple of slivers of smoked fish and then put some on his own plate. Cath ate a mouthful then put down her fork and took another sip of wine.

Mark leaned over to her and whispered in her ear, 'I'd go easy on the wine if I were you. It can have an effect on anyone who is over-tired.'

Cath looked at him. 'It tastes nice,' she said. 'I don't think much of the smoked salmon though. I prefer tinned salmon with a drop of vinegar, myself.'

Mark smiled. 'Squeeze a little lemon juice on it,' he advised.

'I must admit I like tinned salmon too,' his father intervened.

'Nonsense, there's no comparison,' Daphne snapped, then made a determined effort to cover up. 'Nigel, go and call Toby, will you?' She looked across at Cath. 'We are fairly relaxed about lunch on Sundays but Toby would miss it altogether if I didn't remind him.'

'My little sister is a poor eater,' said Cath and felt a pricking behind her eyes and for a few minutes was engaged in willing herself not to cry. Luckily, Mr Drummond came in with Toby causing a small distraction. Toby had grown since she last saw him and his legs beneath long grey shorts were very thin. Still, he seemed wiry enough and he smiled at Cath shyly and said hello. He reminded her of Annie.

Daphne busied herself making him a plate of sandwiches. Cath took an individual dish of trifle when Nigel handed it to her and ate a few spoonfuls but found it too rich and sweet. She drained her wineglass.

'Have you had enough?' Mark asked her. 'Only I thought we should be on our way back to Durham.' He glanced at his mother. 'I have things to do,' he said vaguely.

'That's fine,' she said. 'Will you be honouring us with a visit next Sunday?'

'Probably,' Mark replied.

Cath, who had recovered her equilibrium, made to stand up but somehow her skirt slipped on the shiny leather seat of the dining chair and she found herself falling to the floor. Mark grabbed at her, catching her just before she disappeared under the table altogether and Toby and Nigel burst out laughing though Daphne merely looked pained.

Mortified, Cath struggled to her feet. 'Sorry,' she said. 'I don't know what happened there.'

Toby was having a fit of the giggles and Mark frowned ferociously at him. 'Shut up, Toby,' he said.

'I can't stop,' his brother replied. 'It was funny, you know it was.'

'Come on, Cath, let's go,' said Mark. 'Goodbye all. Don't bother seeing us out.'

Daphne followed them to the door, ignoring him. 'Do come again,' she said brightly. Cath murmured her thanks and went out with Mark holding her firmly by one arm. Her face was bright red and her head was beginning to throb. She felt sick. She was just outside of the front gate when she vomited into the hedge.

Chapter Twenty-two

'Don't worry about it,' said Mark. He was driving along the road to West Auckland on the way back to Durham. 'It doesn't matter.'

'I'm not worrying, I have worse things to worry about,' said Cath. She stared out of the window as the car went past the Eden Bus Company garage and bore right for Bishop Auckland.

'You were so tired and strung out that the wine went to your head,' said Mark. 'Do you feel better now?'

'Yes.'

She did too for, in spite of her humiliation, the smooth movement of the car along the country roads had sent her to sleep. It was only for fifteen or twenty minutes but when she woke up she did feel better. But she barely looked at Mark in case she saw signs of disgust in his face.

'I'm sorry, I disgraced you as well as myself,' she said, looking down at her hands.

Mark laughed. 'You're not used to wine. Neither were we except on special occasions until my parents went on holiday to France last year. Now Mum thinks it's just the thing.'

Holidays in France, thought Cath. The only people she knew who had been to France had been there to fight in the war. She gave him a quick glance. Was he just saying that to make her feel better? He caught her glance and smiled.

'I'm glad you're all right,' he said softly.

Cath looked out of the window as they were coming into the town. The hospital was on the left, the old workhouse buildings at the front looking as grim as ever. For a moment she was tempted to ask him to stop; to go in to try to see Annie again. But no doubt that dragon of a ward sister wouldn't let her in. No, she would come tomorrow night.

It was quiet in the car. They were out on the open road soon enough and heading for Durham. Cath thought about Eric Bowron again, oh, he was a mean-minded man. He had been mean-minded as a lad and he hadn't grown out of it. She could still remember the feel of his hands on her immature body all those years ago, how the other boys had laughed uneasily but done nothing to help her. Only Brian, he had come to her rescue and he wasn't as old as Eric. She must write to Brian tonight, she thought with a stab of guilt. She had to tell him she wasn't going to marry him.

They were approaching Durham, driving past the Cock of the North Hotel. Soon she could see the cathedral perched on top of a hill as they drove down into New Elvet and on to Gilesgate. Mark stopped outside the door and turned to face her.

'If I were you I'd have an early night,' he said. He leaned over and lightly touched his lips to hers. 'I'll see you soon.'

Oh, he was a lovely man. Not many men would have given up their Sunday to run someone about the county.

Pete and Hilda were not about so she went straight up to her room and got ready for bed. She felt washed out with all the strain of the day and lack of sleep the night before. She opened the curtains before getting into bed so that she could lie and watch the moon and the clouds chasing across the sky. She wrote to Brian sitting up in bed with her writing pad propped on her knees. The letter took a while to write even though it was short but at last she was sealing the envelope and putting it on her bedside table ready to post tomorrow.

Dark clouds had covered the moon and soon rain was pattering against the glass. Cath went to sleep with the soothing sound in her ears and slept through until morning.

THE WAR IN KOREA – 38TH PARALLEL BREACHED: Cath read the headlines as she ate her sandwiches sitting at her desk in the Powers-Samas accounting machine room. Normally she would have gone down by the river or into the basement kitchen where the girls normally boiled the kettle and made tea but today she felt like being alone. Besides, since she had been made supervisor, the other girls were not so friendly as they used to be. And if she worked through the dinner hour she might be able to get off a few minutes early to catch the bus to Bishop Auckland. Mr Graves, the new manager, was not so strict as his predecessor and wouldn't mind.

More soldiers and airmen were being sent to Korea, she read. With a pang of guilt she thought of the letter she had posted to Brian that morning. But surely Brian wouldn't be going to Korea, would he? He had weak eyes, he wasn't classed as A1.

'Further reservists have been placed on alert.' Cath thought of Jack and Mark. But Mark wouldn't be called because of his gammy leg, though his limp was hardly noticeable now. Jack though, he might be called. She sighed and sat back in her chair. It was no good she couldn't concentrate on anything now she had allowed Jack to enter her thoughts. Bitter-sweet memories came flooding back to her. How his head looked on the pillow: the way her looked at her through lowered lids sometimes.

All those sickly sweet songs that came out during the war when couples were separated were meaningful now but she despised herself for those thoughts. Restlessly she stood up and went downstairs to the basement to make a cup of tea. The room was blue with smoke although there was no one in it but two comptometer operators; the others must have gone out for fresh air before coming back to their desks.

Cath made a mug of tea and returned upstairs.

The afternoon dragged as she watched the clock for the bus to Bishop Auckland.

At the entrance to the ramp leading up to H Ward, Cath met her mother. Sadie was dressed in a green, close-fitting suit, which showed off her figure and she had a fur cape over her shoulders.

'Now then, Cath,' she said defiantly. 'You see I have come to see our Annie.' She noticed Cath looking at the cape.

'Henry bought it for me last time we went to Newcastle,' she said. 'He thought I looked cold.'

'Very nice,' said Cath, not because she liked the cape but because Sadie obviously expected her to. They paused at the entrance to the ward for Sadie was having second thoughts about going in.

'Come on,' said Cath, taking hold of her mother's arm and pushing open the doors. A staff nurse was standing by the door to the office, checking the visitors.

'Annie Raine,' said Sadie and as the nurse looked doubtful, 'I'm her mother.'

'I'm sorry, Annie Raine has been transferred to Winterton,' the staff nurse said.

'When? What for? Why wasn't I told, I'm her mother for God's sake!'

'Calm down, Mam,' Cath whispered though her own heart had dropped into her boots. Poor Annie! But Sadie was beginning to shout and the staff nurse was getting annoyed.

'Keep your voice down, please, we have people in here who are very ill,' she said sternly in a fair imitation of Sister. 'If you don't, I will call a porter to put you out. Now if you come into the office I will give you the details.'

'Who the hell do you think you are?' Sadie began to rage and her cheeks flamed with anger. 'I'm her mother and nobody told me she was being transferred to the loony bin. I have a right to know, I have a right to be told.'

'Shut up, Mam,' said Cath and dragged her into the office after the staff nurse. Abruptly, Sadie changed. She sank into the visitor's chair and began to cry. 'I don't know what I did to deserve this,' she muttered through her tears.

'I'll give you the number of the hospital—' Staff Nurse began but Sadie interrupted.

'I know the bloody number,' she said. 'It's not the first time the lass has been in you know.' She stood up and marched out of the office. 'Howay, Cath,' she went on. 'We might as well go home. By, I bet our Patsy knew about this. But would she let me know? Not her. I'm just Annie's mother, I am. I tell you what—'

'Mam, shut up, please.'

They were walking down the ramp now and a cool evening breeze was blowing against them. 'I know you think I've got a big mouth, our Cath. But I was worried. By, you're a cold-hearted bitch, you are an' all. I could have gone out with Henry tonight, he wanted me to. But I thought I'd best see Annie. How I'm going to tell him she's been taken to the loony bin again I don't know.'

She rambled on as they walked down the street to the bus stop and after a while Cath simply stopped listening. 'Are you coming home the night? Cath! That's the third time I've asked, have you gone deaf?'

'Sorry, I wasn't going to—' Cath stopped as she glanced at Sadie's face and saw that her mother really was affected. She was upset and she had a hurt, lost look in her eyes. 'All right, I'll come back with you. But I'll have to be out early in the morning, mind.'

She regretted the decision as they trudged up the drive to Half Hidden Cottage and saw Henry Vaughan's car parked by the front door. As they approached he got out and stood waiting for them.

'Henry!' Sadie ran the last few steps and rushed up to him and kissed him on the cheek. 'I wasn't expecting you or I would have been back earlier. Come in, come in, I'm so pleased to see you.'

The change in her mother was spectacular, Cath thought as she followed them into the house. She sparkled and even her accent had softened. Henry had nodded to Cath and she had greeted him in reply but it was as if they both forgot about her as they went into the sitting room.

'I think I'll just go to my room, I'm tired,' she said from the doorway.

'What? Oh, righto,' Sadie replied absently.

Cath ran a hot bath and got in and lay back, luxuriating in the warmth. She closed her eyes and the next thing she knew she woke up shivering for the water was cold. She must have slept for an hour, she reckoned, as she got out and wrapped a towel round her and went to her room. She felt woolly minded and aching as she fell into bed, pulling the bedclothes over her shoulders and falling asleep again in a minute. In her dreams Jack was holding her as his father had held her mother. He was looking down at her and smiling and they had walked up the stairs like that and fallen into bed. She woke in the grey morning light feeling intensely happy and felt the bed on either side of her for Jack but of course he wasn't there. He wouldn't be, would he, he had just been amusing himself with her. It was her own fault, wasn't it? After all, she had known what he was like.

199

Chapter Twenty-three

Cath walked across Elvet Bridge and up the bank to Durham market place. Though it was just past five o'clock it was quite dark and the streetlights gleamed only dimly in the mist that was rising from the river. The damp cold struck through to the bone. She shivered slightly and turned up the collar of her coat as she turned right for Gilesgate. Today was Friday and she was going back to Half Hidden Cottage for the weekend on Saturday morning. The year was almost over; soon it would be Christmas. Fairy lights were going up in shop windows. It was still close enough to the austere war years for Cath to take pleasure in the lights twinkling but she wasn't looking forward to Christmas very much.

She thought about Jack every day and the pain was only a little duller than it had been at first. Yet she was fond of Mark too; she looked forward to seeing him, he was good company and he didn't force himself on her. In fact, he acted that old-fashioned thing, the perfect gentleman. He was very good for her damaged ego, she thought wryly. Being treated as Jack had treated her was humiliating as well as painful.

There had been those anxious weeks when her period was late and she had thought she was pregnant. What would she do if she were? She would have to go back to Eden Hope and the whole village would know that they had been right all along, Cath Raine was no good, just like her mother.

She was heady with relief when she found out she wasn't pregnant after all. She had steeled herself to go to the doctor and been mortified when he gave her a vaginal examination.

'Have you been doing something that makes you think you might be pregnant?' the doctor had asked. (At least he wasn't the doctor from home who had known her all her life. This was a Durham doctor.) Cath had murmured that she had and the examination followed.

'Get dressed now,' the doctor said when he had pulled off his rubber glove and put it into a kidney dish. He had sat at his desk making notes.

'Well, as far as I can tell, you're not expecting a baby,' he had said. 'Try to be more careful next time, young lady.' Her face was fiery red as she left the surgery.

This Friday evening as she passed the policeman in his glassed-in box, watching the screen by which he directed traffic through medieval Silver Street, her thoughts were interrupted. She almost walked into Brian just coming out of one of the shops with a parcel wrapped in Christmas paper.

'Oh, I didn't know you were back,' she exclaimed.

'I'm on leave,' he replied. He looked at her for a moment without smiling then made to walk past her.

'Brian, you didn't reply to my letter,' she said, then felt foolish as he stared at her in astonishment.

'You didn't expect me to, did you? There was nothing to say. My mother told me she saw you with someone. I suppose it was that Mark bloke I saw you with that time. You weren't straight with me, Cath. You're a tart, just like your mother. I should have listened to my mother a bit sooner.' He shrugged, moved past her and went on down Silver Street.

She watched his stiff back for a moment then turned for Gilesgate feeling guilty. Brian had been good to her and she had used him. He was better off without her really.

A wind had sprung up and there was an icy feeling to the air as she approached the house in Gilesgate. As she closed the front door behind her she heard voices from the sitting room. Putting her head round the door she saw Mark sitting on the couch. Pete and Hilda were there too. They were watching the flickering television set in the corner and discussing the news and drinking tea.

'There you are, said Hilda. 'Come in and have a warm. Here's your young man come to see you. I'll just go and freshen the teapot.'

Mark had risen to his feet still holding his cup and saucer. He smiled at her, his dark eyes wrinkling at the corners. 'I thought we could eat out,' he said. 'Then we could go to the rink at Spennymoor, the ten until two session.'

'Oh, I don't know—' Cath began and stopped as Pete shot her a quelling glance.

'I'm listening to the news,' he said pointedly. 'Our boys are giving those North Koreans a hammering.' Pete loved the recently acquired television; he watched everything on it when he was at home.

'We'll take our tea upstairs,' said Cath as Hilda came back in with the teapot.

'A good idea,' said Pete and Hilda frowned at him. But Cath and Mark took their tea and left, grinning at each other as they climbed the stairs. 'We could eat in, I've got some macaroni,' Cath offered as they sat on the edge of the bed and drank the hot, sweet tea. The mattress sagged a little and her thigh touched his and warmth from his body penetrated through her skirt.

'If you like,' he whispered and bent his head to kiss her on the lips. He lifted his head and looked into her eyes and, satisfied with what he saw there put down his cup and hers on the bedside table and put his arms around her and kissed her again.

After a moment or two he lifted his head and looked down at her face. Her eyes were closed and her long dark lashes swept her cheeks still rosy from the cold.

Suddenly, Cath felt strange. 'No,' she said, 'This isn't right, Mark.' But Mark didn't seem to hear her protest.

'No!' Cath repeated, louder, snapping them both back into awareness as she roughly pushed Mark away.

'What? Why?' Mark sounded hurt and angry. 'Don't worry,' he said flippantly. 'I have a French letter. You won't get caught.'

'No, it's not that Mark, I, I don't know, it just isn't right. I'm sorry.' They sat quietly for a moment on the bed, side by side, neither knowing quite what to say.

Then Mark stood up abruptly and looked down at her. 'This isn't about Jack, is it?' he said sharply. 'I know you were keen on him before.'

'No, no,' said Cath, rising from the bed too, keen to reassure him despite her confused feelings.

'Well,' said Mark, feeling a little uncomfortable himself, 'maybe I was rushing you a bit, I'm sorry.'

Cath just felt embarrassed; she had wanted him before, but then she'd wanted to stop, and now she'd made him feel bad.

'Let's go and get something to eat Mark, and then we won't miss the session at the rink,' she suggested brightly, trying to lift the mood.

'Yes, let's,' said Mark, moving towards the door, clearly relieved.

They drove to Spennymoor to the Clarence Ballroom, which was called the rink by everyone for it had begun life as a roller-skating rink. Cath had never felt less like dancing but she knew the two of them couldn't stay in her room all night or Hilda would be knocking on the door to see what they were up to. And she wasn't even sure she wanted him to leave. She just felt confused by the strength of her feelings. What did it matter anyway? Jack was not coming back to her. He had left her high and dry.

There was a big band playing on the dais at the rink. A trumpet player played 'On Moonlight Bay' and other hits and she and Mark foxtrotted and waltzed and even jived through midnight and beyond. Afterwards he drove her to Half Hidden Cottage and pulled up by the front door.

'I'll see you tomorrow,' he said. 'I'll come for you at ten.' He brushed his lips across hers.

'No,' said Cath, 'I have to go to see Annie.'

'When then?'

'Later, in the afternoon.'

'Three o'clock?'

'Yes.'

It was a cold night. A break in the clouds allowed a shaft of moonlight to break through. It sparkled on frost that overlay the grass and the paths and among the branches of the hedge. The car was beginning to cool down already though it was only a few minutes since Mark had switched off the engine. He held her closer. 'I love you, you know,' he said, surprising himself as much as he did her.

'I must go,' said Cath and opened the car door. 'I'll see you tomorrow.' She ran to the front door and let herself in to the hall without looking round. She didn't put on the light but went up the stairs in the dim moonlight from the staircase window. As she did so she heard Mark start the car, turn it round and drive off.

As she lay in bed a short while later she heard someone go to the bathroom, someone too heavy to be Sadie. No doubt Henry was staying overnight. Well, why not? For the first time she felt she understood her mother and Henry too. They were both lonely people.

'Hello, I wasn't expecting you back last night,' said Sadie. She came into the kitchen yawning widely and dressed in an old dressing gown and with her hair all over the place so Cath surmised that Henry must have already gone home.

'We went to the rink at Spennymoor so it was just as easy,' Cath replied. 'There's tea in the pot or I'll make coffee if you like.'

'Tea will do. By the way, Henry will run us to the hospital

but he won't stay,' said Sadie. 'Who's we, any road?'

'Mark. He works at the university. Mark Drummond.'

Sadie paused with her cup half-way to her mouth. For a moment she looked a little strange then she shook her head slightly and took a sip of tea.

'What is it?' asked Cath.

'Nothing. I used to know someone called that, that's all.'

'A lot of people are called Drummond,' said Cath.

'Aye.' Sadie let her careful English slip when Henry wasn't there. 'I suppose we'd best get ready. By, I hate that place.'

'Winterton is a bit forbidding but Annie will be coming out soon, I hope,' Cath replied.

'Blooming heck, what are you doing here?'

Sadie stood with her legs apart and stared at Alf and Gerda and their baby, John. Or Hans, as Gerda insisted on calling him. He was a good-looking child with fine fair hair and blue eyes, large for eighteen months. He looked uncertainly at his mother and father as Sadie stared at him.

They were in the cafeteria in the hospital grounds waiting to go into the hospital for there were ten minutes to go before visiting time.

'I have as much right to visit our Annie as you have, you know,' said Alf then turned to Cath. 'How are you doing, lass? I heard you'd got promotion and were living in Durham city, is that right?'

'Yes. I'm fine, Dad, how are you all?'

Cath felt guilty – she didn't realise how much time had gone by since she last saw her father. She nodded and smiled at Gerda and little John who hid his head in his mother's lap.

'He's shy,' said Gerda.

'You've not bothered much before,' said Sadie, lifting her chin and sticking her nose in the air. She didn't look at Gerda.

Fortunately it was time to go to see Annie so Alf didn't

reply. Cath walked with her father along the tarmac path. Sadie had met up with Patsy and the two sisters walked behind. Cath could hear them bickering but she took little notice. They always bickered when they met.

'John's a lovely baby,' she said to her father. 'I should make more time and get to know him better.'

'Yes, you should,' said Alf. 'I once thought you would come to live with us but you didn't want to.'

'Well, there was Annie—'

'Aye, I know, you had to look after Annie. But you weren't with Annie when she needed you, were you? Aw, I'm not blaming you, lass. You couldn't be with her all the time.'

Still he had hit a nerve. She had always felt guilty that she wasn't there for Annie when it mattered.

They sat at tables in a large hall and waited for Annie to be brought to them. When she was, she seemed to Cath to be like a zombie with dull eyes, pale complexion and lank, lifeless hair. She sat down opposite Cath and looked at her hands, which were clasped together in her lap.

'Are you all right, Annie? Do you like it here?' Cath asked as neither Alf nor Sadie seemed to know what to say. Annie nodded. Patsy had been to the trolley where a helper was dispensing tea and biscuits. She brought back a tray of mugs of tea and a plate of biscuits. She brought back a tray of mugs of tea and a plate of biscuits. Cath glanced up at the other tables. Some of the inmates were tucking into the biscuits as though they were ravenous. Anxious parents watched them. Annie sat and looked at her tea.

'She's all right but she'll be better when I get her home,' said Patsy. Sadie pulled a face and looked as though she was about to argue but changed her mind. Alf looked uncomfortable and Cath took a sip of tea even though she had just had a cup in the cafeteria and it made her feel nauseous.

'Do you want to come home, pet?'

It was Alf who had spoken and Annie looked quickly up at him and down again. She nodded.

After what seemed an afternoon as long as a week, a bell rang and visitors was standing up and saying their good-byes. For the first time Annie showed some emotion. She leaned over to Cath.

'It was that lad,' she whispered.

'What was? Who?' Cath asked, startled.

'You know, the one,' said Annie. Then a nurse appeared and she looked confused. It was as if a blanket had lifted for a few seconds then had fallen again just as swiftly.

The party was quiet as they walked down the drive. A sadness gripped them. All those people locked away. When going about normal life it was as if they didn't exist. But Annie existed and she needed to get her life back. Cath wasn't sure that turning her into a zombie was the way to do it.

Patsy's husband, Jim, was waiting by the car. He had been walking round the grounds to fill in the time.

'I can give Cath a lift if Sadie goes with you,' said Alf. So it was agreed and the family set off for home.

Chapter Twenty-four

'We'll drop you off here if that's all right,' said Alf. They were on the road at the end of the drive to Half Hidden Cottage. 'Unless you'd like to come back with us today?'

Gerda was startled and not at all happy about the invitation, Cath could see, but she recovered and said, 'Yes.'

'No, I won't, thank you very much though,' said Cath. 'Only I'm meeting someone.'

'A boy no doubt,' said Alf, smiling playfully.

'A man friend, yes,' said Cath as she got out of the car. 'I'll come to see you soon, though.' She said her goodbyes and walked off up the drive. Her mother was already home.

'I'm sick of our Patsy acting as though Annie was her bairn,' she greeted Cath.

'Well, you don't want her here, not the way Henry feels. Do you? Annie trusts Aunt Patsy,' Cath replied.

'An' she cannot trust me, that's what you mean, isn't it? By, you have a nasty streak, our Cath.' Sadie sounded bitter. She was sitting at the kitchen table with a glass of stout before her. 'Anyroad, who is this Mark fellow? You kept him quiet, didn't you?'

'I've known him a long time,' said Cath. 'His family live at Staindrop.'

'Staindrop eh? I used to know some Drummonds but they went to the other end of the country.' Sadie took a long swallow of her stout and made appreciative noises. 'Good stuff this,' she said. 'Well, he'll be making better money at the university than down the pit. You could do worse.'

'I'll have to get ready, he's calling for me,' said Cath. It was no good saying anything to her mother; Sadie would never understand.

'Aye go on, leave me alone as usual,' said Sadie.

'You'll be seeing Henry later, won't you?'

Sadie didn't reply so Cath went up to her room. She still kept some things at Half Hidden Cottage and she took a pair of slacks and a roll-necked sweater from the wardrobe. She sat in front of the dressing table and put on lipstick, then looked at herself in the mirror and decided that would do. Pulling her hair back from her face she tied it with a thin chiffon scarf, which echoed the soft, rose colour of her sweater.

She sat looking at her reflection for a while without really seeing it. Her thoughts touched on Jack and a stab of pain shot through her. It was like probing an aching tooth. And yet she was so mixed up. She was attracted to Mark and she knew he was attracted to her. What was the matter with her, she couldn't be in love with two men at the same time, could she? Cath heard the doorbell clanging through the house.

'Cath? Somebody to see you!' Sadie called up the stairs. Cath took up her coat and went downstairs.

Mark drove up the dale to where the moor stretched out on either side and the heather was brown and bending to the prevailing west wind. Though the light was fading already he parked on the top of a rise and turned to her. Clouds were gathering in the sky and below them, in the valley, lights were beginning to twinkle. It was warm in the car and Cath had taken off her coat and as he turned he slid a hand over her left breast.

'Don't,' said Cath pulling away.

'Why not? You like it, don't you?'

'Please Mark, don't.' Cath pulled away from him and gazed out of the car at the rising darkness. There was a moment or two of silence.

'I won't if you don't want to,' said Mark. 'But I thought you did want to.'

'No,' said Cath. 'I'm sorry.'

He moved towards her again and put his arm around her and kissed her gently on the forehead. 'It's fine,' he said. 'Everything is fine.' Moving away he started the car.

'We'll go down to the Black Swan.'

'Can we just stay here for a little while?'

'Cath, what do you think I am? I'm not made of stone.'

Cath sighed. 'Righto. We'll go.'

They drove down Langley Dale and into Staindrop where he pulled up outside the Black Swan.

'Your parents won't be about, will they?' Cath had painful memories of the time she had drunk too much wine at the Drummonds' house.

Mark laughed. 'Don't worry. They bought a television. They won't be able to tear themselves away from it.'

They sat in a corner of the snug and Cath drank lemonade while Mark had a beer.

'They don't do food,' said Mark. 'We can go to—' he stopped short as the door opened and in came his mother and father with another couple. They were laughing together over something and at first, Daphne didn't notice Mark and Cath sitting quietly in the corner. When she did she stopped laughing.

'Excuse me a minute,' she said to the others and walked over to them. Mark stood up.

'Hello Mother,' he said.

'Mark. Were you going to let me know you were in the village?' So far she had ignored Cath but now she looked at her properly. 'How are you, Miss, er, I don't think Mark ever told us your surname?'

'Raine. Catherine Raine,' said Cath. Mark began to

210

apologise for his omission but his mother interrupted him.

'Raine? Where are you from?' she demanded. Then, realising she sounded abrupt, she went on, 'I used to know some Raines from one of the colliery villages near Bishop Auckland, Eden Hope, it was. I don't suppose you are related in any way?' It sounded like a casual question but Cath detected a note of strain underlying her tone and was puzzled. She looked closely at Mrs Drummond. Under her make-up she was very white. Perhaps she was ill?

'Well?'

Cath glanced at Mark then returned to the question. 'I am yes. I was brought up in Eden Hope.'

'Eden Hope?'

'Are you all right, Mother?' Mark moved to his mother's side and cupped her elbow. 'Do you want to sit down?'

Daphne shrugged him off. 'No. No, I don't. Where's your father?' She was trembling with some strong emotion and Cath's heart sank. Mark's mother seemed to hate her.

'What's the matter? What is it?' Nigel Drummond had come up behind his wife and put his arm around her.

'Nigel,' she whispered. 'This – this girl is from Eden Hope Colliery. Her name is Raine.' She looked up at him piteously. 'I want to go home.'

Everyone in the room was looking at them; it had gone very quiet. Mark stepped towards Cath who had risen to her feet.

'We'll go with them, see if there is anything we can do. Get a doctor, perhaps?'

'No!' The cry was loud in the snug. 'I don't want her in my house. Nigel!'

'It's all right, dear. Come on we'll go.'

As they went out of the room with Nigel supporting his wife, he murmured apologies. Mark and Cath followed them on to the pavement.

211

'I'll sit in the car. You go with them,' said Cath. 'I don't mind, really I don't.'

She sat in the car and watched as they walked up the road and over the green to their home. She sat for twenty minutes, then half an hour and then it was a full hour. She didn't know what to do. She considered going to the front door of the house and knocking, telling Mark she would catch a bus to Bishop Auckland and find her way home from there. But she was nervous of doing that.

Daphne hated her for showing up that Sunday lunchtime. Yet it wasn't that, it was something worse than that. It was when she found out what her name was and that she came from Eden Hope. Daphne obviously had heard of her mother's reputation, perhaps of the trouble with Annie. A girl was attacked and a lot of people thought it her own fault, she must have done something to provoke it.

Maybe it was just the fact that she came from a mining village. Some people still thought of the miners as scum. And Daphne was a social climber if ever she saw one. A miner's daughter just wasn't good enough for her son, who had been an officer in the army.

Bitter thoughts chased themselves round and round in Cath's head. She couldn't work out why any of this should make Mrs Drummond ill. She was suddenly aware of how cold she was: stiff and cold. She got out of the car and buttoned up her coat and walked up and down for a while. In the distance she saw the last bus from Barnard Castle to Bishop Auckland coming along the road. It halted at a stop further up the road and she scribbled a hasty note to Mark. 'Caught the bus. Cath.' It was all she had time for as the bus drove up to the stop a few yards away. She pushed the note under the windscreen wiper of the car and ran to the stop.

'Took your time, didn't you?' asked the conductor. 'We want to get home tonight too, you know.'

'Sorry,' Cath replied. 'Thanks for waiting.'

As they drove out of the village and through the darkened fields she gazed at her reflection in the window unseeingly. She was tired and hungry and she had yet to find her way from the town to Half Hidden Cottage for the buses would have stopped running for the night. Well, she would just have to walk. Mark must just have forgotten she was waiting outside the house. Yet he had said he loved her.

Cath took the short cut through the fields to Winton then walked up the old wagon way to Eden Hope. It was very dark but cut at least a mile from her journey and the railway lines were easy to follow even in the darkest patches. She was almost too tired to be nervous. She concentrated on putting one foot before the other and counting the sleepers.

She passed the part where the line divided, one going to Old Pit. She could see the tops of the old houses, now in ruins, as a ray of moonlight came through the clouds and showed them in a break in the trees and overgrown bushes by the line. She shivered and quickened her step. 'Rest in peace,' she whispered as the local children did when they passed.

In spite of the short cuts it took over an hour for Cath to reach the final path that led up through the woods to Half Hidden Cottage. By this time she was exhausted and she paused for a few moments before the climb. Looking back on Eden Hope the only lights seemed to be those of the colliery yard. The miners were working extra shifts as the country was still recovering from the war. As she watched, the winding wheel turned to bring up the cage and soon there was a string of lights twinkling along the streets as the night-shift men made their way home. For all she was going in the opposite direction they made her feel she wasn't quite alone in the night. She turned and plodded steadily up the path. At least the sky had cleared properly and the moonlight lit the way.

Cath had almost reached the point where the path

levelled out and became broader when she thought she heard footsteps behind her. She stopped and listened but after a few seconds decided she must have been mistaken. It was probably one of the miners going to the end houses of the village. Pit boots had steel studs and they were very noisy.

At last she got to the end of the path and was almost on the road. The opening to the drive of Half Hidden Cottage was only a few yards away. Thank goodness for that. She had been mad to come home the way she had. She could have knocked on her father's door and asked for a bed for the night. Gerda would not have been too pleased but she—

'Got you!'

The voice coming out of the darkness behind her shocked her to the core. She pulled her arm away violently but it was held in a vice-like grip. She screamed.

'Nay lass, no one will hear you, not here. And if they did they'd think it was nowt but a vixen. There's a few foxes round about.'

It was Eric. Still in his pit gear he switched the light in his helmet on and the beam fixed on her face and reflected on his. He was grinning, the whites of his eyes gleaming in a face blackened with coal dust.

'Let me go, Eric, let me go!' she hissed at him but for answer he pulled her to him and held her practically immobile. The memory of the time he had held her down on the grass all those years ago came vividly back to her. 'What do you want?' she asked desperately, feeling the hardness of his body and smelling the rank sulphurous smell of damp coal on his clothes. She struggled to free herself but he was too strong for her.

'I just wanted to remind you of what I said before,' he replied. 'I meant it. But mind, I was surprised to see you the night when I came to bank out of the pit. Been out whoring, have you?'

'Leave me alone, Eric.'

Cath stopped struggling, she had to control her fear, had

to make out she wasn't frightened.

'Oh aye, I'll leave you alone,' he said. 'I wouldn't touch you, you filthy bitch.' He held her hands with one of his and ran the other over her body, squeezing her breasts and grasping at her between the legs. She had to move then, even though he twisted her arms cruelly backwards.

'No, I'll not touch you this time,' he said. 'Mind, I'm not finished with you yet. We'll meet again.' Taking his hand away. 'You're not to my taste at all any road. No, I just thought I'd show you what a real man is like.' He pulled one of her hands down and pressed it against his crotch, moving suggestively as he did so.

Cath was suddenly galvanised into action. She grabbed his belt with her free hand and kneed him as hard as she could. Eric let go of her and howled with anguish, bending double with the pain. Cath didn't wait another moment. She turned and ran as fast as she could, her exhaustion forgotten.

It was only minutes before she was pounding up the drive and fumbling with the lock of the front door of Half Hidden Cottage. All the time she expected to hear him coming behind her but she got inside and locked the door and leaned against it until her heartbeat slowed.

She went upstairs and ran a bath even though the water was barely tepid. Getting in she scrubbed the coal dust and the feel of his hands from her body then changed the water and did it all over again. At last she got out and wrapped a towel round her and walked back to her bedroom. As she passed her mother's room she could hear her gentle snore; Sadie had not woken.

Cath climbed into bed and lay in the dark and at last the events of the day crowded in on her, one awful image succeeding another as she tried to push them out of her mind. She hardly knew if she was waking or dreaming as she saw Annie's sad face then Daphne Drummond's, filled with contempt and over all, the grinning mask of Eric's as he said he wasn't finished with her. Towards morning, she began to weep and she wept steadily for a while. Then, as though the tears were the beginning of healing, she fell into a deep dreamless sleep.

Chapter Twenty-five

'What in the world's the matter with you?' demanded Sadie. 'I've asked you twice when you're going back to Durham. Are you going deaf?'

Cath started and turned round from where she had been gazing out of the sitting-room window at nothing in particular.

'Sorry. What did you say?'

'I asked you when you were going back to Durham. Only I'm expecting Henry this afternoon and he won't want you hanging around like a wet week.' Sadie gazed critically at Cath. 'An' another thing, you're losing weight. Your clothes are hanging on you. You are beginning to look like a refugee from Belsen.'

'I'm all right. And I'm going back this afternoon.'

'Good.' Sadie's eyes narrowed as she prepared to continue her litany of complaints. 'You're not having a bairn, are you? Sometimes people go very thin at first—'

'I'm not having a bairn!' The denial burst out of Cath. 'Leave me alone, Mam, please.'

'Well, all right. But before you go get yourself something to eat.'

'Righto.' Cath went into the kitchen and took bread and cheese from the pantry and cut herself a cheese sandwich. She mashed a pot of tea and called Sadie through for a cup. Sadie sat with her elbows on the table holding the cup to her lips and watched while Cath ate the sandwich.

'You should have put some pickle on that,' she observed.

'Mam,' said Cath, putting down her sandwich. 'Mam, has anyone been hanging around lately?'

'Hanging around? Don't be daft, Henry would give anyone short shrift if they hung about here. Go on, eat your sandwich. You're not going until you do. You've had nowt today so far.'

Cath was a bit surprised and touched at the show of concern, it wasn't one of Sadie's characteristics. She was surprised her mother had even noticed what she had eaten. She warmed to her mother.

'Any road, what do you mean?' asked Sadie.

'Well, do you still get any resentment from the folk at Eden Hope?'

'Of course not. I don't see them often. I don't go that way on. Henry and me go to Newcastle when I want anything to wear and he sends me groceries down from the Hall.'

'It's just that Eric Bowron is back from the army—'

Sadie interrupted. 'Oh listen, that's Henry's car. I'll go and let him in.' She put down her cup on its saucer with a clatter and rushed out to the front door.

Cath heard their voices in the hall and then they went into the sitting room and closed the door after them. Well, a nod is as good as a wink to a blind man, Cath thought, as she took the pots to the sink and washed and dried them. She might as well go. In any case, it wasn't likely that Eric would bother her mother, not when Sadie had Henry to protect her. Some good things came out of the relationship after all.

Half an hour later she popped her head round the door and said her goodbyes then let herself out in good time to catch the bus to Durham. As she turned the corner from the drive she saw Eric standing across the road. He was just standing, leaning on the fence with one leg crossed over another and grinning. Fury erupted in her. She strode across to him, not even considering keeping a safe distance between them.

'What do you want? What?' she screamed at him. His grin grew wider.

'By,' he said, 'you're fair stotting, aren't you? And here am I just minding my own business, taking a walk in the countryside on a nice Sunday afternoon. Everything's not always to do with you, you know.'

'I'll have the law on you, I will, I will,' Cath shouted at him. 'And if I find out it was you bothered our Annie and made her—'

'Bothered your Annie? She's the loony, isn't she? I never bothered your Annie in me life.' He looked up the road. 'Were you going for this bus that's coming up the road? You'd best hurry or you'll miss it.'

The bus was indeed coming up to the stop and Cath had to run and wave at the driver to catch it. She jumped on and took a seat, looking out of the window as she tried to catch her breath. Eric was still standing there. He was nodding and smiling and waving his arm as though he was seeing her off. Abruptly she looked away.

Yet her anger had somehow cleared her fear of him. She wasn't going to let him get the better of her, oh no, she was not. As the bus moved away she turned back to him and smiled, a contemptuous sort of smile, she hoped. She did have the satisfaction of seeing his eyes shift before they lost eye contact.

Suddenly she felt ravenously hungry. She rummaged in her bag for the half-bar of chocolate she had left from the last time she'd been to the pictures and ate some of it. Then she allowed herself to fall into a doze, which was interrupted every few minutes as the bus pulled into a stop. She'd had next to no sleep last night. Tonight she would cook a proper meal and go to bed early.

In Gilesgate she went straight up to her room and closed

the curtains to keep out the darkness of the late afternoon. Stripping off her clothes she put on an old nightgown and fleecy bedjacket and looked in the cupboard behind the curtain to see what supplies she had in. Not much, she saw, a tin of Heinz spaghetti and a couple of sprouting potatoes. Well, she'd just have a lie down and worry about food later.

It was warm under the bedclothes and her legs, aching from all the walking she had done the night before, sank into the soft feather mattress. She thought about Mark with an aching sense of loss. Surely he would have come out to her if he'd thought about her at all. She couldn't let her feelings for Mark run away with her. But she was too exhausted to think about it for long, let alone worry about it. Slowly her eyes closed and she slept.

There was a Christmas party at work. Not much of a one, just a few drinks and titbits and it was held in the last hour of the working day so that anyone who lived at a distance from Durham could get home at a reasonable hour. They crammed into the new manager, Mr Graves's, room and he poured glasses of cheap fizzy wine or orange juice for them.

Joan, who had left the year before to get married, came in with her baby in a pushchair and everyone 'oohed and aahed' at the tiny boy.

'You're not courting at the minute then?' Joan asked Cath.

'Emm, well not really,' said Cath, thinking of Mark. But it looked like he'd finished with her.

'Well, you did right to get right of that Brian, he was a drip,' said Joan. 'Enjoy your freedom while you can. This party is likely to be the highlight of my Christmas. My Charlie's not one for going out much.' Joan had married a boy from the Surveyor's Department. She had an air of discontent about her.

Cath took a limp sausage roll from the plate on Mr

Graves's desk and chewed it thoughtfully. 'At least you've got Jimmy,' she said. 'He's a little darling.'

'You should hear him in the middle of the night,' said Joan. 'Charlie doesn't get up, of course, he has to go to work next day. And for a little 'un, Jimmy can pee like a navvy with twelve pints of beer in him. I can't wait to get him potty trained. I'm sick of dripping nappies.'

'Aw, Joan, cheer up a bit, will you? I tell you—'

She was interrupted by Mr Graves who came over to them and began chatting, asking Joan about Charlie and ogling Cath as he had taken to doing lately.

'I tell you what,' said Joan when he had moved on reluctantly. 'He fancies you.'

'A lot of good it'll do him,' said Cath. 'Come on, let's go down to the County, we can take the bairn in there it being a proper hotel. I'll treat you to something to eat.'

'I don't know, there's Charlie's tea ...' But Joan soon changed her mind. 'Beggar Charlie's tea,' she said laughing. 'Howay then.'

By the time Cath got back to Gilesgate her own mood had lightened along with Joan's. They had eaten spam sandwiches with a salad of tomatoes and cucumber, which was all that was available for it was too early for dinner. Jimmy sat in a high chair and made a right mess while Joan fed him bits of bread and cream cheese. They giggled a lot and even Jimmy crowed with delight and waved his tiny fists in the air and beamed at everyone around him.

Cath told Joan about Mark and his snooty mother and how she must have turned him off her.

'If he lets his mother tell him what to do he's not worth it,' Joan counselled. 'You're a bonny lass, there's plenty more fish in the sea an' all.'

'Yes, you're right.'

'Did you sleep with him?'

'No!' Cath looked at her friend, surprised she should ask.

'Well, it's not the end of the world, is it?' And Cath realised it was not.

'Well, I'd better be getting home,' said Joan. She plucked the baby out of the high chair and pulled on his all-in-one suit. It was what they used to call a siren suit during the war, Cath thought, as she watched, invented by Winston Churchill. Come to think of it Churchill looked a bit like a baby in his when he was photographed in his siren suit. She smiled – the little outing with Joan had lightened her mood.

They made vague promises to meet up more often in the future then Cath walked back to Gilesgate. It was a cold night and penetrating damp filled the air and seemed to get through her clothes to the skin. Usually she walked all the way but tonight she caught the bus. She had thought she would go to her mother's but changed her mind and stayed. Mark might ring, or there might be a message. Though why she should think that when it had been over a week since she had seen him she didn't know.

She didn't love him anyway, she told herself. How could she love him and still be in love with Jack? If she didn't love him why was she thinking about him? What did that make her? A flaming fool, that's what. She spent the evening wrapping up presents and had yet another early night.

'Mam, you want to watch out for that Eric Bowron from Winton,' she said as she took off her coat in the hall of Half Hidden Cottage.

It was the afternoon of Christmas Eve and Cath had just arrived. She was lucky to get there at all for a cover of snow had fallen during the night and a north wind blew down from the Arctic creating blizzard conditions. She had had to walk some distance as the road by the end of the drive was beginning to block and the bus had stopped running.

'What on earth are you talking about?' asked Sadie. 'Come on in, there's a good fire in the sitting room and I'll make some tea. You must be nithered.'

But Cath was not to be distracted from what she had to say, she had been thinking of it all the way from the Great North Road.

'Ronnie Robson's cousin; I told you he was back from the army. He's been away doing his National Service. He was waiting for me when I came home last time, waiting at the end of the drive.'

For a change Sadie was listening properly to her. 'Are you sure he was waiting for you? I mean, he could have just been out for a walk, like.'

'He was waiting for me. That wasn't the first time he's threatened me.'

'He threatened you? The sod! I'll give him something to think about. I'll threaten him all right, I will.'

Sadie had gone red with anger. 'Who the hell does he think he is? You're not frightened of him, are you? I'd give him short shrift if he came near me. I've met his sort before, I have.' She was working herself up into a real temper.

'Mam, I'm not frightened. I just think we should be careful, that's all. I think he probably got at our Annie that day at the bus stop an' all.'

'That would explain a lot, wouldn't it? By God, I'll kill him, I swear I will I'll—'

'Mam—'

Sadie was not listening. 'I'll tell Henry, that's what I'll do. I'll tell him. He won't stand for it, I know he won't. He'll turn him out of Winton that I know. He'll send him packing.'

'Mam, he can't.' Cath was amused. 'This is now the second half of the twentieth century, the pits and the houses belong to the NCB. How can Henry turn him out?'

Sadie nodded her head. 'Oh, he can, believe me he can,' she said. 'Henry has contacts.' She had begun to calm down. 'Howay in and I'll warm some soup. I made a big pot for Henry coming tonight but there's plenty.'

'Henry's coming tonight?' Cath's heart sank. When Henry came it usually meant she was banished from the sitting room. Henry liked to have Sadie to himself. Christmas was beginning to look as though it would be even bleaker than she had envisaged.

'He is,' said Sadie. 'We have some news for you.'

'What news?'

'Never mind. You'll find out tonight.'

Cath ate her soup, a thick mutton broth designed to keep out the winter's cold and found it surprisingly good. She spent the afternoon helping Sadie prepare for the evening. Henry had sent over a large Christmas tree and included decorations so they had a good time decking the tree.

She kept glancing at her mother, wondering what the surprise was, Sadie was happy so it wasn't anything bad. Was her mother having a baby? She wasn't too old, not really. Cath's imagination ran away with her. If Sadie had a baby and it was a boy perhaps she would give it away as she had the others. For a brief moment Cath thought of Timmy, her little brother. Had it really happened that they had gone into the Bishop's park and Sadie had given away her baby? Cath pushed the thought out of her mind. It was so long ago and her mother must have had her reasons. Her mother was a weak woman and she wasn't the only one to go wild when her man was away for years at a time.

They were sitting at the dinner table eating trifle made by Sadie with real cream (which did a good job disguising the runny jelly and custard), when Henry dropped his bombshell.

'Catherine, your mother and I are going to be married next year. I hope you are pleased for us.' He smiled at Sadie and put his hand over hers. 'We wanted you to be the first to know.'

'Married?' Cath thought she had not heard aright. When Sadie nodded and smiled the question popped out of Cath's mouth almost of its own volition.

'Are you having a baby?' she asked.

Chapter Twenty-six

Christmas Day dawned clear and bright though the winds overnight had swept the snow from the fields into great drifts against every wall and hedge. It was a cold, silent world that Cath looked out on from her bedroom window. It wasn't too warm in the bedroom either for there was no fire in the grate.

Cath climbed back into bed and snuggled under the eiderdown. Sadly, she wondered what Jack was doing this Christmas. The aching void inside her just didn't get any smaller.

Reluctantly, she got out of bed and went along to the bathroom. The bath water was still fairly hot, so she had a bath and dressed and went downstairs.

'Good morning. Merry Christmas,' said Henry. Usually he went home sometime in the early hours but today he was sitting at the dining table and eating a plate of home-cured ham and eggs. Though rationing was still on, it had been relaxed yet Cath was still surprised to see two fried eggs on one plate. She was even more surprised when her mother came through from the kitchen with two more plates of food in her hand.

'Merry Christmas,' she carolled and kissed Cath on the cheek. The morning was full of surprises. She sat down and started to eat. The food was well cooked and she enjoyed it. This domesticated side of her mother was new to her. Sadie was really trying hard.

Sadie and Henry were chatting together and Cath concentrated on her breakfast. She let her thoughts wander as they did so often these days. The conversation was simply a hum in the background for her. But she was suddenly alerted by the mention of Jack's name.

'I need Jack at home,' Henry was saying, 'I need him to run the estate. I'm no longer young.' He looked across at Cath. 'Your mother and I want to enjoy our declining years together.'

Despite Cath's surge of hope at the thought that Jack might come home and he might, possibly, if she prayed like mad, get in touch with her and tell her he hadn't really deserted her, it was all an unlucky accident. He might tell her he loved her, that he wanted to marry her—

'Besides, I want him to settle down, have a family, it's high time,' said Henry, breaking into her thoughts.

Oh, she agreed with that, Cath thought fervently. Only Henry wouldn't mean her, no, he would have someone very different in mind for Jack. One of the County set, no doubt. That dampened the wild hope down a bit.

After breakfast a tractor from the farm came through with a snow plough on the front and Henry and Sadie were able to walk up to the Hall. Cath declined to go with them and they made little effort to persuade her. She settled down with her mother's *Forever Amber* before the sitting-room fire, but was soon tired of the antics and machinations of the heroine in the court of Charles the Second. She fell asleep as the afternoon darkened and the only light in the room was from the flickering fire.

Cath awoke with a start and sat up, her heart pounding. For a few seconds she couldn't think where she was. And there was a banging noise and then the sound of the bell ringing through the house. She jumped up and went to the front door and almost opened it when she suddenly thought of Eric. He could have seen her mother and Henry leave the cottage and know she was on her own.

'Who is it?' she cried.

'It's Mark. For goodness sake let me in, it's freezing out here.'

Mark! Oh, she was glad to see him. He would have some good explanation for keeping away all this time. Serious illness was it? His mother or himself?

Cath opened the door and he strode into the hall, his overcoat spangled with frozen snow from the brief time he had been outside.

'I thought I must have missed you, you had gone back to Durham or something. The house was dark, I thought it was empty. Where's your mother?'

'A merry Christmas to you too, Mark,' said Cath. She could smell whisky on his breath. She felt suddenly flat.

'Why did you come out on a night like this? Come into the sitting room and I'll get you some tea. Or coffee if you like?'

'A drink would be more like it.'

Mark swayed and looked at her with a strange expression but he followed her into the sitting room and slumped down in the armchair she had just vacated.

'Where's your mother?' he repeated. 'I want a word with her.'

'She's up at the Hall. She and Henry Vaughan are going to be married. They told me last night.'

Mark laughed. 'She has him fooled all right. There's no fool like an old fool as they say.'

Cath chose to ignore this. 'Did you say you'd have coffee?'

'No I didn't, I want a whisky, damn you!'

'Look, you'd better go if you're going to be—'

'I'm not bloody going until I see that bitch, now get me a drink will you? Or have I to get it myself?'

Cath bit her lip. She was nervous of him now – she hadn't seen him in this sort of mood before. She could hardly force him to go physically and any way he was in no condition to drive anywhere in the snow. It was starting to blow again and the path cleared by the tractor and snow plough was becoming obliterated.

'I'll get it. You sit still. And stop calling my mother names,' she said as calmly as she could. She went to the tray, which held Henry's whisky and glasses, poured him a small one and added a generous amount of water. She handed it to him then sat down opposite him.

He took a gulp then spluttered and spat it out.

'What's that? Get me a proper drink,' he shouted at her.

'Mark!'

Cath was horrified, she couldn't handle this. He was so hostile. She didn't even know what she had done. She took the glass and poured more whisky into it and handed it back to him. He must have driven through the gloom to get here – it was a wonder he hadn't killed both himself and any other unfortunate road user he happened to meet.

'Mark, Mark,' he parodied her and gulped his whisky. 'Butter wouldn't melt in your mouth, would it, you innocent-faced whore.'

'What do you mean?'

Cath was trembling. She got on to her knees to mend the fire as an excuse to pick up the heavy brass poker to defend herself. Then she realised she was in a vulnerable position on her knees and stood up, still holding the poker.

Mark leaned forward in the chair. 'I dare bet you know all about it,' he said. His words were slurring more and more. He shook his head to clear it and rose to his feet unsteadily. 'I'll just get another one,' he said.

'You've had enough,' said Cath. 'What is it I'm supposed to know all about?' The look on his face was so dark she thought of edging towards the door; she was still holding the poker.

Mark didn't reply. He poured himself the last of the whisky then he turned to her and his expression changed. He grinned and walked towards her.

'Don't touch me or I'll brain you, I swear,' said Cath and stepped back towards the door, lifting the poker.

Mark laughed. 'Touch you, I won't touch *you*, don't worry about that. It's not legal, didn't you know that?'

229

Cath stared up at him. What did he mean? 'What are you talking about?' she asked.

'Don't you know? Why, incest of course,' said Mark. He grinned but his eyes were glistening with unshed tears. He stopped just in front of her and gripped her arms. 'How about a nice brotherly kiss?'

'Get off me, get off me, let me go. You said you wouldn't touch me,' she hissed at him. His grip on her arms loosened and she pushed him. He was taken off guard and stumbled, tripping on the copy of *Forever Amber* she had dropped by the chair earlier in the afternoon and to fall and land sprawling over the carpet and bumping his head on the brass knob of the fender. Cath was left shaking and staring at him as he lay in a heap, blood trickling down from where the skin of his forehead had been split. The blood dripped on to the white fur hearthrug.

She couldn't move for a moment then she stepped over his legs and bent down to him and felt his pulse. At first she couldn't find it then there it was, a little fast and thready but beating nevertheless.

'Oh, thank God, thank you God,' she murmured. She sat back, not knowing what to do, her thoughts were so chaotic. In the end she ran to the kitchen and got a bowl of water and a clean cloth and went back to him to dab at the wound on his forehead. He stirred and groaned, then sat up suddenly, leaned over and was sick on the hearthrug. The smell of stale whisky filled the air.

'Are you all right?' she asked. 'Let me help you up.' He pushed her away. 'Leave me alone,' he said savagely. He pulled himself upright, groaned again and sat down heavily in the chair. 'What a stink in here. And my head is breaking in two.'

'Here.' She held out the damp cloth. 'Hold this to your head. It's just about stopped bleeding.' She left him clutching at his head as she rolled up the rug and took it out to the back porch. She would have to have it cleaned, she thought dully.

Back in the sitting room she opened the window despite the bitter cold wind and the fire flared up with the draught. He was still leaning forward in the chair with his head in his hands. She sat down opposite him again.

'Now tell me what that was all about,' she said.

He sat back and looked at her. 'I need a couple of codeine,' he said weakly. Cath rose and got some from the bathroom and handed them to him with a glass of water.

'Now,' she commanded.

'I have to sort my head out,' he replied.

'Mark!'

'All right, all right. I suppose it's not your fault. How could you know? You weren't even born.' He paused, evidently searching for the right words but in the meantime the front door opened and Sadie's footsteps sounded across the hall and she came into the sitting room.

'By heck, our Cath, it's blowing a gale in here. It's colder indoors than it is outside,' she said, crossing to the window, closing it and drawing the curtains across. 'It smells an' all. What have you been doing?' Then she turned and saw Mark in the chair. He was sitting bolt upright now and staring at her.

'Oh, your friend's here. That's nice,' she said. 'Hello Mark. You haven't been around lately.'

'Hello, Mrs Raine,' Mark replied getting to his feet. 'Or should I say Mother dear?'

'What?'

Sadie halted in her walk towards him and the fire. 'What are you talking about? Oh, are you two thinking of getting married?' She started to smile, still not realising there was anything strange about his attitude.

'Married? No, I'm afraid we can't do that,' said Mark. He was speaking courteously enough though his words were still slightly slurred.

'Mark, I don't understand a word you're saying,' said Cath. He smiled humourlessly at her.

'I'm sure our mother will explain it all to you.'

Our mother? A terrible suspicion was forming at the back of Cath's mind.

'Did you know Toby and I were adopted? I'm sure your mother must have some idea when I tell her my adoptive mother's name is Daphne Drummond and my father's Nigel.'

'What? It's not true, you're lying. They went to live down south years ago. They said they wouldn't be back.' Sadie had collapsed in a heap on to the sofa in the middle of the room but now she jumped up to confront him. 'You're a bloody liar!' she shouted.

'I see I have a foul-mouthed harridan for a mother,' Mark observed. The wound on his forehead had started to bleed again and blood trickled down the side of his face. He ignored it. His face was very white and his eyes glittered. Abruptly he said down again and closed his eyes.

'It was true, Timmy was not the first then,' Cath said to her mother, her voice coming out in little more than a whisper. She was shaking. 'Oh Mam, how could you do it? How could you give away your babies?'

'You don't know what it was like,' Sadie snapped. 'Don't you judge me. I had no man the first time. Lots of people give their babies up for adoption.'

'Not many sell them,' Mark observed.

'I tell you, I did my best for you,' said Sadie. 'You don't know what it was like having a bairn on your own in them days.'

Mark snorted. Cath glanced at him; he was beginning to look really ill. Her mind was running on two levels, one still in shock and hardly able to take in the revelations that were emerging and the other feeling concern for Mark.

'Mark, you're ill. Leave this now. I'll help you upstairs – you'd be better lying down.'

His eyes flew fully open. 'I'm not staying in this damn house,' he cried. 'I'm going back to Staindrop.'

'No, you can't,' Cath insisted.

With a visible effort he got to his feet but then his legs

gave way beneath him and he would have fallen if she hadn't caught him. She was staggering under his weight and her mother rushed forward to give her a hand.

'Lie him down on the sofa,' said Sadie and they managed between them to drag him over and put him down. Sadie took off his shoes while Cath loosened his tie and his collar button.

'Mind it's a bit since I did this for Alf when he came in pallatic drunk,' said Sadie. 'I can smell he's been sick an' all. Alf was sick all over me new proddy mat.'

'I've put the hearthrug on the back porch,' said Cath. 'I'll get a rug for him.'

When he was settled they sat down in the armchairs and gazed at him.

'Mind, he's made a fine figure of a man,' said Sadie. 'He's a lad any mother could be proud of. He's a university lecturer, did you say? Aye well, his dad had brains, I'll say that for him. Let's go into the kitchen. I'm dying for a good, strong cup of tea.'

'He's my half-brother then,' said Cath as they waited for the kettle to boil. 'Mam, he said he loved me. Do you know what harm you could have done?'

'It's not my fault, none of this,' said Sadie. 'I'll not take the blame. That stuck-up Daphne Drummond said they were going down south to live. I thought it was a good chance for the lad. It was, wasn't it? Then when I met her in Auckland in the war she wanted Timmy. She was staying up here to get away from the bombing. I told her she'd have to go away again, as far away as they could get and she agreed. She wanted our Timmy. And I needed the money.'

She stared at Cath with a challenging expression then it changed. 'Oh God, you didn't, did you? You slept with him?'

Cath looked away, she couldn't speak for a minute. They had been so close to it.

'Bloody incest,' said Sadie. 'Wouldn't that just happen.

By, if I got hold of that Daphne and Nigel Drummond I'd strangle them with my bare hands, I would!'

'But I didn't sleep with him,' said Cath, at last.

'Oh, thank God!'

They were silent for a few moments. The kettle boiled and was ignored. Then Cath got to her feet and took it off the flames. She was reeling. Not only was Mark her brother but Toby was her long lost baby brother, Timmy, whom she had so adored.

'I'd better check on him,' she said at last. 'My half-brother, isn't he, I have to look after him.' She sounded very bitter, very bitter indeed.

Chapter Twenty-seven

'Do you think we should have called the doctor?' Cath asked. It was a couple of hours later and Mark had woken once but he was confused. A bruise had come out on his head and, when he had seen Cath, he had held out his arms to her and wanted her to sit by him. He seemed to have forgotten the reason he had come to Half Hidden Cottage.

'We'd best get him upstairs to bed,' Sadie had said. 'It won't be so hard if we have him between us. Henry said he was staying at home tonight but there's still a chance he might drop in.'

Cath didn't reply to that though her bitterness towards her mother rose further. Sadie was more worried about what Henry might think than about her son. They helped Mark to his feet and he leaned on them as they went out and up the stairs to Cath's room, which was the handiest. They were both panting when at last they got him on to the bed.

'I'll leave you to undress him,' said Cath. 'After all, you're his mother.' Her bitterness showed in her tone.

'Aw, Cath, there's no point in us falling out,' Sadie replied. But she cajoled and eased him out of his clothes and put a pyjama jacket of Henry's on him. When they laid him back on the pillows he fell asleep immediately. Sadie and Cath looked at each other.

'I don't think we'd get a doctor out in this weather,' said

Sadie. The wind was howling outside and snow was piling up on the windowsill. 'Maybe it's just the drink. He could sleep it off by morning. He didn't hit his head so hard, did he?'

'He might have concussion,' Cath replied fearfully. She tried to put his hand back under the bedclothes but it turned and clasped hers.

'Cath,' he muttered.

'I'll just sit here with him,' Cath decided. 'If we think he's any worse we can ring the doctor and ask his advice.'

She sat in a chair beside the bed, still holding his hand while Sadie went downstairs to make supper. She brought Cath's up on a tray. The room was fairly dark with just the bedside light with a cloth over the shade providing a soft glow. Cath studied Mark's face. He looked a little better than he had earlier with some colour in his cheeks, she decided. She stood up and gently took her hand away and put his under the bedclothes. He stirred but did not waken. Now, as she studied him, she could see a family resemblance. The same colour hair, the cut of his lips. Had the attraction he held for her been because of their shared blood?

The wind outside rattled the window frame but no draught got in for Sadie had drawn the heavy curtains.

Sadie came in again. 'He seems better,' she said. 'It was probably just the drink. I'll sit with him for a while if you like.'

Cath's first impulse was to refuse but she was tired herself and in any case she had to do something about the Drummonds. Slipping from the room, she went downstairs to the telephone and tried to ring them though her heart beat fast with apprehension at the thought of it. But it was no good, the lines were down. She didn't know whether to be sorry or relieved.

She sat on the stairs and leaned against the wall holding her head in one hand. She sighed and closed her eyes for a moment. It was all such a mess. He had said he loved her but he would get over it and put it all behind him but it was difficult for her, oh yes, it was, even if she didn't really love him. The wall was cold against her shoulder and she shivered. Rising to her feet, she went back upstairs. Sadie was asleep, slumped in the chair, her head lolling against the bed and her mouth hanging slightly open. Gentle snores sounded through the room. Cath nudged her shoulder.

'What? What?' Sadie asked.

'Howay, to bed Mam. He's all right now, I'm sure, just sleeping it off. I tried to ring the Drummonds but the lines must be down.'

'What did you want to ring them for? It was their entire fault this. They promised me they wouldn't come north again, they promised me faithfully.' Sadie had woken up in a grumpy mood. 'But I tell you what,' she went on, 'I'll tell her, I will, I wish I'd never had nowt to do with her, I do. I should have kept the lads, I know I should, but she offered me money and I didn't know where to turn for debt. But I would have got through. You do somehow. Look at him, isn't he a grand lad?' She began to weep.

'Mam, pull yourself together, will you? You're getting maudlin. Anyway, I know you didn't care much for Timmy so you probably felt the same about Mark. I daresay you would have sold me and Annie an' all if you could.'

'Eeh no, I wouldn't, our Cath. I wouldn't do that,' her mother replied as if the thought was really repugnant to her. 'I can't believe you said that.'

'No. Well, I think you'd better go to bed. I think Mark will be all right until morning.' Cath couldn't bring herself to say she was sorry.

'We'll both go. You can sleep in my bed.'

'No, I'll go in the spare room. Goodnight.' Cath took a nightie from a drawer and went up the corridor to the spare room. It was very cold in there; the curtains were open and she could see snowflakes as big as pennies driving down from the sky and piling against the window ledges. She drew the curtains and undressed quickly then climbed into bed. The sheets were icily cold. She curled into a ball and hugged her knees. She would soon warm up, she told herself, and there was a thick eiderdown.

'I've brought you a hot water bottle,' her mother spoke from the doorway.

'Thank you,' said Cath, amazed. This was the first time in her life she could remember her mother thinking of her comfort.

'Right, I'll go to bed now,' said Sadie, looking uncertainly at Cath.

'Oh, go on then, come in here with me.' Cath held the bedclothes up and Sadie jumped in beside her, snuggling up close for warmth.

'I didn't—' Sadie began to say.

'Leave it be!' said Cath. 'Go to sleep.'

It was quiet for a while and Sadie's breathing became deep and even. She turned over once. 'His name is Matthew,' she muttered. 'Matthew, not—' The rest tailed off and Sadie began to snore gently.

Cath woke early. Though the sky was still dark there was a glow from the white snow when she peeked out of the curtains. She shivered in the cold and dropped the curtain. Though her nightgown was winceyette with long sleeves to her wrists it did little to keep her warm. She went along the corridor to get her dressing gown from behind the door in her own room.

'Oh! Should you be up?' Cath asked as she went in and saw Mark, already dressed and standing by the bed. Quickly she pulled the dressing gown on and tied it round her waist.

'How do you feel?'

'Like someone hit me with a sledgehammer,' said Mark. 'What am I doing here, anyway?' He sat down on the bed with a thump. 'Oh lord, I feel dizzy again.'

'Get back into bed and I'll bring you a cup of tea and a

238

couple of codeine,' said Cath. 'Can you manage or can I help you?'

'No, I'll come downstairs. It's passing now.'

They went downstairs and into the sitting room. Cath switched on a small electric fire and stood it before his chair. The coal fire in the grate was dead. Mark watched her as she moved about, a strange expression on his face. Dreading the time when it all came back to him, Cath went into the kitchen and made tea and toast. She put it on a tray with a couple of tablets and carried it back into the sitting room. While he drank the tea she raked out the fire and built it anew. Then she sat opposite him and sipped at her own cup.

Mark had a bite of toast and put the slice back on the plate. He leaned back in the chair and said, 'I loved you, you know. I still do.'

Cath looked at him, the moment had come. 'I knew nothing about it, Mark,' she said. With his elbow on the arm of his chair he held one side of his head with his hand. There was an awareness in his eyes now.

'No, of course not, how could you?'

'It was a bad time for the mining folk, between the wars. And a woman on her own . . . This wouldn't have happened if your parents had stayed in the south as they said they would. It's not all mam's fault either.'

'I've gone through hell these last weeks.' He laughed without humour. 'All those years I played about with the girls I kidded myself I was immune; no girl could trap me. Then I had to fall for you.'

'Poetic justice?'

'Maybe.'

They sat for a while in silence. The room warmed up and light began to filter through the curtains. Cath rose to her feet and drew them back. The world outside was just an expanse of white.

'You won't be able to get home this morning,' she said. 'Unless you're going to Durham? They usually open the main road and a farmer brings his tractor through with a snow plough along here.' She turned back to him. He was still white and the bruise on his forehead showed lividly against his white skin. 'Probably just as well. You don't look very fit.'

'I'll be all right. I'll just rest a bit longer. Look the sun's breaking through, things are bound to improve now.' He was gazing at her, studying her almost. He cleared his throat and sat up straight.

'I came over yesterday to give you a letter. But I was nervous and stopped at the King William pub in Shildon and had a drink, Dutch courage as it were. One led to another ... I began to get angry and the more angry I got the more I had to drink. The landlord threw me out in the end.' He paused for a moment. 'I was drunk but then you know that.'

'Where is it?'

'What?'

'The letter. Were you just going to write to me and tell me we were brother and sister?'

'No. The letter wasn't from me, it was from Jack.'

'Jack?'

He nodded and winced at the head movement. Cath didn't even notice.

'Where is it?' she asked.

'Here.' He reached into the inside pocket of his jacket and brought out a crumpled envelope. He stared at it for a moment before handing it to her.

The letter was dated the morning after Jack had spent the night with her in Durham – the day she had been expecting him to meet her:

My dearest Catherine,

I have had some surprising news. When I got home there was a letter waiting for me ordering me to report to barracks at Catterick immediately. It is war in Korea, my darling, and I have to go. I am a reservist.

240

It couldn't have come at a worse time for us and I am so very sorry, Catherine. But I'm sure, with the United Nations involved it will all be over very soon and I will be able to return to you and we will be able to plan for our future together. I am entrusting this to Mark and he has promised to deliver it to you. Now I have things to do before I go.

Don't worry about me, Catherine. I will be back as soon as I can.

With all my love,

Jack

Cath read it through then read it again before looking up at Mark. 'Why didn't you give me it? Jack is your best friend!'

Mark shrugged. 'You know what they say, all's fair in love and war.'

Cath erupted. 'How could you? How could you? I hate you, oh God, I hate you! Get out! Get out before I kill you!'

Mark rose to his feet. 'You don't mean that. You're putting me out in the snow? You can't, what will I do?'

'I don't care what you do, just get out of my sight, that's all,' Cath shouted.

'Hey, hey, what's all this? It's a wonder they don't hear you up at the Hall.' Sadie had come in unnoticed. 'Don't be daft, our Cath, Mark has nowhere to go, has he? Besides this is my house, I decide who has to go. Sit down, Mark. I'm pleased to see you looking better, any road. Now, are you going to be civil?'

Mark pulled a face. 'I'm sorry,' he muttered like a small boy with an apology dragged out of him.

'Shall I make some more tea? An' mebbe a bit of bacon? Henry brought some home-cured down the other day.' Mark sat down and Cath stared at him, speechless now with anger.

'Right,' said Sadie. 'I'll away and do a fry up then.'

When she had gone Mark said, 'I was going to give it, really I was. But Toby came over to stay and what with one thing and another I was too busy to get over to Old Elvet. Then I suppose I made one excuse after another to myself not to give it to you until I thought it was too late. I wanted you for myself. And look where it's got me.'

'I suppose you wouldn't have given it to me now if you hadn't found out we're brother and sister.' Cath was still angry, she couldn't believe he had been so underhand. Oh, she had misread his character all right. The memory came back of Jack's contemptuous remark, years ago, when she and Annie were caught trespassing on the Vaughan estate. A pitman's brat, he had called her, or was it a miner's brat?

'So you are a pitman's brat too, then,' she said, wanting to hurt him.

'What?'

'Nothing. It was just something Jack said when we first met.'

242

Chapter Twenty-eight

It was mid-afternoon when the telephone rang out loudly; making them all start for it had been silent for so long. Cath went to answer it – the operator informed them that the line was now back in operation, though the fact that she was speaking on it made that obvious. A few minutes later Henry came.

'Are you both all right?' he asked. Sadie came out of the kitchen and he sighed with relief. 'Oh, thank God. I worried about you ever since the road was blocked again. If we have more snow, I think you should come up to the Hall—' He broke off as he saw Mark standing in the doorway of the sitting room. 'Mark! Have you been here all the time? Do you know your parents have been out looking for you? You didn't say where you were going and when you didn't turn up in Durham they thought you must be buried in a snowdrift somewhere. They rang me twice today. What are you doing here, anyway?'

'I was coming to see you, sir,' Mark said smoothly. 'I wondered what the latest news of Jack was. I thought this way would be shorter than the main drive to the Hall.'

'Well, at least this place was here, any port in a storm as they say. Only the line was down between the Hall and here. I've been pestering the post office to get it seen to.'

'It's all right now,' said Sadie.

'Good. Well Mark, you chose a funny time to visit,

during a snowstorm. Still, I'm glad you're here. I had a letter from Jack on Christmas Eve, he's coming home.'

'Coming home? Why?'

'He was injured and captured by the Chinese, evidently. Before they had time to take him behind the lines, the Chinese themselves were captured by the Americans apparently. Good news, isn't it?'

Cath sank down on the hall chair, suddenly short of breath. Henry was the only one to notice.

'Are you all right, girl?' he asked.

'Yes, just a bit tired. The storm kept me awake.'

'Well, let's go into the sitting room where it's warm,' said Sadie. 'I'm really pleased for you, Henry. That he's coming home, that is.'

'How badly is he injured?' Mark asked the question Cath was afraid to ask.

'He didn't say exactly but it can't be too bad or he wouldn't have been able to write the letter, would he?'

Cath's mind was running on the worst possible injuries as she followed the others into the sitting room. She still clutched his letter in her hand and now she thrust it deep into the pocket of her slacks. Mark, watching her, was the only one who had any idea of her feelings and he felt a surge of jealousy. But we're brother and sister, he reminded himself bleakly.

'What have you done to your head?' Henry asked. 'Looks like you had a fall. You didn't skid in the car, did you?'

'No, I fell here, hit my head on the fender,' said Mark glancing at Cath. 'It's nothing.'

'We had to keep him overnight, Henry,' said Sadie. 'Then we couldn't let anyone know because the telephone line was down.'

'I'll ring them now,' said Mark and went out to the hall.

Cath had lost the thread of the conversation by this time; all she could think of was Jack and how seriously he might be injured. It must be quite bad if he was coming home.

The war was still going on after all. She slipped out after Mark. He was talking into the telephone but she hurried past him and ran up the stairs to her room. It smelled faintly of him and she opened the window to let in fresh air despite the biting wind that made the curtains billow out into the room.

She stripped the bed and bundled the washing out on to the landing then made it up again with clean sheets. Her thoughts were agonised; she should have trusted Jack. Why hadn't she trusted him? She worked furiously, cleaning the room until every sign of Mark was removed. Then at last she closed the window and sat down by the dressing table and brought Jack's letter out of her pocket and read it again and again.

By evening the weather had changed for the better. The temperature went up and water dripped from the eaves and the surrounding trees. Every now and then patches of snow slid from the roof with a whoosh and melted into puddles on the grass and paths. The road was clear.

'Cath, Mark's going now, come on down and say goodbye,' Sadie shouted up the stairs. Cath put down the letter she had just read for the hundredth time and reluctantly did as she was bid.

'I could give you a lift back to Durham,' said Mark as she walked out with him to the car. He glanced at her and looked away quickly. Her face was white and set.

'No thanks, I'd rather get the bus tomorrow,' Cath replied. On the opposite side of the road the sodden trees looked as though they were weeping. Just as I am on the inside, Cath thought dismally.

'We could still be friends,' said Mark. 'I think a lot of you, Cath.'

'You're a selfish pig, Mark,' said Cath. 'If I don't see you again it will be too soon. Give my regards to your mother.'

He climbed into the car and pressed the ignition button

and after a few false starts the engine roared into life. He went off down the drive without looking back. She heard him turn at the bottom and then the sound of the engine faded into nothing.

Cath went back inside slowly. Henry and her mother were in the sitting room. 'When are you expecting Jack home exactly?' she asked him. He looked surprised at her interest.

'I don't know exactly. It will depend on when the doctors let him out. It won't be so long though. He said it was just a flesh wound. By the end of this month with a bit of luck. He'll be home for the wedding at any rate.'

'Oh, good,' said Cath.

At a US army hospital in South Korea, Jack lay back against his pillows. One side of his face was swathed in bandages and beneath them the flesh throbbed and ached and itched at the same time and occasionally searing pain flashed across his cheek. The flashes didn't last long and the pain was not so bad as it had been for he was under sedation but nevertheless his endurance was stretched to breaking point. He looked at the doorway, longing for the medical officer to arrive.

His thoughts returned to home and Catherine. At first, when she hadn't replied to his letter, he had been full of anger towards her. She must have known he loved her, she must have, he told himself. It was just like the old story of her mother though, wasn't it? Sadie Raine had been the talk of the pit villages around when her man went off to the war in the Middle-Eastern desert for a couple of years. The men had sniggered about her, made snide remarks about her inability to do without a man. Like mother like daughter, they said. And so it had proved.

Jack had even written to Mark to make sure he had given her the letter asking her to wait for him. 'Of course, I did,' Mark had replied. 'Why wouldn't I?'

Now Jack had received a letter from Mark saying he and

246

Cath were keeping company. Well, it was not the first time that they had been rivals for a girl. When he got home he would fight for Cath. Though he was handicapped now with his injured face. A slight limp such as the one Mark had from his injury and which he sometimes exaggerated for sympathy was an attraction. A scarred face was not. His Catherine was not so shallow, though, surely?

The doors to the ward opened and the medical officer came in, accompanied by an American army nurse. Jack was filled with relief. At least there might be more pain relief coming his way.

'It's like this,' Captain Seton, the medical officer said. 'We can do an interim operation to clean out the wound properly and then send you back to your own command for them to repatriate you to England. I'm afraid it was badly neglected in your time as a prisoner and repairing your face is not so straightforward as it should be. Or we can deal with it in our own hospital in Japan. This would be quicker—'

'I'll go back home, thank you,' said Jack.

'Very well. We'll send you back to your own command immediately for you can't afford to waste any more time. I'll have to sedate you further for the journey.'

'I will be home soon,' Jack wrote to his father. It was two months after his release from his Chinese captors by the Americans and he was now feeling a great deal better. They had dealt with the infection in his facial wound and at least now the pain was bearable. He had only hazy memories of the journey or at least the beginnings of it for he was under sedation most of the time. What he could remember were the vivid dreams of a Chinese captain screaming propaganda at him and his fellow British soldiers. It went on and on until it became part of the pain. The Chinese were determined to turn them into communists. He would wake up in a sweat of agony and fear until he realised he was safe; the Americans had saved them.

'The surgeons have made a good job of my wounds,' Jack wrote. He paused. The infection had been stopped and the wounds cleaned out. It was true also that the flesh was healing well. Still, he avoided looking at himself in a mirror. The sight of the ugly scar brought him up short. One minute he would be dreaming about getting home and seeing his father and most especially Catherine. He didn't care about anything but winning her back. He had had plenty of time to think about it and he knew he wanted her no matter what had happened between her and Mark. And then he would see his reflection in the mirror when he shaved. He had to study the scar to shave round it properly.

He tried growing a beard but the scar extended above it and in any case hair wouldn't grow on the new skin so that a wide line of puckered pink showed in the middle of his cheek.

'The medics are sending me to a hospital in England next week,' he wrote to his father.

Jack paused and bit his lip. Would Catherine want him when she saw how ugly he was now or would she be repulsed? And there was always the question, would she fall in love with Mark and marry him before he got home?

Jack had written a letter to her; in fact, he had written several and torn them up. But this morning he took it together with the one for his father and put it in the post. He had actually got as far as the post box in the main corridor of the hospital, hesitated only once then slipped them through the opening.

Cath had had trouble getting the address of Jack's hospital in England from Henry.

'Why should you want it?' Henry had asked.

'We are friends,' Cath replied.

'Friends? And this is the first time you've wanted to write to him?' Henry was sceptical.

'We had an argument,' Cath said weakly. 'Please Henry.'

'I don't know.'

Henry had mellowed since he had decided to marry Sadie. He had begun to realise also that the world had changed since the war, class barriers were not so high as they had been. And he had grown to like the girl, Sadie's daughter. Not that he thought there was anything between Cath and his son, of course there wasn't. He regarded Cath critically. She was a lovely girl, with her dark hair and large brown eyes, her soft white skin. Maybe she was just what Jack needed to take his mind off recent horrors.

'All right,' he conceded. 'I'll give you the address. Though I think he'll be moving again soon. Nearer to home, I think. They are going to do some sort of plastic surgery on his face. Well, give me a pen and paper then.'

Cath winced; she couldn't bear to think of what he had been through. She handed him her address book and pen and he wrote it down. She lost no time in going to the privacy of her room and starting a letter to him:

Dear Jack,

I hope you don't mind your father giving me your present address. I'm afraid I pestered him for it. I'm so glad you're coming home though sorry for the reason for it. How do you feel? I hope you are not in too much pain.

Cath paused. It sounded so stilted. A maiden aunt could have written it. It did not convey anything of what she truly felt. She began again:

Dearest Jack,

I am sorry for what happened. Mark didn't give me your letter but I suppose you know that, he said he had told you. I thought you had deserted me, I thought you were glad of the opportunity to get away from me. I was lost and hurt.

249

She paused again and read what she had written through. It was all about her and how she felt and she should be asking about him. It was Jack who was hurt, not her. What a selfish pig she was!

Chapter Twenty-nine

'What do you think? There's been a little girl murdered down your way,' Hilda said as Cath let herself in through the front door.

'A little girl?' Cath echoed, aghast.

'It's on the news at the minute, come through and see,' said Hilda. Cath followed her into the sitting room. As usual, Pete and Hilda had been sitting with their chairs turned to the corner where the fourteen-inch television set flickered black and white images rather than to the fire-place, which had been the former focus of the room.

'The body of a girl aged between eleven and twelve was found in the Bishop's park in Bishop Auckland. It was hidden in a patch of undergrowth on the hillside above the River Gaunless,' the newscaster said. 'The girl's name has not been released as yet until her family have been informed. It appears she was a pupil at Bishop Auckland Girls' County School for she was wearing a bottle-green Burberry rainproof coat and a school hat was found lying nearby.'

Cath listened hardly able to believe what she heard. Her first thought was, thank goodness it couldn't be Annie. But neither could the murderer be Ronnie Robson for he was still an inmate in Winterton mental hospital. So there was a monster at large. She was lost in her own thoughts and fears and at first she didn't hear what Hilda was saying.

'Cath?' the older woman asked. 'Are you listening to me?'

'Sorry, sorry, yes, of course. What did you say?'

'I was just saying, how terrible it is. Whoever she is, she's some mother's bairn, isn't she? What's the world coming to if you can't let your girl out on her own?'

'I wonder who she is, where she's from,' said Cath. She had an awful feeling the girl would turn out to be from one of the colliery villages around the town. Since the 1944 Education Act more and more children from the villages had won scholarships to the grammar schools in the town, both boys and girls. And, whereas before the war, few of the miners could afford for their children to go to such schools, they were making good money now.

The *Northern Echo* had the story next morning, blazoned across the front page. The girl was Carol White, aged eleven and a half and she was from Coundon.

Carol had slung her schoolbag a little higher on her shoulder as she walked up Kingsway in the town. She had to walk home because she had lost her bus pass and she had no money in her pocket at all. She had had three-pence that morning when she set out but she had bought a quarter of bull's eyes at the newsagents in Coundon as she waited for the bus to school. She would share them with the girls in her class and then maybe they would be friends with her. She had eaten only two of the sweets herself and then passed them round and for this she had got a rollicking telling off from Miss Macrae, her form mistress.

But none of the girls wanted to play with her when she went out to the playing fields after dinner. She was one of the last girls out and the ones from her old school, Penny and Margaret, had already disappeared down the far field. Not that they had been her particular friends when she was at Junior School but she still hadn't got to know the others really. A wintry sun shone today and it was fairly warm for February.

Some of the girls were turning somersaults on the grass beside the tennis courts. Gwyneth was there, she was a nice friendly girl.

'Do you know where Penny and Margaret went?' she asked her. Gwyneth shook her head.

'You can play with us if you like,' she offered.

'No, she can't,' said Marjorie White. 'Go and find your own friends. My dad said I hadn't to play with pitmen's children.'

'It's all right, I'm looking for my friends,' Carol said to Gwyneth and walked on. When she found Penny and Margaret at the end of the far field they were with their new friends and didn't really want her, she could tell. Perhaps they had been trying to get away from her by going so far.

Carol had got to the end of Kingsway and crossed the road. The tall wrought-iron gates of the park were still open so, instead of following Durham Road to Coundon, she decided to go by the path through the park. She felt sad; she wanted to be on her own. She and her mam and dad had been so excited about her winning the scholarship to the grammar school and now she was without a real friend. Well, she would just have to get used to being on her own.

The gravel crunched beneath her feet and she hitched her schoolbag higher on her shoulder. It had a strap for both shoulders but she soon realised that the other girls wouldn't be seen dead with both straps in use. It was heavy – she had her French textbook and English and geography ones too. Tonight they had two hours' homework.

'Some girls are skimping their homework,' Miss Dixon, the French mistress had said. 'You should allow forty minutes for translation. I can tell if you try to do it any faster.'

Carol went through the cowcatcher gate, having to

hoist her schoolbag over. She looked back when she thought she heard the gravel crunching behind her but she couldn't see anyone. She quickened her pace and had got quite a long way into the park, past the deer house, down the hill to the wooden bridge over the Gaunless and so far up the other side, when she heard quick footsteps behind her. There was someone about. A man was there. In the failing light she saw, as he got close that it was a man she knew, a work mate from Winton Colliery of her father's.

'Hello Carol,' he said. 'Walking home, are you?'

He was a big man with pale blue eyes and a bristly chin. He slowed his pace to match hers. She began to hurry, anxious to get to the other end of the path where the main road ran to Durham and a side road ran off to Coundon.

'Wait a minute,' said the man. 'I know where there is a badger sett. I'll show you if you like.'

'It's getting dark, I'll be late and Mam will be angry,' said Carol but she slowed. She had never seen a badger, not close up at least.

'It won't take a minute,' said the man. 'See that clump of bushes? It's just behind there.'

It was only a few yards off the path and the man was a friend of her dad's. She was probably being silly. She might not get another chance to see a badger.

'Badgers come out about this time, when it's nearly dark,' he said. 'Howay then.'

Carol looked up the path: it wasn't far to the road and she could see streetlights had come on and were twinkling through the trees. That would be Coundon Gate. He was right, it wouldn't take a minute. She was being silly.

It was a woman from Coundon Gate who had found the little body, or rather, it was her dog. She had crossed the road to the park, letting Gyp off his lead. He rushed about demented before suddenly forgetting what he was there to do and putting his nose to the ground and following it

254

blindly. It led him to an overgrown coppice only a few yards from the path. There he stood, barking and barking and refusing to come to heel as his owned demanded. In the end she had to go and get him.

'You bad dog, Gyp!' she said. 'Now I've got my feet all wet from the grass – what's that?'

It looked like a bundle of dark green clothes and beside it was a leather satchel bulging with books.

'Whatever is the world coming to?' Sadie asked. 'It's not safe out on your own any more.' Cath had rung her to tell her she was coming home this weekend and naturally they had begun to talk about the murder of Carol White. 'They say schools don't allow girls to walk home on their own any more. They have to be in pairs at least. And the girls' grammar school, well, they have started escorting them to and from the school buses.'

'It's a good idea,' said Cath. 'Pity they didn't always do that with the juniors, anyway.'

'They were always perfectly safe anywhere,' said Sadie.

'Annie wasn't,' Cath reminded her. 'Mam, our Annie's all right, isn't she?'

'Of course she is. Now she's out, Patsy watches her all the time.'

'I'll see you on Friday, Mam. Cheerio.' Cath put the telephone down and dropped a sixpence in the box Pete had recently put beside it.

'Charges are getting higher and higher,' he had said when he got the last bill from the post office.

Cath packed her bag for the weekend so that she could take it to work on Friday morning and go straight from the office. She didn't like staying in Durham over the weekend now because by accident or design Mark always managed to bump into her.

'We can have a meal together or go to the pictures,' he would say. 'We are brother and sister and there's nothing wrong in that, is there?' But there was a look in his eyes that made her uncomfortable and she couldn't forget that they had nearly become lovers.

As she took the bus to Half Hidden Cottage her thoughts returned to Carol White's murder. The papers were saying she had been 'interfered with', and a full-scale hunt was on for her attacker. Cath's thoughts turned to Eric Bowron. Could it possibly have been him, not his cousin Ronnie, who had attacked Annie? No, it couldn't be, there had been no attacks on girls for years, not since Annie and there would have been, surely?

Cath got off the bus at the drive for Half Hidden Cottage. There was an outside light now by the cottage, she saw, an imitation old-fashioned street lamp that shone out on to the grass showing that there was already a touch of sparkling frost. It showed something else, the clumps of snowdrops by the gate, and sown at random in the grass, were now scattered about as though someone had slashed at them with a knife or something.

'Mam! What happened to the snowdrops?' Cath called as she went into the house and through to the kitchen where her mother was sitting at the table smoking a cigarette and drinking tea.

'Heck, Cath, you made me jump coming in like that. What are you talking about any road?'

'The snowdrops. Someone has slashed them. They're all dead.'

'How could anyone have done that? I haven't been out all day. Are you sure?'

'Of course I'm sure, come and see for yourself if you like,' said Cath.

Sadie followed her out of the front door. 'Well, blow me,' she said. 'I never heard a thing. It's a bit creepy, isn't it?'

'I told you to watch out. That Eric Bowron has it in for us because of his cousin Ronnie. Next time it could be worse.'

'Aw Cath, stop trying to frighten me, it's likely just some kids done it. Little vandals, all of them. Howay in the warm. By, I don't know what kids are coming to nowadays.'

'But did you say anything to Henry? I bet you didn't.'

'I did. That's why he had the lamp put up outside. He looks after me, does Henry.'

She wasn't worried but disquiet ran through Cath's thoughts. 'Please be careful, Mam,' she said earnestly.

Sadie shook her head impatiently. 'You always were full of doom, our Cath. Come on, help me with the dinner. Henry's coming down.'

Cath had decided to have a word with Henry, tell him of her concern about Eric Bowron. But it was driven out of her mind when Henry came and they went into the dining room to eat the meal – rabbit in herbs, courtesy of Henry and cooked into a stew by Sadie. He walked over to the fireplace and held his hands out to the blaze.

'A bit parky out there,' he commented before his eye fell on a letter propped up against clock. 'Hello, there's a letter here for you Cath. And do you know, it looks like Jack's handwriting.'

Cath went hot and cold all over; she stared at the envelope. Henry was gazing steadily at her; she was aware of that but of little else that was happening.

'Oh yes, sorry Cath, I forgot about it,' said her mother. 'I meant to tell you, it came a day or two ago. I would have sent it on but I knew you would be coming home this weekend probably.'

'Why is my son writing to you?'

For a moment Cath couldn't think of an answer for Henry. Then she said, 'I wrote to him and said I was sorry he had been hurt.'

Henry looked sceptical but said no more. Cath took the letter and stared at it before putting it into her handbag, which was on the sideboard.

'Aren't you going to read it?' asked Henry.

'Later, I think. It won't be about anything in particular.'

'Well, forget about it for now. Come and eat before the food gets cold,' Sadie commanded, coming to Cath's assistance without realising she was doing so. The meal seemed interminable to Cath but at last it was over and the washing up done and she could make her excuses and go to her room.

'Dearest Catherine,' she read when at last she could open the envelope and fling herself down on her bed to read the letter:

> As you will see by my address I am back in England. I was wounded a few weeks ago and the medics have sent me home for treatment in England. Soon I am to be transferred to the RVI in Newcastle. It is nothing serious, just a facial wound but I need further surgery.
>
> I don't know what happened before I left, Catherine, I had to go so suddenly but I sent a message with Mark and I expected to hear from you. Mark told me that he gave you the message, so why? I did not think, Catherine, that you were the sort of girl who would change her mind so easily and so quickly.
>
> I'm sorry, I didn't mean that as a recrimination, but I think you owe me an explanation at least. The weekend we had together meant so much, I thought you loved me, as I loved you. In fact I would stake my life on it.
>
> I do not mean to badger you, Catherine. But please write to me to let me know what is happening with you, if you still think of me. If you are happy now with someone else, then so be it.
>
> With love,
>
> Jack

A surge of joy ran through Cath that he still wanted her.

But it was quickly followed by a rush of fury that Mark should have withheld Jack's letter from her. She felt like murdering him ... She remembered her letter to him – in the end she had not posted it. She ought to have done.

Chapter Thirty

Eric watched from behind a thicket of dense holly as Henry opened the front door of Half Hidden Cottage and frowned at the dead and dying snowdrops scattered over the grass. Though Eric was well hidden he could see Henry through a small gap in the prickly branches. He grinned as he saw Henry's expression of anger.

'I'll catch whoever did this, see if I don't,' Henry said loudly, punching the fist of one hand into the palm of the other. 'I'll have the law on them!'

'It's nothing, Henry, nothing to get upset about. I'll tidy it up and the bulbs will still flower next year.' Sadie came into Eric's line of vision. It was Sadie who had started the witch hunt against poor old Ronnie when the lad hadn't done anything at all to Annie. It was just because the lad was simple. Well, Ronnie couldn't get revenge for himself but he intended to get it for him, oh aye, he did. Sadie would be sorry for persecuting poor old Ronnie, who was still in Winterton and not likely to come out neither. It just wasn't right.

'It would just be bairns from Eden Hope or maybe Winton Colliery,' Sadie was saying. Henry shook his head in disagreement but he bent and kissed her on the lips. Eric shuddered at the thought of anyone, even an old man like Henry Vaughan, kissing the withered lips of an old woman like Sadie Raine.

He waited until Henry got into his car and drove away and Sadie had gone back into the house and closed the door. There now, she was on her own. Eric had seen Cath Raine come out an hour earlier and go off for the bus to Bishop Auckland. He had given the woman a warning last night when he'd chopped the heads off the flowers. It was her own fault if she had taken no notice. He pulled his white scarf up over his nose so that only his eyes were visible and stretched his legs from their cramped position.

Sadie went into the kitchen to begin the washing up. She was happy: her life had improved so much since she had been with Henry she couldn't understand why she had yearned to have Alf back. Gerda was welcome to him. Soon she herself would be mistress of the Hall.

She turned on the portable wireless that Henry had bought her and dance music poured into the room. Her feet moved to the music as she put the last plate on the draining board to dry and spread the teatowel over the edge of the sink. Washing up was no trouble when there was hot water on tap. She switched off the two-bar electric fire that Henry had put in here and went into the sitting room, carrying the wireless with her.

Oh, it was grand, with its comfortable furniture and velvet curtains. She stirred the fire into a blaze with the poker and settled down in an armchair to read the paper. She didn't hear the door to the room open.

Cath came back late afternoon. Letting herself in the front door she hummed to herself as she took off her coat and cosy crochet cap, which came over her ears and was all the rage that year. It was similar to the one worn by Sonja Henie, the ice-skating film star, and framed her face becomingly. She had enjoyed her day. She had bought a new dress in a soft rose colour for her visit to Jack in hospital when he was transferred to Newcastle. It had a V neckline with slight gathering at the V and going down to one side: very figure flattering, she thought.

'Mam?' she called, suddenly realising that there was no sound in the house. It was cold too. Henry had decided not to install central heating as he had planned to do for, after they were married, Sadie would be moving into the Hall.

Cath glanced in the kitchen but it was empty. Of course, Henry must have decided they would go out somewhere. She would just have to wait to try it on when Sadie came back.

She had written another letter to Jack, hoping it would catch him before he left the hospital in the south. Oh, she was so happy. She couldn't wait to see him. Her anger at Mark had faded, she was too happy to be angry with anyone. Jack was coming home and he loved her.

Cath opened a tin of mushroom soup and emptied it into a saucepan to heat on the stove. While she waited for it to heat, she cut herself bread and laid out a tray to carry into the sitting room. There was a television there now, a fourteen-inch screen set in an imposing oak console. She might as well watch the six o'clock news while she ate her meal.

She opened the sitting-room door and with the tray in her hand backed in the room. Switching on the light, she stared in surprise. The fruit bowl was on the floor, fruit scattered all around. A juicy pear was squashed into the carpet where someone had stood on it. Had a cat got in? There were cats up at the farm and in the stables at the Hall and sometimes one wandered down to the cottage. She would have to clean up the mess before it dried into the carpet.

She turned to put the tray down on the occasional table that stood by one of the armchairs but it was overturned and the ashtray was on the floor beside it, cigarette ends and ash scattered over the new hearthrug. Her heart beat fast and furious as she took a good look round the room.

262

Sticking out from behind the sofa were her mother's legs, one slipper still in place on her foot and the other, oddly, balanced on the arm of the sofa.

'Mam!' Cath dropped the tray down on the sofa and the soup slopped out of the bowl on to the tray. She ran round the sofa; her mother was lying behind it, her arms raised as though she were trying to defend herself. Her eyes were closed and on her forehead 'Whore' was written in pillar-box red lipstick, the end of the 'e' smeared down by the side of her left eye.

'Mam! Oh, Mam!' Cath knelt down beside Sadie and cupped her cheek in her hand. Sadie's skin was very cold but then the room was cold for the fire was dead and must have been out for hours. There was a bruise on her temple and a trickle of blood had run down to her ear and dried.

Cath felt for a pulse and found it – after an agonising few moments. She went to the telephone in the hall and called the operator. Luckily Saturday afternoons and evening were usually quiet and she got on straight away and gasped out her request for an ambulance. Then she ran upstairs and got an eiderdown and covered her mother, then put a cushion under her head but took it out again as she remembered hearing from somewhere that that was the wrong thing to do.

Sadie moaned and moved her head. Cath flew to the kitchen for a cloth and came back to clean the lipstick from her forehead before anyone else saw it. She rubbed as gently as she could but Sadie moaned again and her eyes fluttered.

The ambulance didn't come; it seemed like hours since Cath had called. She went back to the telephone and rang Henry. Why hadn't she thought of that before? Oh God, she thought, standing by the telephone in the hall, answer Henry, please answer! After it rang out a few times, he did.

'It's me mam, Henry, she's been attacked. She's un-conscious, Henry!' she blurted then, without waiting for him to answer, put down the telephone and ran back in to her mother. Sadie was still lying in virtually the same position as before.

Henry came just before the ambulance and the police. Cath heard his car racing down the track from the Hall and then he burst into the house.

'What happened? Where is she?' he asked and didn't wait for Cath to answer but followed her glance towards the sitting room and strode through. 'My God!' he cried. 'I'll kill him, I swear I will.'

'Kill who, sir?' A policeman had followed him in and caught Henry's exclamation.

'Whoever did this, of course,' Henry snarled.

'Don't touch her, sir,' advised the policeman as he knelt beside Sadie and patted her face.

'Sadie? Sadie?' Henry said.

'Leave her to us, sir,' one of the ambulance men said and reluctantly he stood up and moved to give them room.

'Is she dead?' he asked.

'No, she's alive. Make way, sir, please', the man replied for Henry was edging forward again.

They put Sadie on a stretcher and covered her with a red blanket before taking her out to the ambulance.

'I'll come,' said Cath.

'No, I will,' said Henry.

'Only one can come in the ambulance. In any case, I need you to answer a few questions,' said the policeman to Cath. 'I'll take you after that, I promise you it won't take long.'

It was a nightmare. Left with the policeman, Cath tried to concentrate on his questions but all she could think of was her mother.

'I didn't think he would go this far,' she said more to herself than the policeman. 'I thought he just meant to frighten us all. I warned her but she wouldn't take any notice.'

Cath kept walking to the door, hoping he would follow

her. 'I can talk in the car,' she suggested. 'My mother might die and you're keeping me from her.'

'Who are you talking about? Mr Vaughan? Do you think it was him?'

Cath was impatient. 'No, of course not, he wouldn't hurt her.' She went to the door again. 'I'm not saying another word until we are in the car on our way to the hospital.'

The policeman gave in. 'All right, we'll go. But I want a full statement from you about this man you were talking about. It is an offence to withhold information.'

'Just let's go!' Cath shouted.

'I understand you are upset,' he said stiffly, as they got into the police car. 'So I will not mention your attitude in my report.'

Sadie was in the end bed of Ward E, Women's Surgical, in a similar cheerless prefabricated hut to the one in which Annie had lain, in the General Hospital at Bishop Auckland. There were screens, too, placed around the bed and Cath was stopped at the door to sister's office by a staff nurse.

'I'm afraid you can't go in, not yet,' she said. 'The doctors are examining your mother.'

A policewoman was at the opening to the screens and Cath stared helplessly. She could hear people talking there and after a moment she heard Sadie's voice, weak and faint. She sagged against the doorpost of sister's office, faint with relief.

'Come and sit down,' said the staff nurse and led her into the office. Henry was already there, his head in his hands. He stood up when Cath came in.

'She's awake,' he said. 'Thank God for that. She'll be all right.'

'I told her, I told her he was after her,' said Cath. 'She said you would protect her.'

The policeman who had driven Cath to the hospital put his head round the door, murmured something about a word with his colleague and withdrew.

265

'I don't know who you mean,' said Henry.

Cath told him about Eric Bowron, about his relationship to Ronnie Robson. She told him about his threats to her and how she believed he had frightened Annie so badly she had taken ill again.

'Mam wouldn't take much notice when I told her,' she said. 'Even last night when he slashed the snowdrops she refused to believe it was him. She said it would just be hooligans from the village.'

Henry was violently angry. 'I'll kill him, I will,' he kept saying. 'Why didn't *you* tell me?'

Cath was saved from answering as a doctor and the ward sister came into the office.

'Well?' Henry barked and the young surgeon looked startled. 'How is she?'

'Mrs Raine has recovered consciousness but she is suffering from concussion. I think she has a fractured rib and I believe her wrist is broken, probably she put up her hand to protect her head and face. We'll know for sure after she has been X-rayed.' He paused and looked at Cath. 'It was a very brutal attack. She is lucky in a way she's not more seriously hurt.'

Henry snorted. 'Lucky? I don't call it lucky. When they catch the fellow who did it I hope they lock him up and throw away the key. I—'

'Yes, well, of course it is a terrible thing to happen. Now I must get on, other patients to see. You may go in to see her for a few minutes before she goes to X-ray if you wish.' The surgeon hurried out and Cath and Henry went into the ward.

Sadie was white and frail-looking with dark smudges under her eyes but she managed a small smile. Cath couldn't speak; she felt so shaken and tearful now she knew that at least her mother was not going to die. She kissed her gently on the cheek and moved back to allow Henry to get near enough to hold her good hand.

'I'll get you a private room,' he said to Sadie. 'It's too

public in here, too noisy.' Though in fact it was quite quiet. 'I'll catch him, my love, I will. Don't worry about that. He'll rue the day, oh yes indeed.'

Sadie said nothing. She looked past caring about anything.

It was Sunday morning by the time the police had finished questioning Cath. Sadie had confirmed that it was Eric Bowron who had attacked her but when the police tried to pick him up he had disappeared.

'Don't worry, we will find him,' the inspector said. 'He can't have gone far.'

The news of the attack was on the radio news and the television. There were pictures of Half Hidden Cottage and the desecrated snowdrops for the snow had melted from the withered grass. There was a picture of Winton Colliery village and also Eden Hope on the television news. The reporter had resurrected the story about Annie and the slow-witted boy in Winterton, Ronnie Robson.

'It will all be the fault of that woman,' the former neighbour of Granny Robson, Florrie Dowson, told the reporter. 'She's been at the bottom of all the trouble in this place. Her and her daughters should have been chased out years ago.' It was the talk of the place, even eclipsing the story of little Carol being murdered.

Cath went back to work on Monday. She was aware that many of the other girls were giving her funny looks but she ignored them. It would soon blow over especially if the police caught Eric. In the dinner hour, she went out with her sandwiches and found a sheltered spot on the banks of the Wear to sit and eat them. It was very cold but the bank behind her, rising to the castle and cathedral, offered some protection. In any case she had needed to get away from the office.

She sat gazing at the river, which was in spate, brown and peaty-looking from the fells of Weardale and with twigs and even small logs rushing down to the sea, as

267

though they wanted to get away from wherever they came from. Just as she felt at present.

'What have you got there?'

Mark was sitting down beside her. He too had a packet of sandwiches. 'I've got chicken,' he said. 'Swap you for one of yours?'

Chapter Thirty-one

Mark had seen Cath walk over Elvet Bridge and up the hill to the market place then down the other side to the river and had followed her. She looked as though she was hardly aware of her surroundings so he knew it was unlikely that she would notice him.

He still wanted her. Oh, he knew it wasn't possible but he couldn't help the yearning. He had heard about the attack on Sadie, of course, everyone had. He didn't care, not for her. She deserved it, he reckoned. Whoever heard of a mother selling her children just because they were the wrong sex? But he knew Cath cared desperately and he cared about Cath, he couldn't help himself.

'What about it?' he asked now. 'A chicken sandwich for an egg and tomato one seems fair.'

'Oh, go away and leave me alone, Mark,' said Cath. She couldn't even be bothered to get angry with him now.

'I'm your brother, aren't I? I just want to help you,' he replied.

'Yes, of course. That's why you stole my letter from Jack, why you told him lies.'

'Well, it was different then, wasn't it? I wanted you for myself then. All's fair in love and war, as they say.' He tried to keep his tone light but it was an effort.

Cath put her sandwich back in the packet and the packet

in her bag. She got to her feet and started to walk away from him.

'Where are you going?' he asked.

'Back to work,' she replied. It would be better to face the others than stay and listen to him.

'No, please don't go,' he cried. 'Come on with me and we'll have a cup of coffee or something. It's very cold and look, it's beginning to snow again. I'm sorry for what I did, I really am but it would be good if we were friends.' He walked beside her all the way to the steps by Elvet Bridge. Snow was indeed already beginning to show, driving up against the stone walls.

'Please, Cath. I've been hurt in this too, you know.'

Cath stopped. She might as well go with him. He would pester her until she heard him out. Besides, there was only fifteen minutes left of her dinner hour and she might as well be in the warm.

'Ten minutes is all you have,' she said and went with him into the little café above the bridge.

Mark ordered coffee and they sat down at a table near a heater. 'Can't we be friends?' he asked after the coffees were placed before them.

Cath stared at him. She couldn't forget that they were brother and sister and that they could have made love. It made her feel a little sick.

'Doesn't it bother you that we kissed? It wasn't love, it couldn't have been love,' she said.

'We didn't know,' said Mark. 'If you don't know, well then—'

'Nevertheless,' said Cath. She put her fingers round the cup and the heat from the coffee seeped into them. 'I think we should keep away from each other as far as we can.'

'Cath, I still want—'

'No, don't say it,' she replied quickly. Rising to her feet she went on, 'I must go now. Don't get up, you stay and finish your coffee.'

*

The following Saturday she went up to Newcastle to see Jack. Henry did not go with her; he stayed at home with Sadie whom he had insisted should go to the Hall when she was discharged from hospital.

'There's no reason why I shouldn't go back to the cottage,' Sadie had argued but she didn't put up much resistance. Her spirits were very subdued by what had happened to her. At the big house she had company; Henry had recently engaged a new couple, Mr and Mrs Thompson, for housekeeping and to help with the estate. The great advantage, from Sadie's point of view, was that they were strangers from over Workington way.

'We'll be married as soon as Jack is allowed home,' Henry told her. 'Then I can look after you properly.'

Cath went up to Newcastle by train from Durham station. Feeling very extravagant, she took a taxi to the hospital from the station.

Her heart turned over when she saw Jack, propped up on backrest and pillows in a side room. His face was almost as white as the bandages that swathed one side of it. He was watching the door anxiously when she came in; his usual self-confidence had deserted him.

Cath stood for a moment at the door, unsure of herself too. Then she walked over to the bed and leaned over him.

'Am I allowed to kiss you?' she asked.

His arm came around her and he pulled her to him. In spite of his injuries his kiss was passionate and filled with the frustrations and pain of their time apart. Cath was filled with joy.

'I thought you had left me for Mark,' he whispered into her hair. 'I love you, Catherine.'

Cath tensed. The mention of Mark had brought her down to earth. Would Jack still want her when she told him the truth about her family; that Mark was her half-brother, that Sadie was the sort of woman who would sell her own children? She dreaded the answer to those questions. Sensing her slight withdrawal, Jack released his hold on her and she

271

sat down in the chair by the bed; she was so unsure now. He took her hand and his fingers curled round hers.

'How do you feel?' she asked. 'I mean, does your face hurt much?'

'Not now.' He gazed at her but she bent her head and studied their intertwined hands. His fingers were long and the nails well shaped; they were capable hands, able to deal with most things.

Jack frowned. Was she avoiding looking at his face even though the scar was covered up with the bandage? He had to know.

'Look at me, Catherine,' he said softly and she looked up at him. 'Are you worried I won't look the same? That my face is deformed? Tell me now if you are.'

'No! Don't think that, I don't care about that at all!'

'Then what is it? Something is bothering you, I can tell.'

'It's nothing.' Now it had come to it, Cath couldn't bear to tell him about Mark, not now, not while he lay in a hospital bed. Later she would. Later, when he came home. Instead she told him about her mother and how she had been attacked and how the police were looking for Eric Bowron.

'How is your mother?' he asked and she said that Sadie was at the Hall where Henry could keep an eye on her. And she remembered the things he had said about her and her mother in the past but surely they were best forgotten? She looked searchingly into his eyes to see if he was angry with Sadie and his father's plans to marry.

'It's for the best,' he said. 'Half Hidden Cottage is too lonely for a woman when there is someone like that on the loose.' He bit his lip. 'I'm not angry with your mother now, Catherine. I'm sorry for what I said. I suppose it was because I had lost my own mother and I couldn't bear the thought of anyone taking her place.'

It wasn't really true, Jack was aware of that. He had changed a lot after his experiences in Korea, the humiliations that had been piled on the prisoners even during the

272

short time he had been one. And there had been the longing for Catherine. But there was something wrong, he could sense it.

The visiting hour was over almost before it had begun for Cath. In the end she went away thinking she would tell him about Mark tomorrow; she would come back tomorrow.

After she had gone, Jack had a nurse unwind his bandage. Covering up was unnecessary now, the skin was healed. On Monday Jack was having his last operation. It was cosmetic and meant to improve the look of the deep scar that ran down one side of his cheek and under his chin.

'It doesn't look too bad,' the nurse said. But then, she would say that, Jack thought. She was used to the sight of all sorts of scars and other hideous sights. Jack was sure Cath would be appalled when she saw his face and be unable to hide her revulsion. He didn't think he could bear seeing her face if that happened.

There was no news of Eric Bowron – he had simply disappeared. Henry was furious and had a word with the chief constable about it.

'We are doing our best,' that gentleman said. 'But you must remember that there is the case of the little girl who was raped and murdered. Most of our available resources are engaged on that particular case.'

'I don't know what this corner of Durham is coming to,' Henry snorted. 'Time was when the worst that happened was a fight between drunken miners on a Friday night.'

'It's the Welfare State,' said the chief constable gloomily. 'I knew it would happen.'

Eric Bowron had indeed disappeared. He didn't go to work at the colliery and his house in Winton Colliery village was empty for his mother had died while he was away doing his National Service. Now he lived there on his own. So people reckoned there must have been something to the story that it was Eric who had attacked Sadie Raine in that cottage that belonged to her fancy man.

No one thought much about it. 'Sadie likely deserved all she got,' Mrs Musgrave said to her neighbour as they stood in the queue at the Co-operative store. 'What I'd like to see is the police find the sod that murdered little Carol White. Now I could cheerfully cut off *his* bollocks myself.'

'Oh aye, I know what you mean,' said Mrs Prescott. 'But I reckon they'll take men off that case to look for the lad that battered Sadie Raine won't they? I mean, Henry Vaughan still has a lot of clout round here. Do you think it really was Eric Bowron who did it?'

'Might have been,' Mrs Musgrave conceded, nodding her head. 'He always was a bit of a bully wasn't he? Still he came back from Korea or mebbe it was Malaya, quiet like.'

'I'm not standing here for the good of me health,' said the girl behind the counter who was waiting for Mrs Musgrave's order.

'Cheeky thing, talking like that to folks old enough to be your mother,' the woman replied, banging her basket on the counter to make her point. 'I'll have half a pound of best butter, if you can be bothered serving.'

Cath went back to work in the Powers-Samas accounting machine room in Durham. The weekend after her visit to Jack, she had gone to see Annie in Shildon for Annie was back living with her Aunt Patsy and Uncle Jim.

Annie was quietly sitting by the fire in the new council house, knitting dolls for the chapel sale of work. 'Look, Cath,' she said, 'they're good, aren't they? Do you think they will sell well? How much do you think I can ask for them?'

'They're lovely,' Cath agreed. 'Oh, I don't know, do you think they would fetch 5s. each?'

'They should, they cost nearly that much for the wool,' Patsy said caustically. Then she motioned to Cath. 'Come out to the kitchen with me while I put the kettle on,' she said.

In the kitchen she turned to Cath. 'How do you think she is?'

'Fine. Loads better,' said Cath.

'Aye. Of course she's still on the tablets but the doctor had reduced the dose so she's not so sleepy. I thought this carry-on about our Sadie might have tipped her over the edge again but we've managed to keep it from her, so don't mention it.'

'No, of course not. Only I'm worried Eric might get to her.'

'He won't. I never leave her for a minute unless Jim is here. An' I wouldn't let the police talk to her. She's not fit, I told them. Then, we don't go out much except to chapel and I don't think that one would go there. Annie lives for the chapel now.'

Cath came away fairly happy that Annie was being looked after. But she couldn't help feeling some heartache at the remembrance of how her little sister had been when they were small. Oh, Annie had always been frightened of everything and everybody but they had loved each other and looked out for one another.

As she caught the Eden bus to Spennymoor and the United from Spennymoor to Durham she felt a little less worried about her young sister though. She began to daydream about Jack and their future together.

If all went well, Jack would be coming home from hospital by the following weekend. He was fine, he said on the telephone when he rang home from the call box in the corridor of the Royal Victoria Infirmary.

'I can't wait to see you, darling,' he said to her and the note in his voice sent shivers down her spine. 'The surgeon says the scar on my face will be hardly noticeable in a few months.'

'I don't care about the scar' said Cath.

'Is that Jack?' asked Henry, coming out of the dining

room of the Hall. 'Here, let me speak to him.' He took the receiver from Cath without waiting for her to say goodbye and began to talk to Jack about the estate. He had decided he was going to take Sadie to the south of France to recuperate as soon as she was well enough. Jack was to take over his work on the estate.

Chapter Thirty-two

Jack drove home from the hospital on a fine day in March, which heralded spring. He wanted to feel the sharp air on his face after all this time with it swathed in bandages, so he had got Henry to drive the MG up to Newcastle and now he was driving his father home again.

'It's too cold with the top down,' Henry grumbled. 'For goodness sake, I'll catch my death and it won't do you any good either. You are just out of hospital, remember.'

Jack sighed and put up the hood of the sports car. 'You win, Father,' he said.

'Are you absolutely sure you want to marry Catherine Raine?' Henry asked as Jack slowed for the traffic lights at Neville's Cross.

Jack glanced sideways at his father. 'Are you sure you want to marry her mother?' he countered.

Henry sighed. 'I know, I know. Neither match is what your mother would have wanted. But she would have wanted us to be happy, so there you are.'

'Exactly.'

Jack pulled away from the lights and drove on past the Duke of Wellington pub and into open country. He remembered how angry he had been with his father when he moved Sadie into Half Hidden Cottage; even angrier when he realised that Catherine was Sadie's daughter. How he had driven off in a fury that time he had brought

Catherine home and found out it was to Half Hidden Cottage. He had felt as though both he and his father were betraying his mother. Now, he thought, he was older and wiser.

Jack put a hand up to his face and felt the outline of the scar that furrowed his cheek. His face was not the only thing that had changed during his stay in Korea. His whole attitude to life had matured. He couldn't understand why Catherine still wanted him after the way he had behaved in the past.

They were turning through the gates of the Hall, when Jack's uncertainty about Cath's reaction to his scar surfaced. As the two men got out of the car and started to walk towards the front door, it opened and Cath came out, running down the steps to him in welcome.

'Jack!' she breathed, 'I'm so happy you've come home.' She lifted her face for his kiss. Henry coughed and picked up Jack's bag and took it into the house.

Jack held her tight, revelling in the feel of her against him, then gently he held her from him.

'Well?'

The question sounded harsh and she looked up at him in surprise. She had been awake all night and on tenterhooks all day waiting for him. She had thought she had heard the car a dozen times in the last hour and now at last he had come home and he was holding her away from him.

'What?' Cath asked.

'My face,' Jack said carefully. 'I have to know if you hate it. It would be better to tell me now if you do.'

Cath put up a hand and traced the furrow across his cheek and down, curving into his chin. Then she put her head on one side. 'It gives you an air of distinction,' she murmured consideringly. 'Now kiss me again or I will think you don't want to.'

'Are you two coming inside? You'll freeze to death out there,' Henry had opened the door again and poked his head out as he called to them. 'I've opened a bottle to celebrate and I'm dying for a drink.'

After a few satisfying moments they did as they were told. They didn't realise that other eyes were watching them. The holly bushes near Half Hidden Cottage had been cleared away on Henry's orders but those on the opposite side of the drive to the Hall were still there and just as dense. Above them, in the beech trees planted in a row by Henry's father to form an avenue, birds were busy, singing as they built their nests but they fell silent as the holly bushes rustled and branches moved.

In the afternoon Jack and Cath walked along the path that ran up the slight incline to the farm and fields beyond. The path was sheltered in the lee of the hill and they walked close together, holding hands. Cath's feelings were mixed: one moment she was so happy she thought she would burst and the next she remembered there were things she had to tell Jack and when she did it might be the end of everything between them. They passed the old outhouses and the ancient earth closet, the netty, and Cath shivered.

Jack sensed that there was something still bothering her and he thought it must be the memory of the time he had behaved badly when she had been looking for Annie. He stopped walking and pulled her to him.

'I'm sorry, Catherine,' he said. 'If I could only have that day back I would. I don't know how I could do what I did. I was mad—'

'Don't, don't talk of those days,' said Cath. 'We have to forget those days. Come on, I'll race you to the top of the bank.'

She set off running and after a moment he followed, easily catching up with her. Laughing and entwined in each other's arms, they set off back down towards the old buildings.

'I though we could knock down the outhouses and build a house where they are now,' said Jack. 'What do you think? It's a good position, sheltered by the hill yet high enough up to have a fairly good view.'

'Oh!' Cath was surprised; she had thought they would live in the Hall, perhaps have their own quarters there. But it would be nice to have their own place, somewhere of their own. 'I suppose,' she said. They had reached the outbuildings by now and she stopped and looked around.

It was quite a good position for a house, very good in fact.

'We would get permission too. I mean where there are already buildings,' said Jack. He left her side and walked over towards the netty. He stood there for a moment, apparently thinking. Then he turned and stepped towards her again.

'No,' he said loudly. 'Perhaps it wouldn't be a good idea. Let's go home. It's turning colder now.'

Cath had turned too and taken a few steps down the hill when Jack turned once more and rushed to the netty, bursting the door open with his shoulder.

'What are you doing?' she cried but he didn't reply. There was a scuffling sound inside the tiny building, a muffled cry, then the sound of a blow and then another. And Jack came out, dragging behind him a man. Cath thought at first he was a tramp but realised soon enough he was not.

His clothes were filthy and his face streaked with black, what could be seen of it for his straggly beard. His hair was standing in tufts of grease and dirt and the smell of him was rank. The man Jack was holding by an arm that was twisted up his back was Eric Bowron.

'Bloody well let go of me!' Eric shrieked. 'You're breaking my arm!'

'I'll break more than your arm, soldier, if you don't stay still,' said Jack. 'And I'll enjoy doing it.'

'Eric!' cried Cath. 'It's Eric, Jack, the man who attacked my mother!'

'I thought perhaps it was,' said Jack grimly. He had Eric lying on his face now, his arm still twisted up his back. 'Just go and call the police, would you mind?'

'No need for that, sir,' a new voice joined in. Sergeant Duffy was puffing a little. Behind him were two constables from the town.

'I'll hand over to you, then,' said Jack, rising to his feet and dusting his hands together before looking at them critically. 'I think I'll just head for home and a bath after that. Coming, Catherine?'

Cath was speechless with the shock of what had happened so quickly. She trembled with it and Jack noticed. He strode over to her and put his arm around her, steadying her.

'I'm sorry, my love,' he said. 'Let's go home now. A nice cup of tea will help.'

'For goodness sake, I'm not a Victorian heroine, I'm not going to faint away!' said Cath, annoyed. 'Why didn't you tell me you knew someone was there?'

'I will call in at the Hall later, Major Vaughan,' Sergeant Duffy intervened tactfully. 'We will just put this one where he belongs first. I will need a full statement from you, of course.'

'Anytime, Sergeant.'

Jack and Cath walked on down the incline.

'How did you know he was there?' asked Cath. Her skin crawled at the thought that Eric had been so close and she hadn't known.

'I could smell him,' said Jack and thought of the times in Korea when he had sensed the enemy was there in hiding nearby. His time in Korea had done some good.

'Hiding in our own old outbuildings?' Henry was enraged, affronted at the idea of the man who had attacked Sadie using his property for cover.

'I don't think he has been there all the time, they would have found him before this if he had,' said Jack. 'No, I think he has come back recently, maybe even just today. I think the police were hot on his tail too, else why should they be here today also?'

'Perhaps they thought he might be going to attack one of us again,' Cath suggested soberly. Jack caught her hand and gave it a squeeze. 'Not while I was here, my love,' he said.

It was the housekeeper's afternoon off, so Sadie came in with a tray of tea and a plate of hot buttered pikelets wrapped in a napkin. Oh, thought Cath, smiling to herself, her mother had picked up most of the ways of doing things as the gentry were used to.

They sat round the fire and ate as the gloaming closed in outside the window. Cath felt an enormous sense of relief; everything had lightened up now that she knew Eric Bowron was safely in the hands of the police. Annie would be safe now, she would get better or at least improve more than she was doing at present.

The telephone rang and Henry went out to answer it. Jack and Cath sat close together on the sofa, holding hands. She would remember today, she would remember it all of her life. The time when she was truly happy.

'That was the chief constable,' Henry announced, when he came back in the room. He settled himself down in his chair and Sadie went out to freshen the teapot. 'They picked up this Eric Bowron's trail a couple of days ago and followed him, guessing he was coming back here,' Henry went on after accepting another cup when Sadie came back in, leaning back against the cushions and stretching his feet out to the blazing fire. 'Someone has been watching the estate for days. I'll have a word about that; I'm not sure I like it – strangers spying on the place, even if they are the police. They could have told me.'

'Oh Henry,' Sadie remonstrated with him. 'What does it matter?' Henry didn't answer.

Jack set off to drive Cath back to Durham after the evening

meal. Of course she could have caught the early bus the following day but they wanted some time on their own. He drove out to the road by way of Half Hidden Cottage and slowed as they came opposite it.

'Let's go in, check everything is all right,' he said. There was moonlight by now and it shone palely on the windows. Jack had picked up the key as he left the Hall. Now he opened the front door and, with his arm around her, ushered her in and switched on the light.

They stood together in the hall. 'Nothing seems to have been disturbed,' he said. 'Let's go upstairs and make sure, shall we?'

They went up to the first floor and glanced in the rooms. He was right; everything was as it should be.

'This is your room, isn't it?' he asked, drawing her in.

'You knew it was all right, didn't you?' she accused him and he grinned down at her.

'I confess I had an ulterior motive for getting you in here,' he said. Bending to kiss her he lifted her up and put her on the bed and proceeded to undress her. Cath closed her eyes and let herself be carried away on a stream of mounting emotion. She forgot everything but that they were together and she loved him and he loved her.

It was morning when she woke. The grey dawn light was creeping into the room. She turned to look at him. Jack was lying on his side with his head close to hers, his arm still around her. She didn't move in case she disturbed him, just gazed at him, loving the feel of his body stretched out beside her. He moved his leg suddenly, putting it over her, trapping her, as though he were frightened she would get away. Cath smiled.

There was no hurry now. Jack would run her into Durham at half past eight, it was now only seven; there was a whole hour and a half together first. She had to tell him about Mark. Now, while she had the courage. First she would make coffee though.

Slipping away from him as carefully as she could, she pulled on an old robe she had hanging behind the bedroom door and went downstairs, shivering in the early dawn.

Chapter Thirty-three

Jack woke with a great feeling of well-being. He turned and realised he was in the bed on his own though he could still catch the scent of Cath. He breathed it deeply for a moment then stretched, got out of bed and pulled on his trousers. He went to the window and looked out. The sun was just coming up over the horizon and birds were singing. Dew sparkled on the grass. Though it was cold, it felt like spring. 'God's in his heaven,' he quoted from the poem.

Suddenly eager to see her, hold her, he ran down the stairs and into the kitchen where the scent of coffee was just beginning to permeate the air.

Cath was pouring coffee. She had turned on the small electric fire to warm the kitchen and the whole atmosphere was welcoming.

'Oh, I was going to bring yours up. Sorry if I woke you.'

'It's OK. Gosh, it smells gorgeous. Shall we go back to bed to drink it?' Jack grinned wickedly and went to kiss her.

'No,' she said.

'No?'

'I mean no, we'll drink it here. It's nice and warm and I want to talk to you.'

'Oh, come on, Catherine my love. We can talk in bed. After other things, of course.'

'No,' said Cath backing away from him and he realised

she was serious. They sat down at the kitchen table.

'Well, what is so important? More important than making love?' Unconsciously, he put a hand up to his cheek and felt the furrow there. His old dread that she wouldn't want him because of it returned briefly and irrationally for she had shown no sign of being repulsed by it. He took a sip of the coffee to cover up the gesture but of course she had noticed it.

'Oh Jack, it's not that,' she said and paused, trying to find the right words. He cocked his head to one side and waited for her to explain.

'It's about Mark,' she said. 'Mark and me.'

She told him everything. How Mark had caught her at a low ebb, how she had thought he, Jack, wanted no more to do with her, how unhappy and worthless she had felt.

'I felt something for him,' she said and Jack gave a low exclamation. 'I didn't know what it was. I felt I knew him. He reminded me of someone. Maybe my father, maybe my little brother. I don't know.'

'What are you talking about?'

Jack got to his feet and went to the window then turned and strode to the door. 'I can't listen to this,' he said.

'Jack, please. Hear me out.'

Jack paused, then turned and came back to the table. He stared at her, she was lovely with her hair falling about her face, tousled after their night together, her cheeks rosy and her dark eyes sparkling with unshed tears. He sat down at the table.

'Right, I'm listening,' he said.

'When I was a child, during the war, I remember my mother taking Annie and me and my baby brother into the Bishop's park.'

'Baby brother?' Jack cut in.

'Please, Jack let me finish. She left Annie and me on the path near the Gaunless and told us to wait. Then she disappeared behind the deer house. Annie cried, I tried to comfort her. When I looked back at the deer house, Mam was coming back without Timmy and I saw someone was walking away towards Coundon.'

'She gave the baby away?'

'She said she was sending him to a nice house where he would be looked after. My dad was in North Africa, I think she was desperate. Anyway, to cut a long story short, she had done it before. Once I think.'

Fleetingly, she thought of the baby Sadie was expecting when she ran away after Keith Armstrong, the Canadian flyer. Best not mention that.

'The first time it was Mark, Jack. The second it was his younger brother. Daphne found out we were going out together and she told him.'

Cath heard Jack's chair scrape back and looked up quickly to see him going out of the door.

'Jack!' she cried, going after him. 'Jack, I didn't know. Please Jack!'

Half-way up the stairs he turned to look at her. 'I have to get away on my own,' he said. 'It's so much to take in. I'm sorry, Catherine.'

Cath caught the half past eight bus to Durham, getting into the office only a few minutes late. This morning the girls were punching the cards for the teachers' monthly salaries; it was a busy day ahead.

Cath was pleased about that at least. So far she had got through the morning with her thoughts and mind in a sort of frozen state of calm. Now the routine of the day would keep her occupied. She handed out the papers to the row of girls. Mary, the girl who usually worked on the card sorter, had rung in sick so she would have to do her job after she had finished the books.

She worked steadily all morning, not taking a tea break and still at her desk at dinner time when the others had gone chattering down to the basement to boil the kettle for tea and eat their sandwiches. She sat back and opened her own packet of egg sandwiches she had bought at the corner shop when she had finished, and took a bite then put it back in the drawer. She might as well get on with sorting the piles that were ready. Standing by the machine as it clacked and clattered away, she stared out at the grey day. In the distance the river ran brown and frothy and the trees above the grass were still bare with hardly a hint of green buds.

There was a great weight in her. This was it, she told herself, she had told him too much, and he couldn't cope with it. He hadn't known how fast to get away from her. He wasn't going to come back. It would be best if she didn't go back home at all. It would only embarrass him if she did.

At five o'clock she closed the office door after the other girls and went out into Old Elvet. For a moment she hesitated, unable to suppress the wild illogical hope that he would be there, waiting for her.

There were crowds of office workers walking rapidly towards the bus station; a few cars pulling out from the side of the broad road and zooming down to the traffic lights. Of course there was no Jack. How could she think there might have been?

Cath thought bleakly of an evening in Gilesgate waiting for the telephone to ring. Then, as she turned to look up New Elvet she saw the bus was standing at the stop only a few yards away. On impulse she ran for it. Not that she intended going to the Hall, of course not. She would hide away in Half Hidden Cottage. At least she would be near him.

Jack sat in his car outside the house in Gilesgate. He had not got to Old Elvet until half past five and the road was empty, Cath's office dark. So he drove up to Gilesgate and waited there. He waited until seven thirty then he climbed the steps to the front door and knocked.

'I was expecting Cath to come this evening,' said Hilda in answer to his query. 'But I think she must have gone home to Bishop Auckland.'

Jack thanked her and went back to his car, started up and headed for the A1. As he drove he thought of the meeting he had had with Mark that day in his lodgings in Durham.

'I suppose Cath told you everything,' Mark said, looking apprehensive. 'Come in, we'll have to talk.' He led the way upstairs to the couple of rooms he rented near the university. He changed to the defensive as he saw Jack's expression. 'It wasn't my fault, you know, I didn't know and nothing really happened. Not until my mother found out who it was I was seeing.'

'You knew she was my girl,' said Jack. His fists were doubling and undoubling by his side. 'I trusted you to give her my letter.'

'I know. I thought I loved her, I thought she might love me. I let her think you had deserted her.'

Jack gazed at his one-time friend; oh, what was the point? The fact was he loved Catherine and he didn't think he could live without her. He had been in Korea a long time and he knew he came back a changed man. Abruptly, he turned on his heel and went out. He would go to see her at work, he thought. There should be time to catch her coming out at five o'clock. There was a traffic jam in the narrow streets and then the traffic policeman in his box in the market place kept the lights on red to allow the jam to clear and in the end Jack missed her.

Cath alighted the bus at the entrance to Half Hidden Cottage and walked up the drive. It was very quiet; the wind soughed in the trees on either side and even the birds were silent. But she wasn't nervous, not now that Eric Bowron had been caught. She stood outside the old cottage, wondering if anyone else would come to live in it now that Sadie had moved into the Hall. It was a nice house. It would be a shame if it stood empty for long.

She walked around to the back, found the big old key to the kitchen door and let herself in. If anyone came past they would see a light in the back, she told herself. She found a tin of beans in the cupboard, heated them and ate them at the kitchen table. The only bread she had was on her sandwiches from dinner time so she ate a sandwich too. Then she went out into the hall and climbed the stairs to the bathroom. The water was cold so she had a strip wash rather than a bath. As she opened the door she was grabbed suddenly from the side.

'Got you!' he cried. 'What the hell are you doing in here? You're trespassing, Catherine!'

Jack stood still, his arms still holding her for a brief moment before releasing her. She was trembling, as much from shock as anything else. She felt a fool standing there in her robe and clutched it to her. She waited for him to tell her it was over between them finally. She tried to move away but he still held her firmly.

'Forgive me, Catherine,' he said, his words muffled as he buried his face in her hair. 'I'm sorry I went away in such a hurry this morning. I had to think.' He paused for a moment before going on. 'Well, now I have and I know I want you more than anything. I want us to be married and settled like any other old married couple. I want it more than anything.'

Cath breathed out air from her lungs she hadn't even known she had been holding. But she still wasn't sure he meant what he was saying. Not after a whole day of convincing herself that he wanted nothing more to do with her.

'And it doesn't matter about—'

'Hush, hush,' he interrupted her. 'Nothing matters except this, nothing at all.' Together they walked into the bedroom.

It was much later when they emerged and went downstairs to see if they could find anything else to eat in the kitchen cupboards. While Cath was foraging through them, Jack rang the Hall to let his father and Sadie know where they were.

'Have you heard the news?' Henry asked. 'It was on at nine o'clock tonight. It was that monster, Eric Bowron, the one who attacked Sadie!'

'What?'

'It was him! I mean it was he who killed that little girl, he's done it before. There was one near where he was stationed in the army and they think it was he who attacked little Annie, not that poor boy in Winterton. All these years that simple-minded boy has been in a mental hospital and he did nothing!'

After Jack put down the telephone he walked slowly into the kitchen and told Cath.

Cath sat down abruptly for she felt her legs would no longer hold her. 'I should have known,' she said. 'Of course I should have known. That poor little girl.'

'Don't feel guilty, my love,' said Jack. 'It wasn't your fault. People can't believe anyone could be so evil, not anyone they know at least.' He sat down opposite her and took her hand over the table. 'It's over now,' he said. 'He won't be hurting anyone else.'

Jack and Catherine were married on Easter Sunday, 1951 in Wesley Church in Newgate Street. It was a quiet wedding for Henry and Sadie were in France where Sadie was still recuperating.

Mark came to the wedding, in fact he was best man. Cath and Jack had talked it over and decided the best thing to do was forgive and forget. Alf gave Cath away and little Hans presented her with a silver horseshoe for luck. Patsy and Jim came, with Annie looking better and prettier than she had in years. She had blossomed in the last few weeks, though she wouldn't put herself forward to the extent of being bridesmaid. Nevertheless she smiled and held up her head and showed no signs of nervousness or fright when the wedding party came out of the church and a crowd gathered round to admire.

Jack put his arm around Catherine and they smiled for

the photographers from the *Auckland Chronicle* and the *Northern Echo*. Aunt Patsy preened in her powder-blue suit and lacy hat and Jim looked embarrassed. But it was Annie who almost stole the picture from her sister and her new husband.

Annie looked like any other girl of her age. She had lost the timid, hunted expression that had been so characteristic of her for most of her life. Her happy smile lit up her face and made her look almost as pretty as the bride.

At the reception in the Queen's Hotel she played with her little half-brother, Hans, who toddled after her followed by his anxious mother, Gerda. Watching her, Cath was filled with gladness for her.

Jack and Catherine slipped away while the party was still in full swing. They had decided to honeymoon fairly close to home for Jack was full of plans for the estate now that most wartime restrictions had finally been lifted. They had booked a suite at the Grand Hotel in Scarborough.

'I love you, Mrs Vaughan,' Jack said softly as he opened his car door for her. Catching her to him he buried his face in her hair and breathed in the scent of her.

'We'll be all right, won't we Jack?' she asked.

'Better than all right,' he replied. And they set off together on their new life.